kitty
RAISES HELL

D1040350

Also by Carrie Vaughn
from Gollancz

kitty
RAISES HELL
Carrie Vaughn

Copyright © Carrie Vaughn 2009
All rights reserved

The right of Carrie Vaughn to be identified as the author
of this work has been asserted by her in accordance with
the Copyright, Designs and Patents Act 1988.

First published in Great Britain in 2009 by
Gollancz
An imprint of the Orion Publishing Group
Orion House, 5 Upper St Martin's Lane,
London WC2H 9EA
An Hachette UK Company

This edition published in Great Britain in 2009
by Gollancz

10 9 8 7 6 5 4 3 2

A CIP catalogue record for this book
is available from the British Library

ISBN 978 0 575 09006 4

Printed and bound in the UK
by CPI Mackays, Chatham, Kent

The Orion Publishing Group's policy is to use papers
that are natural, renewable and recyclable products and
made from wood grown in sustainable forests. The logging
and manufacturing processes are expected to conform to
the environmental regulations of the country of origin.

www.carrievaughn.com
www.orionbooks.co.uk

To Kitty's Pack of Readers,
You Rock

The Playlist

Eric Burdon & the Animals, "Paint It Black"

KT Tunstall, "Hold On"

Thompson Twins, "In the Name of Love"

Pretenders, "Day After Day"

Oingo Boingo, "Just Another Day"

Squirrel Nut Zippers, "Soon"

The Cardigans, "Happy Meal II"

Abby Travis, "Blythe"

Duran Duran, "View to a Kill"

They Might Be Giants, "Istanbul (Not Constantinople)" (*Severe Tire Damage* version)

Garbage, "As Heaven Is Wide"

Cyndi Lauper, "All Through the Night"

I had to admit, this was pretty cool.

Rick had gotten us onto the roof of the Pepsi Center in downtown Denver. We sat near the edge, by a railing on a catwalk near the exclusive upper-story clubhouse. From here, we had a view of this whole side of downtown: Elitch's amusement park to the west, the interstate beyond that, Coors Field to the north, and, to the south, Mile High Stadium. It felt like the center of the universe—at least, this little part of it. We could look downtown and see into the maze of skyscrapers. At night, the sky of stars, washed out in an evening haze of lights, seemed inverted, appearing around us in the lights of the city, in trails of moving cars.

When Rick had escorted me through the lobby and to the elevator, the security guards didn't look twice at us. He had a passkey for the elevator. I'd asked him how he got that kind of access, the key and security codes—who he knew or what kind of favors he'd pulled in—but he only smiled. It wouldn't have surprised me to find out he owned a share in the place. Vampires were like that; at least the

powerful ones were: prone to quiet, conservative invest-
ing, working through layers of holding companies. They
had time.

A constant breeze blew up here. I tucked the blond
strands of my hair behind my ears yet again. I should
have clipped it up. The air had its own scent, particular to
this place and nowhere else: oil, gas, concrete, steel, rust,
decay—usual city smells. But under it was the dry tint of
prairie, a taste of air that had blown across tall grasses and
cottonwoods. And under *that* was a hint of cold, of ancient
stone and caves that sheltered ice year-round. The mountains. That was Denver, to the nose of a werewolf. Up here,
I could smell it all. I closed my eyes and tipped my nose
into the breeze, drinking it in.

"I thought you'd like it up here," Rick said. I opened my
eyes to find him watching me.

I sighed. Back to reality, back to the world. We weren't
here sightseeing. City sounds drifted to me, car engines, a
distant siren, music from a bar somewhere. We had a view,
but I was afraid that what we were looking for was too
good at hiding for us to find from here.

"We're not going to see anything," I said, crossing my
arms.

"You may not see anything. I'll see patterns," he said.
Rick appeared to be in his late twenties, confident yet casual. He tended to walk tall, with his hands in his pockets, and look out at the world with a thoughtful, vaguely
amused detachment. Even now, when Denver was possibly
under assault, he seemed laid-back. "Traffic on I-25's thinning out. Downtown's a mess, as usual. It's like a tide. In
an hour, when the theaters and concerts get out, the cars'll
all move back to the freeway. You watch for things moving

against the tide. Pockets of motion where there shouldn't be anything, of unusual quiet."

He pointed to a hidden corner of the parking lot, tucked near Elitch's security fence. Two cars had stopped, facing each other, the drivers' windows pulled alongside each other. The headlights were off, but the motors were running. Hands reached out, traded something. One car pulled away, tires crunching quietly. A moment later, the other pulled away, as well.

I had a few ideas about what that might have been. It still didn't seem relevant to our problem. "And what does that have to do with Tiamat?" I asked.

Not really Tiamat, which was an ancient Babylonian goddess of chaos. According to myth, newer gods, the forces of reason and order, rose up against her in an epic battle and destroyed her and her band of demons—the Band of Tiamat—and thereby created civilization. Really, I was talking about the whacked-out cult of her worshippers that I had pissed off on my recent trip to Las Vegas. Last week, I found the word *Tiamat* burned into the door of the restaurant I co-owned. I figured the pack of were-felines and the possibly four-thousand-year-old vampire who led them had come to Denver on the warpath.

We hadn't learned who left the message on the door, one of the cult members or someone they'd hired. Rick, the Master vampire of Denver, and I had been keeping watch for another attack, but nothing else had happened yet. I was getting more anxious, not less.

"That? Nothing. I'm just showing you how much can happen under our noses. You said a vampire leads the cult. If a vampire is planning an attack in my city, I'll see it."

That was why Rick had gotten involved at all—the cult

may have targeted me out of revenge, but Rick would take any invasion by another vampire personally. I was happy to have another ally.

I scanned all the way around, searching buildings, skyscrapers, parking lots, roads filled with cars, people walking to dinner, concerts, shopping. Someone laughed; it sounded like distant birdsong. Maybe Rick really could sense the movements of another vampire from up here, but I wasn't having any luck. I didn't have much room to pace, but I tried. A couple of steps along the catwalk, turn around, step back. I couldn't stand the waiting. The modern Band of Tiamat was trying to kill me with anxiety.

"You know what the problem with this is? Wolves hunt by moving. I want to be out there *looking* for them. Tracking them down."

"And vampires are like spiders," Rick said. "We draw our quarry in and trap it. I like the image."

I suddenly pictured Rick as a creature at the center of his web, patiently waiting, watching, ready to strike. A chill ran down my spine, and I shook the image away.

"What do you really expect to see up here?"

Absently, he shook his head. It wasn't really an expression of denial. More like thoughtfulness. "If anything else out there is hunting, I'll see it."

I gave a crooked smile. "I can see you sitting like this in the bell tower of Notre Dame cathedral, looking out over Paris like a gargoyle."

He gave me a sidelong glance, then turned his gaze back to the city. "I've never been to Paris."

Which was an astonishing thing to hear from a five-hundred-year-old vampire.

I sat next to him. "Really? No family trips when you

were a kid? Didn't do the backpacking-around-Europe thing? Did people even do that in the sixteenth century?"

"Maybe not with backpacks. But New Spain sounded so much more interesting to a seventeen-year-old third son of very minor nobility with no prospects in 1539 Madrid."

This was more detail about his past than he'd ever mentioned before. I didn't say anything, hoping that he'd elaborate. He didn't.

"Are you *ever* going to tell me the whole story?"

"It's more fun watching your expression when I give it to you in bits and pieces."

"I can see it now. It's going to be the end of the world, everyone will be dead, all that'll be left are vampires, and you won't have anything to say to each other because you can't stop being mysterious and secretive."

He smiled like he thought this was funny.

I looked at my watch. "Not that this hasn't been fun, but I have to get going. I have the show to do." I headed back toward the roof's access door. "I'll find my way out. You keep looking."

"Break a leg," he said.

"Don't say that when I'm standing on the roof of a very tall building." Werewolves healed supernaturally quickly from horrible injuries, but I didn't want to test if that included the injuries sustained from falling that far. "Let me know if you find anything?"

"Of course."

I left him on the roof, scanning across the night, perched like Denver's very own gargoyle.

*   *   *

For the next few hours I had the show to worry about, and all other anxieties stayed outside the studio door.

At this hour, we had the station to ourselves. Except for a security guy and the graveyard-shift DJ, it was just me and Matt, my engineer, tucked away to rule the night. The studio was like a cave, left dark and shadowy on purpose, most of the illumination coming from equipment: computer screens, soundboards, monitors. Matt had his space behind glass, screening calls and manning the board. I had my space, with my monitor, headset, microphone, and favorite cushy chair. When the on-air sign lit, the universe collapsed to this room, and I did my job.

"Hello, faithful listeners. This is Kitty Norville, and you're listening to *The Midnight Hour,* everyone's favorite talk show dealing in supernatural snark. Tonight I want to talk about magic. What's the true story, what's the real picture? Is it pastel fairy godmothers, is it meditating over a stack of crystals, or is it Faust making deals with the devil? What's real, what isn't, what works, what doesn't?"

Once a week I did this, and had been doing it for going on three years. I'd have thought it would start to get old by now. Conveniently, the world kept producing more mysteries, and the public couldn't get enough of it. As long as that stayed true, I'd still have a job.

The supernatural world was like an onion. You peel back the layers, only to find more layers, on and on, hopelessly trying to reach the mysterious core. Then you start crying.

"I have on the phone with me Dr. Edgar Olafson, a professor of anthropology from the University of Colorado, here to give us the accepted party line about magic. Professor Olafson, thanks for being on the show."

"Thank you very much for inviting me, Kitty."

Olafson was one of the younger, hipper professors I'd had during my time at CU. He was hip enough to appear on a cult radio show, which was good enough for me. He was also a scientist and spent a minute or so saying what I expected him to. "Belief in magic has been with human culture from the very beginning. It's been a way to explain anything that people in early civilizations didn't understand. Diseases were caused by curses, a spate of bad luck meant that something was magically wrong with the world. By the same token, magic gave people a way to feel like they had some control over these events. They could use talismans and amulets to protect against curses, they could concoct potions and rituals to combat bad luck and promote good luck."

"That's still true, isn't it? People still have superstitions and carry good-luck charms, right?"

"Of course. But you have to wonder how many people do these things out of habit, built up in the culture over generations, and how many people really believe the habits produce magical effects."

"And we'll find out about that in a little bit when I open the line for calls. But let me ask you something: What about me?"

"I'm sorry, I'm not sure I understand the question."

I hadn't prepped him for this part. Sometimes I was a little bit mean to my guests. They still agreed to come on the show. Served 'em right. "I'm a werewolf. I've got incontrovertible, public, and well-documented proof of that condition, validated by the NIH. I've had vampires on my show. I've talked to people claiming to be magicians, and some of them I'm totally willing to vouch that they are. While the NIH has identified lycanthropy as a disease, modern medical science hasn't been able to explain it. So. This inexplicable sliver that you have to acknowledge as existing. Is it really magic? Not a metaphor, not habit, not superstition, but really some effect that contradicts our understanding of how the world works." Whew. I took a big breath, because I'd managed to get that all out at once.

He chuckled nervously. "Well, we've gone a little bit outside my disciplines at this point. I certainly can't argue with you. But if something's out there, I'm sure someone's studying it. Maybe even writing a PhD thesis on it."

"I plan on getting ahold of that thesis just as soon as I can. Sorry for putting you on the spot, Professor. I'm just trying to get us a neutral baseline before the conversation goes completely out of control. Which it always does. Let's go to the phones. Hello, you're on the air."

With great condescension, a man started in. "Hi, Kitty. Thanks for taking my call. With all due respect for your guest, this is *exactly* the kind of attitude that's held human civilization back, that's kept our species from taking the next step toward enlightenment—"

Away we went.

I had to butt in. "Here's what I'm wondering: In this day and age, with the revelations of the last couple of years, isn't it a mistake to think of magic and science as two different things, as polar opposites, and never the twain shall meet? Shouldn't practitioners of both be working together toward greater understanding? What if there really is a scientific explanation for the weirder bits of magic? What if magic can explain the weirder bits of science?"

A rather intense-sounding woman called in to agree with me. "Because really, I think we need *both* points of view to understand how the world works. Like this—I've always wondered, what if it's not the four-leaf clover that brings good luck, but *belief* in the four-leaf clover that causes some kind of mental, psychic effect that causes good luck?"

"Hey, I like that idea," I said. "The problem that science always has with this sort of thing is how do you prove it? How do you measure luck? How do you prove the mental effect? So far, no one's come up with a good experimental model to record and verify these events."

Sometimes my show actually sounded *smart*, rather than outrageous and sensationalist. I was hoping with Professor Olafson on board that we'd be leaning more toward NPR than Jerry Springer. So far, so good. But it couldn't possibly last, and it didn't.

"Next caller, hello. What have you got?"

"I want to talk about what's going on with Speedy Mart." The caller was male. He talked a little too fast, a little too hushed, like he kept looking over his shoulder. One of the paranoid ones.

"Excuse me?" I said. "What does a convenience-store chain have to do with magic?"

"There's a pattern. If you mark them all on a map, then cross-reference with the locations of violent crimes, like armed robbery, there's an overlap."

"It's a twenty-four-hour convenience store. Places like that get robbed all the time. Of course there's a correspondence."

"No—there's more. You overlay both of those sets of points on a map of ley lines, and bingo."

"Bingo?"

"They match," the caller said, and I wondered what I was missing. "Every Speedy Mart franchise is built on the intersection of ley lines."

"Okay. That's spooky. If anyone could agree on whether ley lines exist or where they really are."

"What do you mean, whether they exist!" He sounded offended and put out. Of *course* he did.

"I mean there's no quantitative data that anyone can agree on."

"How can you be such a skeptic? I thought this was supposed to be a show about how magic is *real*."

"This is supposed to be a show about how to tell the real from the fake. I'm going to say 'prove it' every time someone lays one on me."

"Yeah, well, check out my web site and you'll find everything you need to know. It's w-w-w dot—" I totally cut him off.

"Here's the thing," I said, long overdue for a rant. "People are always saying that to me—how can I possibly be a skeptic given what I am? Given how much I know about what's really out there, how can I turn my nose up at any half-baked belief that crosses my desk? Really, it's easy, because so many of them *are* half-baked. They're formulated by people who don't know what they're talking about, or by people trying to con other people and make a few bucks. The fact that some of this *is* real makes it even more important to be on our guard, to be that much more skeptical, so we can separate truth and fiction. Blind faith is still blind, and I try not to be."

"Houdini," Professor Olafson said. I'd almost forgotten about him, despite his occasional commentary.

"Houdini?"

"Harry Houdini. He's a good example of what you're talking about," he said. "He was famous for debunking spiritualists, for proving that a lot of the old table-rapping séance routines were sleight-of-hand magic tricks. What many people forget is that he really wanted to believe. He was searching for someone who could help him communicate with his dead mother. Lots of spiritualists tried to convince him that they'd contacted his mother, but he debunked every one of them. The fakery didn't infuriate him so much as the way the fakers preyed on people's faith, their willingness to believe."

"Then he may be one of my heroes. Thanks for that tidbit."

"Another tidbit you might like: He vowed that after he died, he would try to send a message back to the living, if such a thing was possible."

I *loved* that little chill I got when I heard a story like this. "Has he? Has anyone gotten a message?"

"No—and lots of people have tried."

"Okay, let's file that one away for future projects. Once again, thank you for joining us this evening, Professor Olafson."

"It was definitely interesting."

So was his tone of voice. I couldn't tell if he loved it or hated it. Another question to file away.

Matt and I wrapped up the show. I sat back, listened to the credits ramble on, with my recorded wolf howl in the background. Soon I'd have to go back outside, back to the real world, and back to my own little curse, which I didn't have any trouble believing in.

* * *

New Moon stayed open late on Friday nights, just for me.

Restaurant reviews describe New Moon as a funky downtown watering hole that features live music on occasion, plays host to an interesting mix of people, and has a menu with more meat items than one might expect in this health-conscious day and age. All in all, thumbs-up. What the reviews don't say is that it's a haven, neutral territory for denizens of the supernatural underworld, mostly lycanthropes. As the place's co-owner, that's what I set it up to be. I figured if we could spend more time relating to each other as people, we'd spend less time duking it out in our animal guises. So far, it seemed to be working.

The bartender turned the radio on and piped in the show Friday nights. When I walked through the door, the few late-night barflies and wait staff cheered. I blushed. Part of me would never get used to this.

I waved at the compliments and well-wishes and went to the table where Ben sat, folding away his laptop and smiling at my approach. Ben: my mate, the alpha male of my pack. My husband. I was still getting used to the ring on my finger.

Though Ben could pull off clean-cut and intimidatingly stylish when the situation required it, most of the time he personified a guy version of shabby chic. He was slim, fit, on the rough side of handsome. His light brown hair was always in need of a trim. He could usually be found in a button-up shirt sans tie, sleeves rolled up, and a pair of comfortably worn khakis. If you went back in time to a year ago and told me I'd be married to this guy, I'd have laughed in your face. He'd been my lawyer. I only ever saw him when I had problems, and he scowled a lot when I did.

Then he landed on my front door with werewolf bites on his shoulder and arm. I took care of him, nursed him through his first full moon when he shifted for the first time and became a full-fledged werewolf. I'd comforted him. That was a euphemism. It had seemed the most natural thing in the world to fall into bed with him. Or so my Wolf side thought.

Over the months, my human side had come to depend on having him in my life. Love had sneaked up on us rather than bursting upon us like cannons and fireworks.

Sliding into the seat next to him, I continued the motion until I was leaning against him, falling into his arms, then almost pushing him out of the seat. Our lips met. This kiss was long, warm, tension-melting. This was the way to end a day.

When we drew apart—just enough to see each other, our hands still touching—I asked, "So, how was it?" The show, I meant. Everyone knew what I meant when I asked that.

He smirked. "I love how you work out your personal issues on the air. It must be like getting paid to go through therapy."

I sat back and wrinkled my brow. "Is that what it sounds like? Really?"

"Maybe only to me," he said. "So, are you okay? Everything's all right?"

"I'm fine. Nothing's happened. I still haven't learned anything new."

"What's Rick been doing?"

"Sitting on rooftops being gargoyle-y. He says he can see 'patterns.'" I gave the word quotes with my fingers.

"He's just saying that to make himself look cool," Ben said. I kind of agreed with him.

"Is there anything else we ought to be doing?" I asked.

"The restraining order against our friend Nick and the Band is filed. There's not much more we can do until something happens. Maybe this—this emotional harassment—is all there is."

"Wouldn't that be nice?"

Nick, a were-tiger, was the leader of the Band of Tiamat. He also led an animal and magic act in Las Vegas—only the animals were all feline lycanthropes. The whole act was a front for the Tiamat cult, and when they weren't using the Babylonian-themed stage and sets in their show, they were using them to conduct sacrifices. Their preferred victims? Werewolves. Dogs and cats, at it again. Nick himself was certainly hot and sexy enough to front a Vegas show. He was also an evil son of a bitch. I got chills just thinking about him.

Ben moved his arm over my shoulder, and I snuggled into his embrace. "I wish I could just go back there and . . . beat them up," I said.

"We've been over that. They didn't manage to kill you last time. It's best if we don't give them a next time."

Especially since I wouldn't have quite the same backup if I faced the Band of Tiamat again. Evan and Brenda, the rather uncomfortably amoral bounty hunters who'd saved my ass, had had to leave Vegas in a hurry to avoid awkward questions from the police. They couldn't help me.

And the one supernatural bounty hunter in the world I actually sort of trusted was still in jail.

"Grant's keeping an eye on things for us," Ben continued. "If they do anything funny, we'll know it."

Odysseus Grant was a stage magician in Las Vegas, a niche act who'd made his reputation with a retro show featuring old vaudeville props and reviving classic tricks that had gone out of fashion in the age of pyrotechnics and special effects. That was the public face, at least. I still didn't entirely understand the persona underneath. He was a guardian of sorts, protecting humanity from the forces of chaos. It sounded so overwrought I hesitated to even think it. But, having encountered some of those forces firsthand, I was grateful for his presence.

I had allies. I should have felt strong. I had a whole pack behind me, and a vampire, and a magician. The Band of Tiamat didn't stand a chance against all that.

It had to be enough for whatever they threw at us. It just had to be.

chapter 2

What did people ever do before the Internet? Could you really go to the library to find out that the hit TV show *Paradox PI* was coming to Denver to film a couple of episodes? Because the show's producers certainly hadn't chosen to let me know.

I found this information after searching on Harry Houdini, trying to learn more about him. What I found, I liked. He traveled, did thousands of performances and demonstrations of stage magic and escapism. He loved debunking fakes. He claimed that he wanted to believe—he was desperate for proof that the mediums and séances he discredited could actually reach the "other side" and communicate with the dead. But every one he encountered used tricks and stagecraft. When Houdini was alive, the supernatural was still hidden. It kept to shadows and refused to draw back the curtains. I had a theory: You could tell who the real mediums and psychics were because they didn't advertise, they didn't brag, and they certainly weren't going to look for attention from someone like Houdini. Ironically, in his search for the real deal, Houdini drove the real deal away, deeper into hiding. He'd have loved this day and age.

As Professor Olafson had said, Houdini promised that if it was possible, he would deliver a message after his death. Despite hundreds of mediums and séances attempting to help him to do that, the world was still waiting.

Paradox PI did an entire episode on the search for Houdini's message from beyond and didn't find anything. Now they were coming to Denver.

I'd seen a few episodes of the show. They specialized in paranormal investigation, especially haunted houses. Went in, set up all kinds of cameras, microphones, infrared scanners, motion detectors, seismographs, and so on, hoping to record some evidence of spectral activity. They usually found something small and indeterminate—heavy breathing in a room where no one had been, the flash of a shadow on a camera, or a drop in temperature in a hallway. The on-camera team—two men and a woman (the woman had beautiful, flowing raven hair and tended to wear tight shirts and jeans)—would stand around, regarding the "evidence" and nodding sagely, and happily inform the haunted establishment's owner that while they couldn't *prove* the place was haunted, this looked pretty cool. The whole thing had a reality-TV aesthetic, lots of shaky video footage of people talking, the occasional expletive bleeped out. It promoted a sense of artificial urgency. They'd never come up with something as definitive as an image of Jacob Marley rattling his chains, but they always pretended that they might. Bottom line: It was a TV show, not paranormal investigation.

Since the emergence of the supernatural—the government acknowledging the existence of vampires and

werewolves, my own show exploiting the topic merci-
lessly, dozens of others jumping on the bandwagon—the
fakes had been having a field day. When you'd seen a werewolf shape-shift on live TV, the psychic hotline somehow
seemed a lot more reasonable.

I wanted to know what side of the line *Paradox PI* fell
on: sensationalist TV show exploiting interest in the supernatural, or genuine paranormal investigators? I wasn't
necessarily going to try to expose them as fakes. But getting a story out of them would be icing.

Now I just had to figure out how I could crash the
party.

I brought all my powers as a prominent media figure to
bear in my quest. Well, basically, I sweet-talked a production assistant at the company into giving me the Denver
filming schedule. It took me about three tries, calling at
different times of the day, before I hit on the right person,
but it worked.

They'd already been in the area three days, covering
some of the more famous locations like the Brown Palace
Hotel in downtown Denver, and the Stanley Hotel sixty
miles north in Estes Park. On day four, the PI gang was
scheduled to examine Cheesman Park. Of course they
were. This was the classic haunting that had supposedly
inspired the movie *Poltergeist,* not that the latter bore any
resemblance to the former. About a hundred years ago, a
cemetery had been cleared of its headstones and spruced
up to make way for a park and fancy neighborhood. And
no, the bodies hadn't been moved. Or they had, but by

cut-rate labor that had dumped them together and swept them under the carpet, so to speak. Since then, reports of angry spirits flourished: headless women in Victorian gowns searching for their skulls, ghosts rattling shutters and doors, that sort of thing. No little girls getting sucked into TVs, though.

I arrived at the park before the TV crew did, so I waited, parked along the winding street in my hatchback.

A half hour later, with about an hour to go before dusk—very scenic and photogenic considering the subject matter—a functional white van pulled alongside the curb and parked some fifty yards behind me, near the picturesque fountain area. They might have been plumbers on a dinner break, but a couple of guys got out, opened up the back, and lugged out a camera, a high-end video job. They spent about fifteen minutes setting it up, then one of them spoke on a cell phone. Ten minutes later, a shiny black van with the show's logo painted on it pulled up and parked on the street, and the cameraman filmed it all. Stock footage, the PIs' arrival, with the lovely backdrop of golden westering sun slanting across the park. Rapt, I watched.

The guys filmed the *Paradox PI* team getting out of the vehicle. Then they lowered the cameras, and everyone milled for a moment.

I made my move.

I jumped out of my car and strode toward the cluster of people and vehicles. I had my sights on Gary Janson, the show's front man both in front of and behind the camera. Tall, maybe six-five, and burly, he had an intimidating presence, but his dark trimmed beard hid a bit of paunch. He'd probably spent more of his life in front of computers than running from poltergeists.

If I had gotten all the way to Janson without anyone stopping me, that would have told me something about how this show was run. But I didn't, which told me that this wasn't a bunch of amateurs. They had a professional production staff. One of the techs climbed out of the white van and intercepted me, jogging slightly, a bit of panic in his eyes.

He held his hand out at me. "I'm sorry, we're filming a TV show. Can I ask you to stay on that side of the park?"

"I know you're filming. I was hoping I could talk to Gary and the gang. I'm Kitty Norville." I gave him my biggest "gosh, gee" smile and offered my hand.

His eyes went round and a little shocky.

"Hey, I recognize you! You're that werewolf!" This came from a woman by the dark van—the show's raven-haired hottie, Tina McCannon. Seeing her in person, I was even more convinced she'd been chosen for her model-quality looks, measurements, and preternaturally tight T-shirts rather than any of her other abilities. She pointed at me with the same urgency someone might have when saying, "She's a witch! Burn her!" I gritted my teeth behind my smile. Being the country's first celebrity were-wolf had its more interesting moments.

Out of the corner of my eye, I noticed the tech guy had signaled to the cameraman to film this. Groovy. If I could be charming enough, they might end up with a very special episode of *Paradox PI,* guest starring Kitty Norville. The publicity opportunity was mouthwatering. Their audience was bigger than mine.

"Hi!" I said cheerfully. "You're Tina, right? You're much taller in person."

She blinked at me, confused.

The third member of the on-camera team, Jules Simpson, came around from the other side of the van, watching with interest. He was dark-skinned, with short-cropped hair and wire-rimmed glasses. He dressed in a sweater and slacks, an intelligentsia hipster. He was British, and his accent played as well on TV as Tina's figure.

"What are you doing here?" Tina said, still confused. She didn't seem to know what to make of me, which was pretty funny considering she was supposed to be a paranormal investigator.

"I was hoping I could interview you, maybe have you come onto my show. I know I probably should have called first." My shrug was perhaps exaggerated. "But I was in the neighborhood and thought I'd stop by."

Gary, who'd been regarding me more studiously, arms crossed, back to the van, said, "And how did you know where we'd be?"

"Psychic?" I said, not very convincingly.

Donning a determined expression, the head of the group came to some decision. "Tell you what: Let us interview you, and then we'll return the favor. Deal?"

Of course he gave me no time to think about this. But I wasn't one to turn down camera time. Not anymore.

"Sure. Sounds great." I gave him a wolfish smile. He probably didn't interpret it as anything but friendly.

Turned out they didn't have anything exciting planned for this session of filming. The Paradox team wandered through the park, followed by the camera, collecting atmospheric stock footage. Gary talked about the history of the park, a canned speech that had been written beforehand outlining the more lurid details while gesturing across the expanse of lawn. *There's where a hundred*

*headstones were ripped from the earth and tossed aside,
there's where cut-rate gravediggers dumped a dozen skel-
etons into one undersized coffin* . . . It seemed more like a
tale of bureaucratic terror than a ghost story. I stayed out
of the way and watched.

Tina kept looking at me like she expected me to growl
and sprout fangs. It made me nervous. The more I glanced
back at her, the more nervous *she* got, which created something of a feedback loop. I finally just tried to ignore her.

If Gary was the leader and did most of the talking and
directing of cameras, and Tina was support crew and eye
candy, Jules seemed to be the brains of the outfit. He paid
little attention to me, the cameras, or even Gary and Tina,
focusing instead on a handheld device, a little metal box
with some kind of dial on the front. He moved slowly,
careful not to jostle it, and seemed to be making a circuit
of the area.

Tina was looking at me again. Instead of ignoring her
this time, I faced her directly. "What's Jules doing?"

"EMF readings. You need me to explain that?" Her
tone was suspicious.

I seemed to remember something about it and thought
I could show her up. "Some people believe an increase
in electromagnetic activity in an area might indicate evidence of supernatural activity. Some people . . . don't." I
smiled with fake sweetness. Jules certainly seemed very
serious about it.

"So you have done some research. Nice." Thoughtful,
she walked away to join Gary and the cameras, before I
could get the last word in.

To the naked eye, the only thing haunting the place
were a couple of unsavory-looking kids with skateboards

and a guy with a dog running across the sloping lawn. I returned to the vans and waited, watching.

When the cameras were off and everyone had gathered again by the parking lot, the sun had almost set. Gary and crew would return tomorrow during daylight hours to set up an array of high-tech gadgetry and sensor equipment. Tomorrow night, the fun would begin, or so they hoped.

"So, is it haunted? You picking up any creepy vibes?"

I'd done enough reading on the topic to not be surprised when Gary didn't give me a straight answer. None of these guys ever came right out and said yes or no.

" 'Creepy vibes' aren't a very reliable indication. But the history of activity in this location is so well documented, over such a long period of time, it's difficult to ignore that kind of pedigree."

"But do *you* think it's haunted?" I tried again.

Tina interrupted. "You're a bona fide, documented werewolf. Do you sense anything? You ought to have some kind of awareness or sensitivity. You tell us."

So many things and creatures fell under the heading of paranormal, it wasn't surprising that someone would blur the lines. Even someone who should have known better.

"I didn't have any psychic abilities before becoming a werewolf, and I'm afraid I didn't get any after. I'm just your garden-variety creature feature."

Gary actually chuckled, which made me warm to him. He said, "You're a werewolf who talks like a skeptic. That's pretty ironic."

I loved it when people made assumptions. "Oh, I believe in ghosts. Maybe not the rapping-on-tables, mists-in-the-night kind of ghosts. But I believe that something lives on and sticks around, if it has a good enough reason to."

"Sounds like there's a story behind that," Jules said. "You have a location where we could go, try to get a few readings?"

"No, I don't," I said flatly. He was right—there was a story. But they didn't need to know how I'd watched my best friend, T.J., die, and how one of the things that kept me going was believing he was still watching over me. Still, I wasn't convinced any disembodied spirit would obligingly stamp an imprint on something as mundane as the light and sound of a camera or microphone.

Gary intervened. "We could talk more about this over dinner. You know a good place to eat?"

I couldn't have hoped for a better opening. "As a matter of fact, I do."

Of course I took the gang to New Moon.

A semiprivate dining room in back gave us a little quiet.

"Why Denver?" I asked, while the staff brought out glasses of soda and water.

Gary said, "I'm hoping the show lasts long enough that we get to every major city eventually. Apart from that, Denver's got some good stories. Some classic hauntings are here."

"Have you found anything good yet?" I said.

"The Brown Palace," Gary said.

Tina leaned forward. "There's this story about a ghostly waiter in an old-fashioned uniform leaving the service elevator. We did a bunch of readings there. The EMF numbers were through the roof—"

"The trouble is," Jules said, "it's an elevator. Of course there's going to be increased electrical activity."

Tina continued, undaunted. "We got a recording of a baby crying. There's been reports of a ghostly baby crying for years—"

"But we checked the guest register and there was a baby staying in the hotel that night. The sound could have carried," Jules said.

Gary shrugged. "This is how it goes. As long as there's a plausible, mundane explanation, we can't call our findings conclusive."

I said, "How do you deal with skeptics? When things like ghost photography have been pretty much debunked—"

Gary gathered himself, lacing his fingers on the table in front of him and taking a breath in preparation for a long speech. Tina rolled her eyes, like she'd heard this a thousand times. Jules smirked.

"There's the supernatural, then there's really the supernatural. There's proof, then there's proof. Once you've explained, discounted, and debunked every piece of evidence you possibly can—there's still something there. Something that can't be explained. That's what we do. We go in, try to explain away everything about these phenomena we possibly can. Then we look at what's left. That's as close to proof as we'll get. We're scientists, not spiritualists."

"'When you have eliminated the impossible, whatever remains, however improbable, must be the truth,'" I quoted Arthur Conan Doyle.

"Sherlock Holmes. That's right," Gary said.

"You know Arthur Conan Doyle believed in fairies? He

didn't think it was possible for a couple of little girls to fool everyone with a cheap camera and paper cutouts."

"You know the other side of that story, right?" said Jules. His British accent was regional, distinctive. From somewhere in London, maybe. "That the girls really saw fairies. They just couldn't get anyone to believe them until they did up those photos. Funny, isn't it?"

"You can ask for proof all you want," Gary said. "But can you trust it once you have it? That's the tough part. Especially where the paranormal is concerned. So much of it is taken on someone's word."

"At least until the day we can get a ghost to sit in front of the camera for an interview," Tina said. They all made noises, huffs and groans, like this was a long-running joke. In fact, I remembered a scene on a past show: Tina pointing the camera at empty space, asking silly questions, *And what made you decide to become a ghost? How's the food? Any word from Elvis?*

I decided the *Paradox PI* guys weren't just the stars of a TV show—they were in earnest about their work, and I could take them seriously. We were on the same page, and I wanted to get them on my show more than ever.

"How'd you all get interested in this? Ghost hunting, paranormal investigation, whatever."

Gary, it turned out, lost his brother when he was young. Since then, he'd been searching for some kind of hope, some evidence, that his life hadn't simply ended. If I recalled correctly, Arthur Conan Doyle became obsessed with the paranormal when he lost his son. The same story playing out. Conan Doyle had turned to mediums and séances. Gary turned to science. Tina told a story of a ghostly encounter when she was a little girl, a young woman in antique clothing appearing in the attic of their old New England house. She was a believer through and through, but Gary's methods appealed to her more than those of the table-rapping set.

"That, and I like trying to scare people," she added with a grin. "It's amazing: Someone can be the most hard-nosed skeptic in the world, but you tell them something's definitely there, you can actually watch their hair turn white. It's awesome."

"Jules has the real credentials here," Gary said. "He's a fifth-generation member of the SPR—"

"Which is—"

Jules answered in a patient, humoring-toddlers voice. "Society for Psychical Research. The oldest and most respected group of its kind."

"Except for maybe the Catholic Church," Tina said.

"That's different," Gary said.

I leaned forward. "Slow down. What's the Catholic Church have to do with paranormal investigation?"

Again, the humoring-toddlers voice, from Gary this time. "We hunt ghosts, they hunt demons."

This conversation just went around the bend for me. But I'd sort of asked for it. I sat back and let it happen.

Jules said, "The society has always tried to bring scientific reasoning to bear on the subject of the supernatural. With varying degrees of success . . ."

"They believed the fairy photos, didn't they?" I said.

"Only some of them," he said, almost pouting.

"The society represents a lot of experience," Gary said.

Tina, I noticed, had started staring off, distracted, through the French doors to the main area of the restaurant.

"Tina," I said. She flinched a little, startled. "Are you okay?"

She looked at me, looked back through the door. Pursed her lips and furrowed her brow like she was trying to figure out a problem. "Yeah. It's just this place is really . . . I don't know. There's something weird here." She shook whatever thought it was away. "Do you know if there have been any reports of activity?"

Like, besides all the activity that goes on in a busy restaurant? "You mean ghosts? I'm not sure."

"It's just . . ." She set her jaw, and I caught her looking out at the dining room again. Specifically at a couple sitting at the bar, and another by a table in the corner. Back and forth, then at me. Like she was comparing.

I had a lightbulb moment. Tina was looking at all the other lycanthropes, werewolves who were members of my pack who were here. She was looking at them the way she'd looked at me earlier—nervous, tense. Could she see what we were? I'd have to find a way to get her alone and ask her about it.

"I think it's just this building," Tina said dismissively. "It looks old. I bet it's haunted." She looked around at her colleagues hopefully for confirmation.

"I don't know," Gary said. "You know the history of this place?"

"Not a clue," I said. I wasn't about to blow my friends' cover by announcing that it was popular with werewolves. "Now. Tell me what I have to do to get you guys to come on my show. Hey, I've got a great idea. You'll still be in town Friday, right? How about this . . ."

Two birds with one stone. I'd come along on one of their haunted-house trips, broadcast my show remotely, and talk to them about paranormal investigation. At the same time, they'd interview me as part of their show—the supernatural's take on the paranormal, if that wasn't too confusing.

Jules looked across the table at Gary. It was a sinister look. "How 'bout we take her to Flint House?"

Gary gave a low chuckle. "Oh, that'll be perfect." Tina nodded in agreement. They all had eager gleams in their eyes.

"What? What's Flint House?" I was starting to feel like the butt of a joke. "I've seen that look on people's faces before a really brutal hazing."

"Tell her," Jules said.

Gary said, "It's an old house, an old neighborhood. It has a long history of well-documented activity. Somebody died there—"

"I thought that was one of the prerequisites for a haunted house," I said. "Somebody died there. Ergo, ghost."

"This is different. This was just a few years ago, and the person who died was a paranormal investigator. Some of us think the house killed him."

And I couldn't complain, because I'd asked for it.

Our plans set, I saw the PI crew off and headed for home.

I'd parked a couple of blocks down from the restaurant. Night was full dark now, and the air had turned cold. I kept looking over my shoulder as I walked. It had occurred to me more than once over the last week that maybe no one was out to get me. Maybe the Band of Tiamat hadn't sent anyone to kill me, they'd just gotten someone to burn that message on the door, and that was all. I'd done the rest myself, assuming it was a warning, an opening salvo, and that something worse would be along soon.

Nights like this, though, chill and dark, I could convince myself that I heard footsteps. Heavy steps on the concrete, claws scraping with every movement as some hulking beast stalked me. Since Vegas, I'd done a lot of reading on Tiamat and her band of demons. None of it was pretty. She was supposed to be the mother of the elder gods, one of the creators of the cosmos, a personification of salt water, who blended with Apsu, the personification of fresh water, to create life. It was all very symbolic and Freudian. Then war came, with the founding gods and the newer gods trying to destroy each other. Tiamat created a horde of serpents, dragons, and monsters to do battle for her. They were defeated. She was cut in half to form heaven and earth, and her tears formed the Tigris and Euphrates rivers.

I had to ask: Was this supposed to be literal? Did this really happen at the dawn of civilization, inhuman demons lumbering across the landscape, doing battle? Or was it a metaphor, and if so, a metaphor for what? I'd spent a lot of time discovering how many of those old stories of gods, demons, witches, vampires—werewolves—and magic were true. Not all the stories were. So much of an ancient myth like this was metaphor that was repeated across stories and cultures. What metaphor was the Tiamat cult worshipping? How far would they go to get me?

I had to get my mind off this or I'd completely freeze up. I pulled out my cell phone and hit speed dial.

"What's wrong?" Ben said, before hello, even. Just the sound of his voice made my shoulders relax a notch. He was okay, no one had gotten him.

Smiling, I said, "You always assume something's wrong."

He chuckled. "Because it usually is."

"Nothing's wrong. This time," I said, hating the whine in my voice. "At least, I don't think it's anything. It's dark. I got lonely."

"Are you on the way home?"

"Yeah." Finally, I reached my car. I took one last look around, up and down the street, at parked cars, hunched buildings, and weird shadows cast by old streetlamps. Anything could be hiding here. Rick's patterns, waiting to strike. My nose wasn't helping. All I smelled was oil, concrete, city.

"Nothing's gone after you yet, it probably won't start right this minute," Ben said. He was a lawyer, always the practical one, able to rationalize just about anything.

"It's waiting for me to let my guard down."

"Is your guard down?"

Safe in my car, I said, "How would I know? Though if my guard was down, I suppose I'd stop thinking about it. I kind of like that idea."

"Just hurry home. I haven't seen you all day." I heard the twinge in his voice. He couldn't hide it. He was nervous, too.

"Roger," I said and waited for him to hang up before I did.

We were a pack, and we needed to be together, so I raced home, maybe a little faster than was safe. Wolf needed her pack, after all.

chapter 3

A couple of days before my next show, when I would tag along with the *Paradox PI* team, we had a full moon to get through.

I stood at the front door and called back to Ben. "Aren't you ready yet?"

"Stop nagging, I'm coming." He marched from the bedroom, with no revealing evidence of what had delayed him.

"I'm not nagging," I complained. Nagged, actually. We were late. The sun was setting. We were due in the mountains soon. With my luck, we'd get stuck in traffic on the way there. Shift into wolves behind the dash of my hatchback. Wouldn't that be exciting?

"Yes, you are." Ben joined me and dropped a kiss on my forehead.

"You think that makes everything better?" But the warm flush in my gut said that yes, it did make things quite a bit better.

What all the stories and romances don't say is that happily ever after doesn't just happen. You have to work at it. You have to keep working at it.

We still argued.

"I don't want to do this," he said as we made our way to the car. By "this" he meant the full-moon ritual that drew our werewolf pack together, to Change, to run, to hunt. To stop being human.

"You say that every time."

"And it's true every time."

"But do you have to keep saying it?"

"If I didn't know better, I'd say you like it," he said, almost cutting.

"So do you, and that's why you insist on saying you hate it."

"Ah, in with the pop psychology."

"That's me," I said happily. He grumbled wordlessly.

We drove in a stretch of silence until we reached I-70.

"I miss the old days," Ben said suddenly. "When it was just the two of us."

The old days. Our pack of two. We'd Change, run, hunt together as a pair. Sleep curled together, wake human, naked, in the great outdoors. Aroused, inhibitions lowered to nothing—we'd spent some very nice mornings together, after full-moon nights.

"Maybe we can sneak off for a little while. The rest of the pack won't miss us." I smiled thinking of it.

Ben wore the same dreamy smile. "Hmm. Makes me almost look forward to it."

On the drive into the mountains, I watched the rear-view mirror, waiting to see someone following us. No one did, and we arrived at our destination. One of these days someone in a uniform was going to discover this wooded field at the end of a remote dirt track filled with cars at midnight on full-moon nights. I hadn't figured out a better way to get the pack to wilderness. Charter a bus, maybe?

My skin itched, every square millimeter, every pore. The car parked and silent, the world dark around us, I sat in the driver's seat. Ben sat beside me. Outside, people lingered at the edges of the field, waiting for us.

"I don't like this," I said. This was the first full moon since we found the word *Tiamat* defacing New Moon's door. "I can't get rid of the feeling that someone's watching us."

Ben shook his head. "We're a pack. Nothing can get to us if we stick together."

That didn't make me feel any better. "You're supposed to tell me that nothing's out there, that I'm being paranoid and everything's going to be fine."

"Everything's going to be fine," he said unconvincingly.

Sighing, I got out of the car.

"Hey," Shaun called to us from the trees. Shaun was, for lack of a better word, our lieutenant, our right-hand wolf. He also managed New Moon for us. Brown-skinned, dark-eyed, he wore a T-shirt and jeans and went barefoot. He was rubbing his arms like he was nervous.

"Is everything okay?" I said. "You see anything, smell anything?"

"Seems clear." But he shook his head and sounded uncertain.

The forest didn't look any different. The conifers stood tall and black against a sky painted deep, deep blue by moonlight. The moon sang to my sensitive ears. *It's time.* Maybe it was a matter of expectation. We were expecting something to happen, something wrong and dangerous, and so we looked through the trees and saw more danger than was really there.

Some of the pack members had left their clothing in their cars and walked out naked, like ghosts, moving with purpose. Others had already Changed; they were larger than natural wolves, waist-high, padding forward, heads low to smell for scents, tails out like rudders. Becky, Mick, Tom, Kris. The first ones to Change tended to like being wolves, or weren't able to control themselves as well. They came to our territory, with the moon shining on them, and the wolves took over. These animals trotted to me, their backs at my hips, heads and tails low, looking away. I reached out, hands spread, and let their bodies pass under my touch. My fingers left tracks in the thick velvet of their fur. Grays, browns, tans, blacks. Their eyes glinted yellow and amber. I pressed my lips in a smile.

The ones who were more comfortable in their wolf skins seemed to revel in these nights. The few of us who lingered by the cars, kept our clothing on, our human trappings, still resisted, even though most of us had lived this life for years.

All of them, wolf and human, showed deference to me. The bowed heads, slumped backs, tails flattened between their legs when they looked at me. They didn't look *at* me, but around me, glancing away, not daring to meet my gaze, to offer challenge. All of this was body language that said, *You lead, we'll follow, we trust you.* So much trust shown in a few gestures. Almost, it was comforting—I didn't have to guess what the wolves were thinking about me. In the human world, someone could act like they adored you even as they planned to stab you in the back.

Eighteen of us made up the pack. We'd lost a few people

over the last year to fighting, battles for dominance, all the crises that happen to a pack in transition. I didn't want to lose anyone else. I was desperate not to. I wanted to justify the reverence the others showed me.

I wanted to justify what I'd gone through to become alpha of this pack.

It was my job to keep them all in line. To keep everyone safe—from enemies, from each other. From attention. We came here, to the wild, where no one would get in our way. Where we couldn't hurt anyone. By touch and look, I replied: *Thank you. I will lead, I will keep you safe.* I was more confident on these nights than any other. I had to be. They had to believe me if they were going to feel safe.

A couple more of those still human among us hunched over, skin blurring, bones stretching, fur growing, muscles straining, voices groaning. Their transformations called up something in me. The itching turned to fire. *Time to run.*

The wolves of my pack paced into the woods, to the wilds of our territory.

Ben stood at my shoulder. He kissed my neck. "Ready?"

"No," I said. "I'm never ready for this."

"Yeah." His voice was tight, and I knew what he was feeling. Wolf clawed at my insides, howling, *It's time, it's time.*

We walked farther into the woods, some of us human, some of us wolf, to the place where we made our den. A beautiful spot for a picnic, I always thought, shaded over with trees, a well-worn rock outcropping, lichen-covered granite forming a sheltered space. Plenty of space for a dozen and a half wolves to curl up and sleep. It smelled safe, despite my misgivings. We stripped.

A few steps away, Shaun had taken off his shirt. He looked through the trees, his gaze distant, vacant. His breaths were deep, fast. He grimaced and hunched his back.

A wolf howled, and around us human flesh melted, slipped, morphed into something else. Fur grew on smooth skin, bones stretching. Think of snowmelt becoming a rushing stream.

I quickly hugged Ben. All my muscles tense, I clung to him for a last lucid moment. "I love you," I said.

He kissed me mouth to mouth. Then he fell, groaning, and I fell with him, and the wolves around us surged and whined, hungry, celebrating. I shut my eyes, clamped my jaw, let my mind slip away—

Her mind is torn. Senses in one direction, thoughts in another. Two-legged thoughts, from the other world. Worried, uneasy. But the fear has no shape, and she can't focus on it. Her senses tell her that nothing is wrong. But the tension is there, shared among the whole pack. Tails twitch, ears flicker. Watchful. This is what the furless human world does to them. The pack's children, weaker ones whom she must protect, are especially fearful, slinking close to the ground, whining.

She remembers how that felt, fearing all. She nips and nudges them, encourages them. This is their night. Must not fear.

Her mate is at her side, silver and burning. They bump shoulders, trot side by side, circling around, searching for scent. Hunting.

She stops. Ears up, tail straight. Hackles grow stiff like reeds. Whole body stiff. Because finally she smells it.

Too late, she smells it.

Sulfur, carbon, banked flames from hot coals. The two-legged self provides the names for what she smells. The names don't matter; it's wrong. She whines, yips—at her side, her mate bumps her, flank to flank. They look in all directions, but see nothing. Gather the pack, she thinks. Run. But where? The fear is confused, direction-less. The scent doesn't have a track. It's everywhere. It simply appears.

A wolf yelps, high-pitched, pain-filled.

She hears it and feels rage. One of her pack is in danger, hurt, something has attacked—

She and her mate together—he is at her shoulder—race, bounding in huge strides over brush and bracken until they find their threatened brother.

Not one of the weak ones. A strong male, the beta, able to take care of himself, yet something pins him to the ground, a weight on his back. He yelps and snaps, struggles to twist his mouth around to bite, to free his claws to slash at the thing. He only scratches at dirt. There is a scent of scorched fur.

Nothing attacks their kind. Unless they corner desperate prey, they have no enemies except for two-footed death—enemies from the other halves of their beings. This is something else. Maniacal, deadly, a shadow rising from the earth itself to swallow them.

She attacks. Her mate follows from the other side. Jaws open, throats rough with snarling, they can't see what they attack, they only know something must be there.

But nothing is. They crash into each other and fall to the ground at their brother's side, stunned.

Something sinks against her, pressing her. Human hands, but they're too large, too strong, and too hot. In a panic she lurches, claws into earth, struggling to escape. Writhing with every muscle, she manages it, cries out, and then all her wolves are running. A burning smell fills her and drives her to panic.

They can run very, very fast when they need to.

She nips at flanks, pins her ears at the slow brothers and sisters, urging them on, faster. This is for their lives. The forest becomes a blur, the moonlight a tunnel through which they fly. Lungs pumping, hearts pounding, mouths open to take in air, tails straight out. Miles pass effortlessly. The pack together is a sea of motion.

The smell of sulfur fades. Soon she senses only forest, pine and damp, earth and life, as if the danger has never happened. She lopes around her pack and gives a signal to slow, to settle. The wolves mill, uncertain, panting, ears back—frightened.

So is she. She can't hide it. But she'll watch out for them.

She leads them to a place if not as comfortable as their usual den, at least defensible. It's a space of sheltered trees on the side of a hill, open on all sides—she can watch anything that approaches, smell the air all around. They have plenty of chances to escape. She paces, counts her wolves by scent. All here. All safe, though shaken. She settles in to patrol. To keep watch until morning.

She watches the sunrise. The pack sleeps around her— naked, furless. They've all slipped back to their other halves. It's sad, seeing them like this. But they still smell of pack, of family. Exhausted, sleep is heavy in her eyes, but fear keeps her upright.

Her mate wakens, and his furless hands reach for her. She sniffs him, wet nose tracing his limbs.

"Kitty." His voice is thick, anxious. "You have to sleep. Come back to me, please."

She licks his face, saying, But I'm here, I'm right here.

Others wake, moving slowly, groaning. Some of them flinch, looking around wide-eyed.

She yips. I'm standing guard, you see? I'm keeping watch.

"It's our turn, Kitty. Let us watch. Sleep now." He bends his face to her shoulder. She squirms under his touch. His fear increases hers.

"What's wrong?" another asks.

"She won't sleep."

"Can't say I blame her."

Her mate again, almost desperate. "Shaun and Mick are keeping watch, okay? You can rest now."

He whispers by her ear, soothing. Strokes her flanks. Urges her to sleep. Shelters her with his presence.

Her eyes close. She can no longer stand. When she sleeps, she's curled up tight, stiff with worry.

I convulsed with the feeling of falling. My muscles twitched in anticipation of pain.

But I lay on solid ground, the earth of a forest, and with a great, frightened heave of breath, my lungs filled with Ben's scent.

His embrace tightened around me. "Shh, shh. You're okay. It's okay."

The morning was bright around us. Late morning, by the look and smell of things. I was usually up much earlier than this, the day after running. But Ben and I were both still naked. He held me close, his front to my back, his breath stirring my hair. We weren't in our usual den. His whole body was taut with anxiety.

"What happened?" I sat up, struggling free of him but still keeping hold of his hand, his arms. I still smelled burning coals, like the woods were on fire. But all around me was calm.

"I'm not sure," Ben said. "Something came after us last night."

"Is everyone okay? Where is everyone?" We were alone in our shelter.

"I sent most of them home. I thought they'd be safer away from here. Mick and Shaun are still here."

Watching our backs. Memories returned—images, emotions. We'd all been terrified. How far had we run? I didn't recognize this place. I started shivering and cuddled closer to Ben.

"You're freezing," he murmured. But I couldn't get dressed, because my clothes were back at the old den, miles from here. I looked around, dazed, trying to get my bearings, glancing over my shoulder for something that burned.

Mick and Shaun returned. Fully clothed, they might have been anyone. They'd walked out, studying the area between here and where the attack had come, looking for any evidence of what had happened. They brought our clothing with them. I dressed quickly, trying to get warm.

"What's out there?" I said.

"Nothing," Shaun said, shaking his head. "Just that smell."

The smell of a burned forest. Unseen, a bird called, the sound echoing.

"Shaun—you're okay?" I remembered an image: Shaun was the wolf who'd been attacked first.

"I'm fine," he said, but he looked tired and seemed to be favoring a shoulder. All I remembered from the attack on me was shock and anger.

"Could you tell what it was? What do you remember?" I asked.

He shook his head. "It's blurry. Things are always blurry the morning after—you know. But I could have sworn it had hands. Like it grabbed me and shoved me. It was strong—it must have been huge."

"But did you see anything?"

"No, nothing. But the smell—"

"Fire," I said. I could still smell it, and the odor triggered a feeling of fear.

"Something's hunting us. I don't like it," Mick said, scowling and surly. He was short but stout, built like a brick wall and just as tough. Dark hair in a buzz cut, black eyes looking out. Still gleaming with a little wolf. He and Shaun were some of the first to back my takeover of the pack. I couldn't have a better pair looking out for me. I might have been the alpha, but I couldn't do it without them helping me. I didn't rule by force, but by friendships.

"Let's get back," I said, urgent now, hurrying. I wouldn't let go of Ben's hand. My mind was coming back to me, and the pieces of my body clicked back together after shifting. "I need to make some phone calls."

The four of us went back to the cars.

"You think this is connected to the Tiamat cult?" Ben said. "That this is the attack we've been waiting for?"

"The burned door, the smell of fire here—what else could it be? It was waiting. All this time it was waiting for the full moon."

"Maybe it's a coincidence. Maybe it's random," Ben said. Even he didn't sound convinced.

"That would be worse, don't you think?" I said.

Because then I wouldn't know where to start with trying to figure this out.

chapter 4

First, I called Odysseus Grant.

We'd kept in frequent touch since the message appeared on New Moon's door. He'd been keeping an eye on the Band of Tiamat on their home turf. He didn't believe any of them had left Vegas, which meant the group of lycanthropes that had kidnapped me, and the vampire priestess that had tried to sacrifice me to her goddess, had sent someone—or something—else to leave that note at New Moon. And, I believed, whatever had come after us last night. I told him the latest news.

"The full moon was the trigger," Grant said, after I told him what happened. "I can't say that I'm surprised."

"We should have expected it, is what you're saying." I paced the living room, holding my phone to my ear with one hand, scratching my greasy hair with the other. I was still feeling stiff and cranky, off-balance, Wolf's shadows lurking in my mind. The bars of the cage she lived in most of the time hadn't quite closed yet. I didn't feel quite human, and I didn't want to be talking on the phone. I hadn't even showered yet. This seemed more important.

"Maybe. But there's more to this. You said no one was hurt but that this thing was powerful. You could have been hurt."

"It sure seemed like it. It came out of nowhere. We outran it."

"Anything else you remember? Any detail at all?"

"Fire. The smell of burning coals. And a shape, something with hands that could fight. I don't know. It's not very clear. It's all in wolf senses. Makes it hard to remember."

"I understand. They've sent something after you, that much is obvious. I'll learn what I can. If we can identify it, we can get rid of it."

I already felt better. Right up until he said, "Whatever it is will strike again. Now that it's exposed itself, it won't go back to hiding."

"What does it want? To scare us? Or to kill us?"

He paused before admitting, "I don't know."

This was my fault. I'd brought this thing here. "I don't suppose you know of any cool charms that might work against something like this. Holy water, old Indian arrowheads, that sort of thing."

"Can't hurt to try," he said, as close to encouraging as he ever got. "I'll call you when I learn something."

"Okay. Thanks. I'll talk to you soon." Sooner rather than later, I hoped.

That evening, I called to tell Rick about the new development. We agreed to meet at New Moon to discuss.

The first time Rick came to New Moon, I had to invite him in.

I shouldn't have had to. The legend about having to invite vampires in applied only to private residences. Public places, where people were free to come and go at will, were open to vampires. But Rick had come to New Moon and stopped at the threshold.

He'd looked at me through the glass doorway, only mildly perplexed, like this wasn't the biggest problem he'd faced all day. "This is awkward," he'd said.

"What? What's the matter?" I'd said through the glass.

"There's something odd about this place."

I'd gotten a big grin on my face. Crossed my arms, regarded him smugly, and seriously considered not inviting him in.

"That's because it's not yours," I said. Then I opened the door and invited him in, because when all was said and done, he wasn't just the Master vampire of Denver. He was my friend.

"Arturo never would have let you get away with this," he'd said.

Arturo was the previous vampire running Denver, and this was a place within his city where lycanthropes had power.

"Well. Thanks for not being Arturo."

This night, we sat in the back, at what had become my usual table. Rick leaned back, looking over the thinning late crowd. We were down to barflies and a birthday party in the far corner.

I was distracted, tapping my fingers, waiting for the building to burn down. "You ready for me to tell you what happened last night?"

He made a palm-up gesture, giving me the floor. I told the story again, and it seemed even more vague and less likely than when I told it to Grant. The whole thing was turning into a dream. Rick listened thoughtfully, attentively, brow slightly furrowed. In a lot of ways, of all the vampires I'd ever met, Rick had stayed the most human. He could still engage in the problems and concerns of mere mortals. At least, he could make it look like he did, finger tapping his chin, his dark eyes thoughtful.

I finished, and he sat back in his chair.

"You didn't get a good look at it? You don't know what it was?"

"I don't know. I don't remember seeing anything, only what it felt like. Maybe it wasn't a thing, but a force. You've been around for five centuries. Does stuff like this happen a lot? Have you ever heard of a monster that likes to attack werewolf packs on full-moon nights?"

"And also could be summoned by a vampire," he said.

"Or has something to do with Tiamat. Maybe this isn't a vampire thing."

"I think this goes beyond the Tiamat cult," Rick said. "The cult leader might be using this as an opportunity to get a foothold in this territory."

"Rick, just because the cult is run by a vampire doesn't mean this has anything to do with vampire politics. Does it?"

He glanced away, seeming to ponder, and didn't answer. And wasn't that just what I needed right now, to worry about vampire politics, as well?

Sighing, I said, "We wanted something to happen so we'd have information. So we'd have something to work with. But I feel like we're worse off than before."

"We both have contacts," he said firmly, decisively, in a

way that was probably meant to sound reassuring. "We'll do our research."

"Like standing on rooftops, looking for patterns?"

He seemed to be scanning the crowd. It made me nervous, because I could never forget what he was, and the look in his eyes was appraising. I didn't want him treating my restaurant like *his* restaurant. He absently tapped a finger on the table.

I was about to say something catty to him when he said, "I called Dom. To ask his opinion, for old times' sake."

Dom, the Master of Las Vegas, was only a figurehead. I wasn't entirely clear on the situation, but he was there to divert attention from the real powers there. Like the priestess of the Tiamat cult.

"What did he say?"

"He told me I'd be better off if I stayed out of it and suggested I'd be happier if the local alpha werewolf wasn't so uppity. You seem to have made an impression on him."

"Dom doesn't know anything," I said.

"I know. He refused to talk about the vampire priestess of the cult. Whatever we're up against has him cowed."

Hell, it had *me* almost cowed. This wasn't anything I didn't already know. "How does that fit into your pattern?"

"I know Dom. It would take more than a two-bit cult to cow him."

I hadn't been that impressed with the guy, but Rick had known him for at least a hundred fifty years. Maybe there was more to him. What I didn't want to hear was that we were dealing with something more powerful than a two-bit cult, though it certainly didn't feel two-bit to me.

I rubbed my hair and sighed. "I just don't want anyone to get hurt."

"I know. We'll do our best."

Our best didn't always keep people from getting killed.

When my phone rang at work the next day, I jumped at it, hoping it was Grant with a glorious revelation, or at least a piece of news that would help explain what was after me and the pack. But it wasn't. I didn't recognize the voice.

"Is this Kitty Norville?"

"Yes, can I help you?"

Anxious, the man asked, "I was wondering if I could ask you a few questions about Ted Gurney."

"Ted Gurney? I'm not sure—" But then the name clicked, and the world around me lurched. My stomach froze in the same moment the caller said, "Theodore Joseph Gurney."

T.J.

T.J. had been my best friend. He'd protected me, saved my life, helped me adjust to being a werewolf when I was new to it all. He showed me how I could use the lycanthropy, how it could make me strong, if I could learn to integrate both sides of my being. He'd died in my arms, his heart torn out of his chest by the alpha male of our pack. The pack I had taken over, after watching that same alpha die by the claws of a dozen angry wolves.

Revenge was supposed to make me feel better.

Grief for him had turned into something like a land mine. It would lie quietly for days, weeks even, me not thinking of him, not dwelling. But then something would come along to set it off. Then his death felt like it happened yesterday.

I couldn't hide my suspicion. Why was this land mine bringing up T.J. now? "Why do you want to know about him? Why are you calling me?"

He sounded like he'd prepared the speech. "I have a copy of a police report of a murder that happened outside your apartment a little over a year ago. You're listed as a witness, and you named Ted Gurney as the murderer."

Here was a ghost. Metaphorical, but here he was. I could see T.J.'s face appearing before me.

"Who are you?" I demanded, half rising from my chair, ready to growl.

He hesitated. I could almost hear him swallow. "My name is Peter Gurney. I'm his brother."

That knocked the wind out of me. I sank back, trying to figure out what to say, what to think. T.J. never told me he had a brother. I didn't know anything about his life before I met him.

Peter Gurney filled the silence. "I'm looking for my brother. I've spent the last year tracking him down. It hasn't been easy, I know he doesn't want to be found. But I really need to find him. The trail dried up here, and the last sign I can find of him anywhere is this police report. I need to know: Do you know him? Did he really kill someone? Do you have any idea where he is?"

He didn't know T.J. was dead. I didn't know how I was going to talk to this guy.

"Where are you? Are you here in Denver?" I said.

"Yeah."

That made it harder, and maybe a little easier. I wanted to look him in the eye. For T.J. "Can we meet someplace? I can answer your questions, but I'd rather do this in person."

"Yeah. Okay." He sounded nervous. He had to suspect what was coming, didn't he? "Just tell me where."

I sent him to New Moon and met him there half an hour later.

Peter was waiting just inside the front door, glancing around like he wasn't sure he wanted to be here. He was younger than I was expecting. Twenty, maybe. Lanky, boyish, scuffing a nervous foot on the floor. But I spotted him right off. He looked like T.J.: dark hair, sharp face. A young T.J., like he might have been as a teenager. Weirdly, though, his scent was different. T.J. worked on motorcycles and always smelled a little like grease. He also smelled like wolf, of course. He smelled like all the familiar little parts of his life. Peter didn't have that. He smelled like travel: fast-food restaurants, gas stations, clothes that needed washing. No wolf at all.

I greeted him as I walked in. "Hi, Peter? I'm Kitty."

"Oh. Hi." We shook hands.

"Let's sit in back." I gestured him to my favorite table in the back of the bar, where we wouldn't be disturbed. "You want anything to drink? Soda, tea . . . double whiskey?" My smile, like my humor, was weak.

"Just water," he said, and I relayed the request, water for Peter, soda for me, to one of the staff while we settled in.

We looked at each other across the table. I had so many questions. I didn't know anything about T.J.'s past. Nothing of him remained after I'd lost him. Suddenly, here was a connection, answers—evidence that he'd ever lived at all. I wanted to cling to Peter, but he wouldn't have understood any of that. At least not until I had a chance to explain what had happened to his brother. Which I didn't want to do. I didn't want to be the one to extinguish his hope.

Peter spoke first. "Kitty, can you tell me where my brother is?"

There was no way to soft-pedal this. Out with it, that was all I could do. Calmly, methodically, I started in on it.

"How much do you know about him and what he was doing here? When was the last time you talked to him?"

He hesitated a moment, editing his response maybe, like he didn't want to tell me anything. "It's been a long time. I know he moved out here a while ago. He doesn't have a regular job—he fixes bikes. I know he's hiding, but I need to find him. I know he'll want to see me." He was tense, leaning on the table, desperate. And he didn't have a clue.

I said, "Did you know he was a werewolf?"

He chuckled, disbelieving. "What?"

"T.J.—Ted—was a werewolf. Like me. We were part of the same pack. He was my best friend."

He stared. "You're not serious."

I soldiered on. The words were cotton in my mouth. I just kept spitting them out. What else could I do? "There was a fight. It happens sometimes, like with natural wolves. They—we—have fights for dominance. Your brother was killed. He died protecting me."

Stricken, he murmured, "I don't believe you."

"I'm sorry. I'm sorry you had to find out like this. I

wish—" Of course I wished it had all turned out different. That wasn't the right thing to say. I shook my head. "T.J.—everyone here called him T.J.—never told me anything about his family. I didn't really know anything about him, other than his life here. It never occurred to me that he was hiding. I have so many questions—"

"Do you have proof? Is there a grave? A death certificate? I should have been able to find a death certificate."

He'd died in a werewolf battle, in the hills. The body had vanished, dropped by the other wolves down some dark hole where no one would find it. The pack cleaned up its messes precisely so there wouldn't be a trail for the police, or people like Peter, to follow.

"No. I'm sorry."

"Why didn't you tell the police this?" He was growing angry, his face flushed, puckered from grief, from a struggle not to cry. So he did believe me, deep down. At some level, he must have suspected how his search would end.

"Because it wasn't their business." I smiled sadly at the harshness of my tone. What a bitter assessment of the situation. It must have sounded shocking. "Because they'd need the same kind of proof, which I didn't have. I didn't want them to keep asking questions."

"But if he was killed, if someone killed him—"

"The man who killed him is dead, if that helps."

By the stark expression of shock he wore, I guessed it didn't. No—I'd watched the man who killed him die, and it didn't help me at all.

I was about to ask him more about T.J.—where had he come from, what other family did he have, why didn't he want to be found? But Peter, his gaze down, pushed away from the table. I wanted to hear everything, but I'd had a year to live with T.J.'s death. Peter had just learned about it. He wasn't ready.

"This is crazy," he said. "I'll find out what happened. What really happened."

His long strides carried him to the front door in moments. I let him go. What else could I do?

I stayed put to finish my soda, but I was having trouble getting even that past the lump in my throat. I covered my eyes with a hand when the tears started.

"Hey, you okay?"

Through a gap in my fingers I saw Shaun standing next to me.

"Headache," I muttered.

By his smirk I could tell he wasn't convinced. I scrubbed my already reddened face and looked at him full on. "That guy who was just here?"

"Yeah? Hey, if he hurt you I'll—"

Aw, wasn't that sweet? "No. Apparently, T.J. has a younger brother. That was him."

"Oh. Oh, shit." He sank into the chair opposite me.

"Yeah." I smiled stiffly. Shaun had known T.J., too.

An unplanned moment of silence, of grief, followed.

Shaun said, "What did he want?"

I sighed. "To find his brother. I told him he couldn't. The guy has a right to be upset."

"What are you going to do?"

"Not a lot I can do. But if he stops by again, be nice to him."

chapter 5

I had a lot to put out of my mind before the show on Friday. T.J.'s brother haunted me—like T.J. I tried to imagine his story, to make up the background that built their lives. What made T.J. leave his family, disappearing so utterly that his brother had to turn detective to find him? What drove Peter to go through the trouble? The stories I came up with were all unhappy, and it made me unhappy to think of it. T.J. had always been so levelheaded. I couldn't imagine him in that kind of life. I didn't want to. I wanted to let him rest, to preserve the memories I did have.

The Band of Tiamat's recent attack was at the front of my mind, aggravating because of how little I could do about it. All I knew: They had sent something against me, and it involved fire. And maybe a vampire conspiracy, if Rick was right. I had to hope Rick or Grant found something out. Or wait until it struck again and we learned more about it.

I thought about calling Gary and canceling the Friday gig with the *Paradox PI* team. Maybe the house was really haunted, maybe it wasn't. I wasn't sure I could deal with another confrontation with supernatural weirdness, in either case. But as cliché as it sounded, staying home and cowering would have felt like losing ground. Would have admitted that whatever attacked us had gotten to me. I didn't want to do that.

If we ignored it, would it go away? Despite what my mother told me about my big sister's teasing, that never worked. But I hadn't yet let the scariness in my life interfere with the show. In fact, I sometimes thought having the show to focus on saved my sanity. I needed my sanity right now.

Ben insisted on coming with me to meet the Paradox crew. I didn't even have to ask. Safety in numbers. We could watch each other's backs.

I did a little research about Flint House on my own before heading out on Friday night. The death of the investigator hadn't made it into major news outlets, so it took some digging into publicly released police reports to discover anything about it. A short investigation determined that the death was accidental—he'd fallen down the stairs. That sort of thing didn't draw any attention or raise any eyebrows, but the paranormal community jumped on the story and ran with it.

The usual background applied: The house was a hundred twenty years old, a stately Victorian, built by a silver mogul with more money than sense, and bad luck followed him. Several of his children died of illness or injury. His wife committed suicide. He went mad and died young. The house was sold, and the new owner immediately began reporting the usual haunting symptoms: strange noises, drops in temperature, voices in rooms where nobody was talking. That owner moved out and rented the house to a couple who within the year died in a messy murder–suicide situation. The house was sold again, and again, and now it had stood empty for almost ten years, because no one was willing to live there.

The body count piled up over the years. Every death could be attributed to normal, nonsupernatural causes, but this went beyond the law of averages or mere coincidence. Consensus among those who studied these things: The house was killing people.

It stood in an older part of Denver, west of the freeway, in one of those neighborhoods that started out as the wealthier side of town, lined with lots of Victorian houses; then went downhill, the houses falling into disrepair and the yards becoming choked with weeds; then became the really bad part of town; then slowly underwent a gentrification that was turning it into the artsy part of town.

The house wasn't the nicest on the street, but it wasn't the worst. The pale green exterior could have used a coat of paint, and rather than lawn the yard held a forest of shrubbery that hadn't been pruned back in a decade. Two stories and an attic, with a round window, looked out on the street. The place was dark. I wished the Paradox crew hadn't told me it was haunted. It would have looked perfectly normal, otherwise. Now it did look rather sinister.

The *Paradox PI* vans were already here, and a camera crew was already filming background footage, a few shots of the team poking around the yard and wrought-iron fence. A wrought-iron fence complete with spikes lining the top—of *course* the place was haunted.

The KNOB van, black, with the station logo painted on the side in big letters, was also here, with Matt and one of his minions waiting in the front seats. We had a few hours before we needed to set up, but I wanted to watch the team work and record a bunch of material to play back later.

We emerged from the car, and I got to work, gathering the gang over and making introductions. "This is my husband, Ben." It still felt weird saying that, but people smiled, and no one else acted like it was unusual.

Gary said, "Ben, I know this is personal, but I have to ask, what's it like being married to a werewolf?"

I was outed. Ben wasn't. We looked at each other. With great interest, I waited for the answer. He pressed his lips in a wry smile, filled with everything he *might* say. What he *did* say when he looked back at Gary was, "It's a howling good time, I suppose."

Ben tried to wink at me. It looked kind of leering. I winced and shook my head. There were groans all the way around.

Tina gave Ben a narrow-eyed, suspicious look, like the one she wore at New Moon the other night, and like when she looked at me, as if she knew something, or at least suspected something. I *really* needed to talk to her privately.

The film crew asked Ben to wait in the van and had me get back in the car so they could film me stepping out and walking up to shake hands with Gary and company—twice. That was reality TV for you.

Gary filmed an opening narration while Matt and I taped my own introduction.

Gary spoke at his camera in the no-nonsense, explanatory tone his viewers had come to know and love. "The house was originally built by George Flint, a silver miner who struck it rich. He raised a family here, but they had a lot of tragedy in this house. One daughter died of pneumonia. A son was trampled by a horse right outside, about where the streetlight is now. The ghost stories started almost immediately."

My own narration was a little different. And, I could admit, a little more sensationalist. "I'm here at Flint House, the house that kills people. Or maybe it's just haunted. Or maybe it's just stories. I'm here at the special invitation of Gary Janson of *Paradox PI*. I get to tag along while the crew tapes a show, and we'll see if anything happens, and maybe get some insight into the world of paranormal investigation."

We trooped into the house next. The interior was as sadly faded as the outside. It gave the impression that it had been beautiful, once: dark red carpeting, now worn down and threadbare; wood paneling gone black with age; peeling wallpaper; wires hanging out of holes where light fixtures should be. No evidence remained that this used to be anyone's home.

It took a couple of hours to film the gang setting up all their equipment. Jules did a lot of the on-camera work, although a couple of off-camera assistants helped. Tina did her usual posing. Gary discussed timing with one of the show's tech guys.

It all looked so much more tidy on the finished episodes.

I had my own thing going, following Gary around with a microphone, asking, "What's this do? What's this do? Why are you doing this?" Patient guy, was Gary.

Jules, not so much. "We're not going to get anything with her babbling on," he muttered. "We're likely to scare off anything that's here."

I overheard and couldn't help but comment. The cameras and my microphone were picking all this up for posterity, which pleased me immensely. "What? You're afraid of scaring the house that kills people?"

"Would you stop calling it that?" he said, scowling.

"Am I going to offend it?"

"You might. If this place is haunted, nobody really knows why. Was there an original triggering event, unfinished business of the original owners? Or has the negative energy built up over the years? But if there is a presence here, you don't want to aggravate it, do you?"

I shrugged. "We want to see some activity, right? Maybe we do want to rile it up a little." Though based on what was happening in my own life right now, I ought to be a little more careful. I ought to be walking on eggshells.

And I really shouldn't be standing in a house with a reputation for killing people. I suddenly wanted to step outside for some air.

All the monitors, heat sensors, cameras, and microphones were in place. We retreated to the *Paradox PI* van, set up in grand cinematic CIA glory. Banks of TV monitors relayed what the cameras showed us. Speakers hissed and cracked with static—background noise inside the house. But wouldn't it be cool if chains started rattling and a voice moaned? Jules sat at the far end, headphones crammed over his ears, staring intently at a monitor. Tina sat nearby, a little less intent, gaze flicking from one screen to another. Gary sat with me. A smaller camera mounted in the interior recorded all.

As we approached midnight, my own show started broadcasting live. Which meant I got to watch everyone sitting around staring at monitors, and I had to describe it in a way that made it sound interesting. I whispered and hoped it came out sounding spooky and cool. During quiet moments, Matt could switch to my prerecorded interviews with the team to avoid dead air, then come back to the live broadcast if—when—anything happened.

"I'm in the *Paradox PI* command center looking at about a dozen TV monitors and waiting for something to happen. What? Can't say. My expectations are completely open. Gary—you guys normally film the stakeout here in the van all night?"

We spoke in hushed voices. "You never know when something's going to pop up, so, yeah. We tape it all and do a ton of editing."

"Now, this may sound boring to you all at home, but it's actually pretty exciting. There really is this sense that anything can happen. Would you say it's like this every time, or does it get boring after a while?"

"It doesn't really get boring, per se. We do this because we love it. We always hope we'll get some good activity. But I'll admit, we've staked out places that we're pretty sure aren't haunted—there's a cat making noise, or some kind of electrical effect. In those cases we just want to get some evidence of what's really going on, something we can show the owner to say, look, nothing's here."

"What do you think we'll find tonight?"

He blew out a breath and shook his head, a gesture indicating that all bets were off. "I hesitate to make any guesses."

"You're preempting us," Jules complained at one point. "This isn't going to air on our show for a month."

"Are you kidding?" I said. "All my listeners are going to be dying to watch your show to see what this really looks like. Your ratings will triple."

"You have that many listeners?" Gary said.

"Er . . . maybe?" Actually, I probably exaggerated a bit. The ratings of a cult radio show like mine didn't amount to much against a popular cable show like theirs. But I knew after listening to all this, *I'd* want to watch the show.

Nothing happened. I had a schedule to keep. I could sit here and make observations, such as how much patience it took to be a real paranormal investigator, and prompt the crew for comments for maybe twenty minutes before this all become intolerably boring. So, before then, I'd head out to my own van and take a few calls to shake things up a little.

I was glancing at my watch, thinking, *Just another minute*, but Gary and I had been reduced to trading war stories. I had resisted bringing up my one and only ghostly encounter, because it was personal, and it wasn't even a ghost, not the way they defined ghosts. When you sensed the spirit of your dead best friend hovering, looking out for you in times of crisis or uncertainty—that was just wishful thinking, wasn't it? Even when a professional medium tells you it isn't your imagination.

I wondered if they knew a way to summon T.J.'s ghost to tell Peter what had really happened to him. A good old-fashioned séance, like the kind Harry Houdini liked to debunk.

"You guys do séances, right?" I said. "I was just think-ing about the Harry Houdini episode you did. Trying to contact him."

The three exchanged glances, sharing an inside joke shorthand like I'd seen them do before. Brows raised, I waited for an explanation.

Gary said, "We don't do traditional séances—"

"Depends on what you call traditional séances, there, mate," Jules said.

"What if I want to talk to a specific dead person?" I said.

"Because you saw how well the Houdini episode worked out," Tina said.

Jules leaned forward and pointed his hand like he was going to start an argument with Tina, who had a "bring it on" look in her eyes, but Gary gestured and they both calmed down.

"While there've been lots of documented incidents that suggest communication with the Other Side"—he really did say it like it had capital letters—"is possible, it's not as simple as making a phone call."

I said, "Oh, I don't want to make a phone call, I just want—"

"Did you hear that?" Tina said, straightening, her eyes growing round.

We went silent, and a beat later, a noise came over the speakers, a series of thumps like a body rolling down the stairs. Everyone leaned toward the monitors. Jules cranked up the volume on a piece of equipment.

But I watched Tina. Because none of us had heard anything before she asked the question. There hadn't *been* anything. So—had she heard it before it happened?

Matt came over my own headset, his voice tense, hushed. Scared, even. "That came through on the broadcast, Kitty. Everyone heard it."

Okay. Cool. I didn't say anything. I cringed inwardly at the silence, anathema on the radio. But this wasn't a talk show anymore, this was drama, and we all waited to see what would happen next.

After a tense moment, the talking started.

"You recorded it?" Gary said.

Jules flipped a couple of switches, peering at the equipment through his glasses. "Yeah, of course."

"There's nothing on the cameras," Tina said, checking all the monitors. "I was looking right at the staircase, there was nothing."

"So nothing fell. Nothing's out of place." Another manic search of all the screens.

I asked Tina, "What did you hear?"

"What do you mean, what did I hear?" She pointed at the speaker. "That thudding. Like something falling over on the stairs. You all heard it."

"No, I mean before you said anything. What did you hear that made you ask if we'd heard it? Because I know I have better hearing than anyone here, and I didn't hear anything before you spoke."

Now everyone was looking at her.

"Tina has good hearing," Gary said after a moment.

"Not as good as mine," I said, my smile a bit toothy. A bit lupine. "She's not a werewolf."

Gary said, "Tina? Did you actually hear it before it happened?"

The ratings hound in me was jumping up and down. Had I scooped a story here? Was I about to expose one of the *Paradox PI* crew as actually being paranormal herself? Clairvoyant or something? How cool would that be? I still needed to ask her about what she saw when she looked at me, at Ben.

But Tina was stricken, looking back and forth between her colleagues and shrinking as far as she could against the wall of the van.

"I don't know," she said. "Maybe I saw something on the monitors. Whatever made the noise, I must have seen it. We'll go over the footage later. It'll be there."

But we'd all been looking at the monitors. Nobody saw anything.

"Can we talk about this later?" she said, almost shrill.

Another thumping came over the speakers, drawing us back to the task at hand. It sounded like the first noise, a rapid, arrhythmic series of hollow thumps, like something falling, or like a herd of children running downstairs.

"Shit," Jules murmured. The hairs on the back of my head stood up. I quelled an instinct to run.

"Do random, unidentifiable noises like this happen often?" I whispered to Gary.

Slowly, he shook his head. "It never happens like this."

It came louder, and closer, if that was possible, rattling the speakers. Still, nothing appeared on the monitors. No visible source in the house was producing the noises. In defiance of the laws of physics, these noises seemed to come from nowhere.

The thudding grew louder again, until the van started vibrating, like now the children were running on our roof. I could feel it in my bones.

"Is it an earthquake?" Jules said. "Maybe it's not the house at all."

"Does Colorado get earthquakes?" Gary asked. His voice was taut, anxious.

"Sort of," I said. "Little tiny ones. You can't actually feel them."

"I've lived in LA for ten years," Tina said. "This isn't an earthquake."

Something odd occurred to me. "What if it's just the speakers?"

"What?" Jules said.

"The speakers. Unplug the speakers."

Jules and Tina were still gawking at me like I'd sprouted a second head, so I lunged over them and pulled at the speaker units mounted above the bank of monitors. Custom jobbies, wires looped into the back of them.

Of course, either way, pulling the wires would stop the noise. Right?

We still didn't see anything on the monitors, which were bouncing on their shelves now. The noise had changed to a steady pounding, like someone was beating on the van. This wasn't happening on the house—this was happening right here.

I almost had to shout. "The other option is to go into the house and see if this is going on in there, too," I said, growing exasperated. I was ready to pile out of the van myself, one way or the other.

When no one said anything, I yanked the wires.

The beating, pounding, thudding noise stopped.

We all held our breaths, waiting for it to start again.

Jules's shoulders slumped. He grabbed the speaker out of my hand. "Don't tell me that was an equipment malfunction? Christ."

In the midst of grumbling, I paused, nostrils flaring. I smelled something. It pinged a memory, but I couldn't quite catch it. Something recent. Something bad, dangerous—

Sulfur and fire. Brimstone. Attack in the forest. In the back of my brain, Wolf howled.

I bit back a growl and lunged for the door.

"Hey—"

The van tipped over.

Chaos rocked us, objects falling, monitors smashing, bodies tumbling. People shouted, cried out with surprise. I wrapped my arms around my head, over the headset I was still wearing. Then movement stopped. We ended up sprawled on the van's side, picking ourselves out of the mess of shelving and gear that had been stored there.

I didn't wait. I could move, I didn't hurt, except for the panic and anger burning in my gut. I lunged for the back door, shoved it open, and spilled out.

The van was on its side, in the middle of the street. The windshield had smashed, spreading sparkling pebbles of glass across the asphalt. The metal side looked slightly crumpled, as if there'd been a collision. One of the tires was spinning slowly.

Matt and Ben were jumping out of the KNOB van and sprinting toward me. Something in me identified them as friend, so I ignored them. Shoulders tight, hackles stiff, I circled, looking for the enemy, waiting for the thing to attack again.

"Kitty?" Ben caught my body language and looked around with me, searching.

It was *here,* I knew it was, I could smell it. Any minute it would pounce. I couldn't talk. All I had in my throat were growls. Wolf stared out of my eyes.

Ben held my arm, took a scent. His grip tightened. "You smell that?"

"Yeah," I said.

The three investigators had picked themselves out of the van, brushed themselves off, and looked each other over, cursing.

The exterior cameramen, along with the crew, was coming toward us in a hesitating panic. Jules yelled at one of the camera guys, "What did this? What did you guys see?"

"Nothing," one of them said. "There was nothing there, it just fell over."

Gary looked at me. "Is she okay? Is she in shock?"

"No. Nothing like that," Ben said.

A minute ticked on and nothing happened. The panic faded. Wolf crept away, and I was fully me again. Blinking, I shook my head and looked around. We were standing in the middle of the road, staring at the wreckage of the van. This felt like the aftermath of a car accident. Which it kind of was.

A pair of cameras focused on us, capturing every moment for the show. I was still broadcasting, as well. This was going to end up making a pretty good episode for both of us.

But this was far, far too personal for me to be thinking of that.

"Is everyone okay?" I said.

"Cuts and bruises," Gary said. "What the hell was that?"

"Full-on poltergeist, I'd say," Jules announced, sounding excited.

"But why us and not the house?" Gary said.

"Didn't like us looking at it? She really did tick it off. I dunno." His accent had gotten thicker. He started picking through the wreckage for something. "I've got to get some readings. EMF, temperature, infrared. This is unbelievable. Where is everything?" No one moved to help him.

The rest of us were standing around, shell-shocked. Waiting for the second round, possibly.

"What do you know about this?" Tina said. She was rubbing her arms, obviously chilled, looking around like she expected something to drop out of the sky. "You act like you know something."

I didn't know. It was just the smell, the same prickling on my skin I'd felt the other night. But it was gone now. Only a lingering scent remained. I said, "This is about me, it's not about the house. There's something after me."

"Now that's a story I want to hear," Gary said.

I chuckled. "Got a few hours?"

"Will somebody *please* help me with this?" Jules demanded, still digging through the wreckage for equipment.

Matt called out, "Kitty, you're still on the air. You've got five minutes."

Shit. The KNOB van was still upright. I wondered how long that would last.

I adjusted the microphone on my headset and moved away from the group to pull myself together and get my show back on track. Not that this was getting off track— I'd been waiting for something exciting to happen, hadn't I? Anything more exciting than this and I'd be done for the night. I wondered how this was sounding to my audience.

"Right, okay. What just happened? I believe, in paranormal-investigation parlance, we've just seen some activity. Yeah, right. The freaking van tipped over, and we don't know what did it. If you watch *Paradox PI* when this episode airs, you can check it out, because they caught it all on camera and I imagine it looks pretty good. Hey,

Gary—tell me again you've never seen anything like this."

Loudly, he announced, "In my twenty years of investigating, I have never seen anything like this."

"What's next for you guys?"

"We go over the footage with a fine-tooth comb. Make sure there aren't anomalies, some other reasonable explanation for this. Monitor the area. Wait to see if anything like this happens again. Are you sure you don't get earthquakes here?"

Tina said, "If it was an earthquake, all the cars would have tipped over. There'd be more damage. This was localized."

"Everything's wrecked," Jules said, still in his own world of picking through gear. "We're going to have to replace a lot of this if we want to do any more tonight. Not to mention get a tow truck over here."

Gary sighed. "Just pull out some of the equipment we put in the house. Those should work."

"But what about monitoring the house?" His temper was right on the edge.

"I don't think we have the luxury of choosing our battles right now. It's either the house or the van."

I tried to come up with some kind of wrap-up, some way to put all this in context or expound on some nice greeting card conclusion, but my nerves were shot.

"Well, folks. I wish I had something pithy to say, but I'm kind of at a loss to describe what's going on here. I'll be the first to tell you that the universe is filled with some pretty wild, unexplained phenomena. Me, for example. I'll also be the first to say it's still a good idea to take things with a grain of salt. But I'm all out of salt right now. Something happened here tonight at the old haunted house, but it didn't happen in the house, and I'm not convinced it was a haunting. Whatever it was, it sure wasn't happy. Tune in next week when, hopefully, I'll have a little more to give you. I'll also go back to taking calls so you can tell me about some of your own unexplained, unexplainable, experiences. Until then, this is Kitty Norville, and this has been *The Midnight Hour.*"

Matt was in the van, pushing buttons, working his own brand of arcane wizardry. He gave a curt nod, which meant we were done. Finally.

I pulled off my headset and threw it into the van. Then I found Ben and got clingy. I wrapped my arms around his middle and hugged him close as his arms closed over my shoulders.

"Why do I get the feeling this is going to get worse before it gets better?" he said.

"Because it usually does," I answered. "Maybe it's just trying to scare us." After all, no one had been hurt. Yet. There was always a yet.

"Isn't that enough?"

Tina walked up to us. I lifted my head from Ben's shoulder just enough to face her.

"You going to tell us what you know?" she said. "*Something's* going on here, and it has to do with you."

What the hell. Maybe they knew something that could help explain this.

"Okay. But not on camera."

chapter **6**

Gary called a tow truck for the van, and the *Paradox PI* camera crew stayed behind to clean up the equipment. Their producers would probably have conniptions over the damage when they saw it. But think of the *ratings*.

Not much was open this late, so we ended up at an all-night coffee shop downtown, five of us—the three from the Paradox team plus Ben and me—crammed in a corner booth, away from prying ears and eyes. None of us even thought about starting the explanations until we had steaming mugs in our hands. Tina's hands were still shaking.

The rest of us were just doing a better job of hiding it.

I told them the condensed version of my confrontation with the Band of Tiamat, leaving out the more sensational bits. Like me being chained to a wall by a pack of lycanthropes. Even the edited version sounded crazy; but out of anyone, the professional paranormal investigators ought to be open-minded, right?

Jules stared at me. "You mean to tell us you're being

haunted by an ancient Babylonian goddess that practices human sacrifice?"

"No," I huffed. "I'm being harassed by a cult that worships an ancient Babylonian goddess and practices lycanthropic sacrifice. I thought you of all people would be sensitive to these nuances."

Gary said, "But you don't know what's doing the harassing. If they somehow found a way to summon a poltergeist, or are using some kind of astral projection, or if they've laid some kind of curse on you."

My head was spinning. "This isn't exactly my area of expertise."

Jules turned to the team's leader. "Gary, this is hearsay, occult nonsense. Not the subject for a proper investigation. We need to look at the evidence."

Gary stared into his coffee cup, shaking his head. "I don't know what to make of it."

"I just don't want anyone to get hurt," I said. "And if this keeps up, someone—either me or someone close to me—is going to. I have to stop this thing."

Tina had a gleam in her eyes and a serious set to her jaw that were at odds with her on-screen persona. "I might be able to help. I'd like to try something."

"What?" Jules said. "Video? Infrared? We had all that at the house and didn't catch anything."

"No, this is different." She was blushing a little and sounded nervous.

"Like what?" Jules said, insistent.

"You'll laugh at me if I tell you. I'd rather wait and show you." She turned to me and said, "I'll need your help. You willing to play along?"

"I'm game." Like Ben said, we had to do something about this.

"Wait a minute, what are we trying to do here?" Jules said. "Find evidence of hauntings or go chasing after a phenomenon that may not even exist? That may all be a figment of *her* imagination?" He pointed at me.

"Do you have any other idea how that van tipped over?" I said. Ben squeezed my hand, and I took a breath to settle down.

"Electromagnetic phenomenon," he said, his face perfectly straight. "Seismic activity. Telekinetic event."

I rolled my eyes. "He talks telekinesis, and I'm the crazy one?"

"Telekinesis has far more documentation than the activities of Babylonian cults," he said.

I had a feeling Jules was starting to not like me. I addressed Tina. "I'd really appreciate any ideas you have."

"This is shaping up to be an episode of an entirely different show," Gary said.

Tina said, "None of us started out with these investigations because of the show. We're in this because we want to *know*. Whatever's happening, it's obviously dangerous, and if I can help discover what it is—I have to at least try. Let's meet again tomorrow night. That'll give me time to get supplies together."

"Where?" I asked.

"Where did you say this first started? That graffiti at New Moon? Then let's go there, after closing."

This sounded ominous. Ominous and intriguing. Ben and I glanced at each other and nodded in agreement. Sighing, Gary shrugged, indicating he'd lost control of proceedings but wasn't interfering. Jules slouched with his arms crossed and wouldn't look at anyone. So much for keeping an open mind.

Full of coffee, if not any more settled, we went our separate ways to get some sleep. Tomorrow was going to be another late night.

The next morning, my mother called. I was too dazed, confused, and exhausted from the previous night's chaos to be irate. Or even worried. I worried about Mom a lot these days, and every phone call from her—especially when it didn't come at her usual Sunday phone-call time—had the potential for disaster.

I answered brusquely. "It isn't Sunday, Mom, why are you calling?"

"Well, good morning to you, too, Kitty," she answered in that put-out voice that instantly made me feel guilty.

"I'm sorry. I'm just . . . I'm a little stressed out right now," I said, hoping she wouldn't ask any questions or try to fix everything, or invite me over for a dinner of macaroni and cheese. She still did things like that.

"That doesn't seem at all surprising. I listened to your show last night."

I braced, because I knew she was going to ask questions I couldn't answer. I didn't want to expose her to what was happening; I'd already told too many people about the attacks. I was afraid that telling them about it exposed them to danger.

She continued, "I'm not sure exactly what happened, but it sounded serious. Are you all right?"

"I can't believe you're asking me that when you're the

one who has cancer," I said, when what I wanted to say was, *No, come and take care of me, please.*

"That may be true, but at least the cancer is under control."

Months of chemo will do that, I supposed. And how could she be so calm about it?

"Why were you even listening to the show? You never listen to my show, it's on past your bedtime!"

"How do you know I never listen to it? And I think you're just arguing with me to avoid answering my question. Are you all right?"

Could I never win an argument with that woman? Ever? Though if I had to be honest, a little childhood part of me was jumping up and down with joy: Mom listens to my show.

I took too long deciding how best to answer her question, and every moment I delayed would only make her more worried. I didn't want Mom to worry, not when she was still sick. Not when there wasn't anything she could do about it. "I'm fine. Nobody got hurt last night. We're trying to figure out what happened, and I have some pretty good leads."

"Nothing like that is going to happen again, is it?"

Good question. "I don't know. I hope not. But if it does, I think we'll be better prepared."

Mom gave a frustrated sigh. "Kitty, I worry about you."

So do I. "Thanks, Mom. But I wish you wouldn't."

"I'll tell you what: I'll stop worrying about you if you stop worrying about me."

Wasn't going to happen, of course. We both wanted assurances from the other that everything was going to be okay. Just fine, hunky-dory, we weren't in trouble, no way. Neither of us could guarantee that.

"I'll be fine. Really. Everything's going to be fine." I didn't expect her to believe it, any more than I believed her half the time. But she played along, because the conversation obviously wasn't going to go any further.

"You'll let me know if there's anything I can do to help, won't you?" she said. The usual gambit at this point in the conversation.

"Absolutely," I said. After a few more empty assurances like that, I coaxed her off the phone.

I called all my wolves, every member of the pack: Was everyone safe? Had anything else happened last night? Had any of them noticed any more signs of what had attacked us?

The answer was no. But no one had been sleeping well. Mick had gone out to the woods to Change and run off his anxiety for a few hours. I berated him for that, but only halfheartedly. He wasn't out of control if he could get himself to wilderness first. And if it made him feel better . . . well, then.

I understood the impulse.

Ben and I arrived at New Moon after closing, at a bright and early two a.m., to meet the *Paradox PI* team.

"Do you know what Tina's going to do?" Ben asked.

"No, but there's something weird about her. I think she's psychic," I said.

He chuckled, but the sound was nervous. "Like, she can read minds? Tell the future?"

"Nothing like that, but have you seen the way she looks at us? I think she can tell what we are. I think she really did hear that noise before it happened. There's something going on with her."

"I suppose if anyone can help, a psychic can. But it feels like grasping at straws."

"They're professionals," I argued. "I'll take any advice, help, or straw grasping I can get."

"I guess it can't hurt," he said. I felt the urge to rap on the wooden doorframe.

The street had quieted, traffic thinning to nothing after bar hours, when the *Paradox PI* van—the unsmooshed one—parked on the street in front of New Moon.

Gary had the camera crew along, as usual—"never waste an opportunity to collect material for your show" was a philosophy I wholeheartedly endorsed. By the same token, Jules wasn't going to waste an opportunity to collect data, so he got to work setting up his standard array of cameras, microphones, and sensors in all parts of the restaurant. Just in case, he said. Tina asked us to help her clear a space in the middle of the dining room. There, we set up a large round table with five chairs. Then Tina went to the van to retrieve her equipment.

"Jules," I said while we waited for her. "What's she going to do? What equipment does she have that you guys haven't already used?"

Jules grumbled. "I haven't a clue, but this is looking suspiciously like a séance. I can't believe we're getting suckered into this."

Tina returned, carrying a big plastic shopping bag. Now I was really intrigued. We—Ben and I, Jules and Gary—gathered around as she set the bag on the table.

"Out with it, Tina," Gary said. "What are you doing?"

Sheepish, she winced. "I guess it's sort of going to be a séance." Jules rolled his eyes. Gary just watched, reserving judgment.

"What kind of séance?" I said, keeping my own skepticism in check. "Holding hands, table rapping—"

Jules snorted. "That's just what we need to earn a little respect, some good old-fashioned table rapping."

"No, not exactly like that," Tina said, still wincing, still sheepish.

She took a long, flattish box from the bag and started pulling off the plastic shrink-wrap that sealed it. It looked like a board game. I didn't catch the title until Jules groaned and rolled not just his eyes, but his whole head, in a gesture of disgust.

"You're joking!" he burst. "I'm not going to be a party to this. Gary, tell her. This is ridiculous. This is *insane*."

It was a Ouija board, brand new, smelling of fresh plastic and cardboard.

"Hey," I said. "We used to play that at sleepovers in the third grade."

Glancing at me while she opened the board on the table, Tina said, "These can be really dangerous. You were lucky nothing happened. I assume nothing happened?"

"Not really. We always caught Susan Tate moving the thing around on her own. On the other hand, did you ever play Light as a Feather, Stiff as a Board? Now that was freaky."

Gary said, "That's a simple trick of minor hypnotism."

"Ah, another childhood illusion shattered. But you're telling me the Ouija board is real."

"I've had a little luck with it," Tina said.

"And what do you mean by *dangerous*?" I asked.

She said, "Quite a few cases of suspected demon possession have been linked—"

"It's rubbish!" Jules interrupted. "If we broadcast this, it'll ensure that no one from the legitimate paranormal investigation community ever takes us seriously again."

"I know what I'm doing," Tina said. "Trust me."

It was easy to discount her as just a pretty face—and I really should have known better. The others stared at her, like they were thinking the same thing. Like they'd never seen her like this before.

"What aren't you telling us?" Gary said, wary.

"I've been using these since I was a kid," Tina said. "It might be a way to find out what's really going on."

Whether or not a person could actually use something like a Ouija board to communicate with the beyond, or whatever, I found it hard to believe you could do it with a piece of mass-produced cardboard straight out of the packaging.

I said, "The commercial version works? Shouldn't you be using one made of ancient wood, hand-lettered by gypsies from the Orient or something?"

She threw me a look. "The trouble with the old ones is you don't know where they've been, what they've been used for. We know this one's clean. Besides, it's not the tool, it's the person who uses it."

"Jules, if you don't want to be a part of this, you can watch the monitors in the van," Gary said.

"Fine," Jules said, getting up to leave.

"And keep an eye open."

"Of course," Jules said brusquely. "I'm a *professional*."

He marched outside to the van, where the team had set

up the monitors and speakers they'd salvaged from the previous van's wreckage.

The rest of us took seats around the table, with Tina facing the board. The planchette sat right in the middle, pointing toward her. I'd never have thought of her as a leader, but she took charge of the group without hesitation.

"Right. Here are the rules. Don't move, don't speak. I'll do the talking. If you hear anything, see anything, stay seated. Don't look, don't move, don't scream. As long as we stay in this circle, we're safe. Got it?"

Scream? Gooseflesh sprung out on my arms, and I'd have sworn a draft passed through the room. The low chuckle of a demonic voice. Of course, everything Tina had just said was *exactly* what you'd say to people sitting around a Ouija board when you wanted to totally freak them out.

Gary was studying Tina, his brow furrowed. "There's definitely something you're not telling us."

"Are we doing this or not?" Tina said. She was a little flushed. Nerves. Anticipation. Her fingers, resting before her on the table, almost seemed to be straining toward the board.

I had to admit, I was a bit giddy with excitement. I couldn't wait to see if this really worked. And if it didn't, this felt like those third-grade sleepovers. With less giggling.

"I'm sure you all know the drill," she said. "Two fingers of each hand on the planchette. Only touch it. Take a deep breath and relax."

We leaned forward, stretching toward the board. It was crowded, four grown people squished together to maintain contact with the plastic doohickey. You could fit a dozen third-grade girls around one of these things.

This was where séances traditionally got a little bombastic, when theatrics played a part in setting the stage and inducing a state of anticipation in the participants. *Oh, spirits, we ask you to cross the veil of death to speak with us, yadda yadda.* Tina didn't do that.

"Right. We know something's out there. We're pretty sure it has an interest in at least one of us, and that it's willing to go to violent lengths to make its presence known. Now, if that presence wants to talk to us, we're here. Why don't you come out and have a chat?"

We sat like that for a long time. The room was almost quiet. I heard faint clickings, hissings—the refrigerator under the bar, emergency lights, other electrical background noise. A car going by outside. My nerves stretched taut, waiting for some other sound, for ghostly laughter, for the scrape of plastic over cardboard. Everyone breathed quietly, almost holding their breaths, only drawing breath when they couldn't hold it anymore. My arms, raised over the board, grew tired waiting for something to happen.

"Come out, come out," Tina said in a taunting voice, like she was mocking any lurking spirits, daring them to show themselves.

The plastic thingy gave a little static shock and slipped out from under my fingers.

It was the strangest feeling, not at all like Susan Tate yanking it away from the rest of us and then insisting she hadn't done anything. The plastic gave a quick jerk, just a few centimeters, then stopped. I didn't think anyone was moving it, unconsciously or otherwise, because all of us were sitting there, our hands in midair, fingers splayed and not touching the plastic. My skin tingled with the tiny static charge. I was sure I'd imagined it.

The little arrow pointed to YES.

"Gotcha, sucker," Tina said, lips curling in a sly smile.

"Who did that?" Ben said. "Someone moved it."

"Quiet," Tina said. "Everything's under control."

"If this is some—"

"Quiet," Gary added. Ben clamped his lips shut and glowered.

"Let's try this again, shall we?" Tina said.

The familiar and safe surroundings at New Moon suddenly became odd, strange. Unwelcome. I regretted coming here for this experiment. But maybe Tina would tell us what was causing this, and we could stop it.

I wasn't sure I wanted to touch the thing again, but with Tina's urging, we all did. My nerves were quivering, waiting for something to happen.

"Right," Tina murmured. "I want to know who we're talking to. Who are you?"

The plastic zipped out of our grips again. I had to admit, part of me was ready to leave the room right there. But I definitely wanted to know what was going on. Had to know.

Our hands hovering, the planchette resting untouched, we looked. The arrow pointed to NO.

"You're willing to reveal yourself but not willing to talk to us, is that it? Not good enough," Tina said. "What are you?"

The thing didn't move again.

Tina shook her head. "*Something's* here. I'm sure of it."

"We can't document gut feeling," Gary said.

Closing her eyes, Tina touched the planchette, which slid slowly across the board. She wasn't trying to be subtle—she might have been moving it herself. But it still seemed strange. The air temperature seemed to drop a few degrees.

With her eyes closed, unable to see what she was doing, she spelled out a word: F–I–R–E.

Maybe she'd practiced and could do it by feel; maybe this wasn't for real. I wondered, though: If this really was working, was it because some spirit was moving the planchette? Or because one of us here believed it was? And was, in effect, subconsciously, psychically, telekinetically, whatever, moving it around because of it? Was a four-leaf clover lucky because the bearer believed it was?

Then there was fire.

A cloud of red flames billowed from the kitchen in cinematic glory, like it should have been a special effect in a movie. It washed through the room, pushing air and heat in front of it before dissipating. The table tipped, flew, and hit a wall. Ben and I dove for each other, crouching over and protecting each other. The Ouija board flew away, the planchette careening off another wall. Chairs launched and scattered, and Gary and Tina seemed to fly with them. Feeling cornered, I wanted to snarl. Wolf wanted to burst out and face the enemy. But there was no enemy, at least not one we could see. Not one we could face.

I wanted to say it was a gas-line explosion, that somebody had lit a match near a leaking stove. Old building like this, anything could happen. Funny that it chose that exact moment to ignite.

"Everybody out, get out!" Ben shouted. He grabbed my shirt and shoved me toward the front door.

"Where's Gary? Gary!" Tina wailed.

"Tina! Come on!" It was Jules, clutching at her like Ben was clutching at me. He'd rushed in from outside.

"Gary's hurt!" Tina called.

I saw Gary curled up by the wall, unconscious. He might have landed wrong, might have hit his head. Tina went and crouched by him, trying to pull his arm and drag him toward the door, but she didn't have the strength. Jules helped her. The two of them pulled his arms over their shoulders.

Fear rattled me, and Wolf said to run, run. I looked back, saw flames in the kitchen, felt the heat, smelled it growing stronger, and despaired. Something in me snapped: No, this wasn't going to happen, not my haven. This was my territory; I had to protect it. It couldn't burn, I wouldn't let it.

I squirmed out of Ben's grasp and lunged for the fire extinguisher behind the bar.

"Kitty!" Ben shouted.

The walls were exposed brick. They wouldn't burn, not right away, but the furniture and fixtures were another story. The blast had been quick, more sound than fury, but flames had taken hold, crawling toward the shelves of alcohol. I did battle, spraying foam wherever I saw fire. I wasn't even thinking, so lost in the moment, the smells of fire, chemicals, and panic, to think about what I was doing. To think about the heat scorching my hair and roasting my skin.

Ben wrapped his arm around me and hauled me back. "We have to get out of here!"

"No!" I screamed. No explanation, no pleas about how I couldn't lose this place. Just no. I fought him, kicking and elbowing as the chemical spray from the extinguisher bobbed and faltered. I was at the door of the kitchen now, where a dozen small fires ate away at whatever combustible material lay exposed: aprons, boxes and bags of ingredients, cooking supplies, blackened and disintegrating. Fires from hell. I couldn't identify what fueled the flames; I just wanted to fight them.

Then Ben was standing beside me with a second extinguisher from the door of the kitchen.

I didn't know how long we fought to save our restaurant and haven. The next thing I knew, a pair of firemen had grabbed hold of us and hauled us out of there. No arguing with them, but Ben snarled, like his wolf had come to the fore, and I bared my teeth. We were tired by then, hurt, and I at least used all my remaining strength to keep Wolf under control, no matter how wild I felt.

Outside, Ben and I huddled together.

"You okay?" he said, his voice shaky, scratching from the smoke.

I needed a moment to answer. "You keeping it together?"

"Yeah, I think. But I want to claw something."

"Yeah."

Paramedics started pawing at us, and I tried to push them away. Even if I was hurt, I'd heal soon enough; I'd come to appreciate that part of being a werewolf. They insisted on putting masks over our faces and feeding us oxygen, and I did feel burned. I felt hurt. But the pain, the sensations, were detached. I didn't dare look at myself—seeing the burns would make them start hurting. So I ignored them.

I looked for the Paradox crew.

They had sprawled on the sidewalk nearby, gathered around Gary, who lay flat on the sidewalk. A bloody spot was visible above his brow. He must have hit something hard on his way down, but it seemed to be clotted, matted with hair, rather than gushing blood. I hoped that was a good sign. A couple of paramedics were working on him, without the urgency that would have meant his situation was critical. And yes, the camera crew was still filming.

Jules wandered over to us.

"How is he?" I asked.

"Alive," Jules said. "Probably a bad concussion. They're taking him in for X-rays."

We all looked parboiled, skin red and sweating, streaked with soot, hair and clothing singed and smoking. We looked shell-shocked. Disaster survivors.

"Why the hell didn't you get out of there?" Jules said.

"I couldn't lose the place," I said and realized I was crying. The tears carried soot and smoke from my eyes. I could feel the grit scratching at me.

"Stupid," Ben grumbled at me. "It was stupid, Kitty. It's just a place. We can rebuild a place."

"And a few burns aren't going to kill me."

"Being a werewolf is no excuse for staying inside a burning building!" Ben said.

"What happened?" I said. "What the hell happened in there? Did anyone see anything? Did the cameras pick up anything?"

Jules shook his head. "I don't know. It happened fast. There was a fireball from the kitchen."

"Gas explosion," Ben said, echoing my earlier thought.

"Maybe," Jules said.

"But not really," I said.

"Of course not," Jules grumbled. "Coincidence only goes so far."

Paramedics loaded Gary into an ambulance, while Tina and Jules left for the hospital with him. Yet another guy in a uniform poked at me, and I had to concentrate not to snarl. I was still sitting on the sidewalk, in the dark, listening to water spray and firefighters holler at each other. The oxygen mask lay in my lap. I'd dropped it.

Wolf was cowed. Far past wanting to shape-shift and run away to protect myself, I was in shock, numb, hugging myself. It had been a while since Wolf was so scared and confused that quivering seemed the best option.

"Ma'am, you need to go to the hospital."

"No, I don't. I'll be fine."

"You've got second-degree burns on your arms, ma'am."

"Really?" I looked. My arms were red. Very red. Bad sunburn red. But didn't second-degree mean blisters?

The paramedic stared at my arms, as well. He blinked a couple of times. Then he shook his head. "I could have sworn that was a lot worse a minute ago."

"Maybe you're just stressed," I said. He went away, shaking his head.

The fire was almost out, and the building itself remained intact. The investigators had already had their first look and gave us their impression: There hadn't been an explosion, so it probably wasn't a gas leak. Just fire. I hoped all this meant we could make repairs and reopen quickly. But how was I going to explain this to Shaun?

Ben talked to the police and fire investigators about what we were doing here and proved that we owned the place, so no one would get hauled off on trespassing or vandalism charges.

"The police want to take a look at all the video footage, to see if they can figure out what happened. I have to say I'm looking forward to reading that report," he said.

"I'm not sure how much more of this I can take," I whined. My fury had drained away along with the rush of adrenaline. "It's going to keep coming after us. It's going to keep . . . *destroying* things, until . . ." Until it destroyed *us*. I didn't want to say it.

He put his arm around me, tucked my head on his shoulder, kissed my hair. "I wish I had some suggestions. But this is way out of my league. All I really want to do right now is go *run*." His body was stiff, hands clenched even as they rested against me from the tension of keeping his wolf under control. He hadn't gotten to the numb stage, apparently.

I didn't want to sit around and wait to see what disaster happened next. "Come on," I said, pushing myself off his shoulder to stand up, then tugging on him to get him to his feet. "Let's go see how Gary's doing."

chapter 7

Gary Janson had a concussion. He hadn't suffered anything as serious as a skull fracture or bleeding in the brain, but the length of time he'd spent unconscious had the doctors worried, so they were keeping him in the hospital under observation. Before we arrived at the hospital, he'd woken up, been aware of his surroundings and of his team gathered around him. But he didn't remember what had happened, and he'd seemed confused at some of the doctor's questions. He hadn't been able to answer the classic "How many fingers am I holding up?" for example. Still, the doctor expected him to recover, given time and rest.

The cameras had followed us to the hospital and spent time getting video of the doctor explaining Gary's injuries. I wanted to corner the show's cameramen and ask if they were really wanting to put all this into the show. It seemed sensationalist, even by my standards.

We found Tina and Jules in a nearby waiting room, sitting hunched in their chairs, looking bereft. Jules had taken off his glasses to rub his eyes. I hated to break the mood, but I was still under attack, and my restaurant had almost burned down. I had to find out if Tina's little experiment had accomplished anything.

"So," I said, scuffing my feet. "Can I assume the Ouija board just pissed this thing off?"

They looked at me like I'd turned green. Ben had wandered off to read a public health notice hanging on the wall—pretending like he didn't know me. Then they sputtered with laughter. Tina held a hand over her mouth and turned red, almost crying from trying to keep from laughing, and Jules just shook his head.

"Bloody *hell*," the Brit said. "I have *never* seen anything like that!"

Either this was a lot of pent-up stress getting loose, or I was confused.

"I can't believe it. When I said it was dangerous I was talking demonic possession. I've never had anything like that happen before," Tina said, gasping for breath. "We almost *died*. And Gary—oh, my God!"

Stress, I decided. I wondered if I should say something.

"And you—" Jules pointed at his colleague. "What *was* that? What *are* you, some kind of psychic? Medium? Have you been holding out on us?"

Tina stopped laughing. Because Jules reminded us of what had happened right before the fire.

The room went quiet, and Jules stared at her. She stared back, looking like she'd been hit by a truck. Jules's eyes were wide with revelation.

I stepped in. "Maybe we should all talk about this over coffee." I raised my brows hopefully.

The hospital cafeteria had just opened—it was something like five in the morning—so we went there.

Jules, completely sober now after whatever post-traumatic hysteria had gripped him, almost sounded betrayed. "Tina, I've never seen *anybody* work a Ouija board like that."

"And you can tell what I am just by looking at me," I said.

Jules again, even more insistent: "What's your angle on all this? What aren't you telling us?"

I felt like I had a front-row seat to my own private reality-TV show; too bad the cameras hadn't followed us here.

They communicated by stares. Jules leaned over the table, demanding an explanation from Tina with his accusing gaze. Tina turned sullen, like she was a kid who'd just gotten in trouble for something.

"I've been doing it since I was a kid," she said at last, voice soft, all humor gone. "And not just with the board, but with dowsing, automatic writing, runes, most of the old tricks. It all works. I walk into a house, and I know if it's haunted or not because it talks to me. Things talk to me. I sense things. Ghosts, spirits. Whatever."

The old tricks Tina mentioned—using rods or pen and paper to communicate with the spirit world, reading tea leaves, shapes in a plume of smoke—they *were* old tricks exactly because they must have worked for someone, at some time. But it wasn't a science, because the results weren't reproducible. The methods worked for some people and not for others, and even those people with talent didn't have it all the time. With the Age of Reason and rise of science, what couldn't be dissected and explained was discredited and abandoned. Still, the tricks lingered, and thousands of people clung to them, used them—or abused them—because they so desperately wanted them to work.

What happened when someone like Tina came along? Someone who actually could make the tricks work? And what did that say about the world?

We stared at her.

"Really," Jules said flatly.

"Really," she said, echoing. "I don't advertise it because of people like you, who assume everyone who picks up a forked stick or holds a séance is faking it."

I bet she used her looks and humor, as well, to distract from those moments when she stared out into space, as if listening. She was the show's eye candy; she couldn't *possibly* be its resident psychic.

Paradox PI had a resident psychic. A real one. I *so* wanted to be the one to break that story.

"So, Tina," I said, trying to sound encouraging. "I'd love to have you on the show next week to talk about this, how you discovered this, what it's been like to live with it—"

"No," she said. Didn't even think about it.

"Why does everyone always tell me no like that?" I said. "Am I really that bad?"

Ben patted my hand. "I think it's the predatorial gleam in your eye when you ask them."

"What gleam?" I grumbled. Okay, so there might have been a *little* predatorial gleam.

"Gary doesn't know?" Jules said. "All this time you've had this information, this access, and you've let us mess around with our cameras and microphones and infrared monitors and EMF readings?"

"Because even if you and Gary believed me, I have no

way of proving what I know. So I keep my mouth shut. So the legitimate paranormal investigative community will take us seriously, as you're always saying."

"Then why reveal yourself now?" he said. "Why give away the secret now?"

"Because this isn't about the TV show anymore—this thing is dangerous. I thought I could help. That I might be able to do some good." She crossed her arms and looked away. I wondered if she regretted revealing herself.

Jules sat back, rubbing his face and staring into space. "God. God." I worried that something in his brain might have snapped.

"Jules? You okay?" I said.

His smile was sad. He spoke to Tina. "You know, I'm not surprised. I've worked so hard, searching for evidence. I've tried to be so thorough. But you've always seemed to have this talent. That's why the show works, not because of my methodology, but because of your talent. Things just *happen* when you're around. What I wouldn't give for an ounce, a microgram, of what you have. To be able to touch it, just a little bit. I've been looking for it my whole life, and I'm as far away from it as ever."

"Try walking into an old church, and the whole thing just *presses* on you like a weight because there's so much there," Tina said. "I hate it, Jules. I'd give it to you in a heartbeat."

And that was how we all grew closer and learned to share in a very special episode of *Paradox PI*.

"I hate to interrupt," I said. "But we're still not any closer to figuring out what it is that's after me. Did you get *anything* out of that séance?"

"Besides the fact that there's some seriously pissed-off mojo floating around you?" Tina said.

"That's obvious and not helpful," I said. "Did you sense *anything*?"

"Yes. No." She furrowed her brow and shook her head. "I've never felt anything like it."

"Well, we know a few things about it," Jules said. "It's violent, destructive, and associated with fire. I could do some research. I'd need to get back to some of my books, contact some people I know in the SPR."

Tina smiled the smile that had probably helped get her the job on the show. "See, we need you!"

"Huh?" Jules said.

"You were worried that we didn't need you because you aren't psychic, but you know way more than the rest of us. I could never do that kind of research."

Jules smirked. "Thanks for the pep talk."

I said, "Tina. You felt this thing, or whatever it is that psychics do. What's it like?"

Tina shrugged. "Probably nothing you don't already know about it. Heat. Malice. Fire. Destruction. It's what ties all this together, isn't it?"

My head ached, I was so exhausted. I seemed to remember eating something today, but I couldn't remember what. And I was scared to go home. Scared to stay here. Just scared.

"Maybe we should get some sleep," I said. "Maybe this will seem clearer in the morning." And maybe pigs would fly.

"It's noon in Britain," Jules said. "I'll make some calls and see if some of my contacts have any information."

"I'll go check on Gary," Tina said.

We parted reluctantly, even though we all needed to sleep, even though no amount of hashing it out over coffee would solve the problem. But there was safety in numbers. Comfort in the shared experience. We could look each other in the eyes and know that it really happened, that we weren't going crazy. We promised to leave our cell phones on and call the minute, the second, anything weird happened.

When we arrived home, I half expected to see the condo spewing flames and surrounded by fire trucks. But it was quiet.

The best part about having Ben around—rather, one of the best parts—was finding myself in his arms at the end of a really rough day. Assuming, of course, that arguing with him hadn't been part of what made the day rough. Usually, though, I could count on him to hold me and tell me everything was going to be fine. Even if the tone in his voice wasn't convincing. That night, he was cold and clinging to me as much as I was clinging to him. Neither of us fell asleep easily, and we woke up far earlier than we wanted to.

Not able to fight my way back to sleep, I left Ben in bed, pulled on an oversize T-shirt, and wandered to the living room.

My head pounded, and my eyes were caked with grime. My hair smelled like soot and fire. *Fire.* No wonder I felt boiled and limp. I didn't want to see what New Moon looked like in the daylight. Seeing the damage in detail would probably break my heart.

I checked my phone. It hadn't rung, which I took as a good sign.

The first person I called was Shaun. I needed to tell him what had happened before the lunch crew showed up for its shift and saw the damage firsthand. We needed a plan to get the place repaired and functional.

As the phone rang, I squeezed my eyes shut really tight. I still didn't want to tell him. Like if I didn't say the words "New Moon almost burned down," I didn't have to believe it.

Shaun picked up. "Kitty."

"Hi, Shaun. How are you?"

"I don't know—how are you?" His voice was coy.

Deep breath. Had to get it out. "Not good. There was an accident at the restaurant last night—"

"I know," he said. "It was in the paper this morning."

"What?" I was relieved and chagrined. I didn't have to explain, but—he was going to yell at me for not calling him last night, wasn't he?

But he didn't. "Is everyone okay?"

"One person's in the hospital," I said.

"Shit," he said. "What are we going to do?"

"Make repairs. Reopen as soon as we can." We had to continue, onward and upward. What choice did we have?

"Does the fire have anything to do with that thing that went after us the other night?" His voice was numb, like he didn't want to believe it had really happened, either, and didn't want to give voice to the truth.

"Probably," I said, wincing. "It had the same smell."

"When's it going to stop? How are we going to stop it?"

Saying *I don't know* would have been the truth. But it would also be a sign of weakness. It would be admitting that I was floundering. And I couldn't show that kind of weakness and still keep the pack together. I had to be the strong one. If the others lost confidence in me . . . well, I didn't want to go there. It didn't matter if I had any confidence in myself. I just had to convince them I did.

"I'm working on it, Shaun. I'm sorry I don't have a better answer than that."

"Let me know if there's anything I can do."

"I will. Thanks. I'll talk to you soon."

He hung up without saying goodbye. I'd make it up to him, I promised myself. I'd make this right.

Next I called Tina for an update on Gary. Jules answered her phone.

"We're still at the hospital," he said. "Tina finally conked out, so I'm letting her sleep."

"How's Gary?"

"Awake, but groggy. He doesn't really remember what happened. But he's going to be okay."

I repeated my promise to myself: No one was going to die. We'd figure this thing out.

"Any other news on your end?" I said.

"Not yet. I'm waiting to get replies to some of my e-mails and calls. We still need to talk about what we're doing next. We could meet this afternoon, if you like."

"Sounds good." We agreed on a time and place—the hospital cafeteria—and said our farewells.

I made another call. Grant picked up on the first ring.

"You're probably getting sick of hearing from me," I said.

The barest hint of a smile touched his voice. "If I were, I wouldn't answer the phone."

Ah, the magic of caller ID. What did we ever do without it? Strangely enough, I was comforted.

"What's happened?" he said.

"There was a fire."

I told him, starting with the incident with the van, even including the part about the Ouija board, even though that was a little embarrassing. I didn't want to leave anything out in case it turned out to be important. But we'd had enough attacks now to discern a pattern: heat and fire. Something invisible that struck suddenly and left no trace.

"It's rare finding someone who can read anything through a Ouija board. It's not the most efficient tool."

And I'd been worried that he'd make fun of me for going along with it. Grant seemed to take everything seriously.

"What *is* an efficient tool?" I said.

"Oh, this and that."

The trouble with the real-deal psychics and magicians is they didn't like to talk about what they could do. Like Tina covering it up because she wanted her colleagues to take her seriously.

"What does something like this?"

"I'm starting to get some ideas," he said.

"What are we supposed to do in the meantime? This thing is getting more violent. I don't want anyone else to get hurt."

"What do you know about protective magic?"

"You can crush St. John's Wort pills and scatter them with breadcrumbs to get rid of a fairy," I said.

After a pause, he said, "I didn't know that. Interesting."

Hey, my side gets a point on supernatural *Jeopardy*. That was a switch.

"But that's probably not going to be useful here," Grant said.

Oh well.

"Try this instead." Grant gave me directions: "Take the dust from a ruin—"

"Ruin? Like old temple, Roman aqueduct? How am I going to get—"

"You live in a city—what's been knocked down recently? An abandoned shed going to weed will work just as well. Mix it with blood—"

"How much blood? Human blood? I'm trying *not* to kill people here—"

"Cow, sheep, pig, chicken. Special order it from a butcher shop. Not human."

Grant was being very patient with me. "Oh. That makes sense."

"Mix the dust and blood, then sprinkle the mixture around whatever you need protected. Probably the homes of everyone who's involved. Any other structures. You can even carry a jar of it with you, to use in a pinch."

Kind of gross. But I wasn't going to question it. "What kind of spell is that?"

"I adapted it from an old Egyptian potion. Ideally, it'll form a protective barrier."

"And it works?"

"In at least one case it did, yes."

Now, there was a story I needed to get. But later, when this was over and we were all still alive.

"Thanks. We'll give it a try."

"This still won't stop it," he said. "This isn't an ideal solution. I'll try to come up with something better."

"I appreciate the help."

"I took it upon myself to keep that group from causing trouble. Much of this is my responsibility."

Grant was usually calm, emotionless, a good guy to have at your back. But he was sounding downright frustrated.

"There's only one of you and like a dozen of them. Just think how much damage they'd be doing if you weren't there."

"It's kind of you to say so."

I tried to sound cheerful. "Let me know when you come up with anything else. I'll talk to you later."

"Until then."

We clicked off and I felt better, because now I had something I could do. I started thinking about taking a shower.

By this time Ben had gotten up and was making phone calls of his own, in bed, a pen and notepad beside him.

I said, "Grant has this protection spell I want to try, but I have to get ingredients. Do you want to come?"

He glanced up. "Do you need me to?"

"No, I guess not." We were married, after all. Not attached at the hip.

"I still have to call the insurance company and try to figure out what we're going to do about New Moon. I called the fire department a little while ago. They're going to inspect the building for structural and gas-line damage, but if it checks out we should be able to make repairs and open back up in a couple of weeks."

Which was good news. We were still in the game.

"Call me if anything happens," I said.

"You too. Be careful."

Which, when Ben said it, also sounded like "I love you."

chapter 8

It turned out you really could go to the butcher shop and get blood. It wasn't easy—I had to call all over town to find one that could special order it from their slaughterhouse. But I found one that was willing—and they were certainly willing to charge me for it. I also got a couple of steaks to go along with the blood. Any excuse.

For the ruin, I went to where a set of 1920s townhouses was being—tragically, in my opinion—torn down to make way for high-priced lofts. I had always wondered what made a place a loft rather than an apartment or condo. I figured it had to be the outrageous price. Around back, the crews weren't watching, so I was able to get to the roofless, half-knocked-in building and scoop up a bucketful of dirt and debris.

When I mixed the two ingredients, I ended up with a dark, sticky, smelly paste. Plaster of Paris from hell. The stuff reeked. I separated it out into a dozen mason jars, hoping it would be enough. I hadn't realized how much I had to protect.

The first place I anointed was New Moon. The building

was still intact, after all, even though the doors had yellow tape sealing them off and a sign from the fire department declaring that the building was awaiting inspection. I stared at the facade a long time. From the outside, no damage was visible. Lycanthropic vision was pretty good for seeing in the dark, so I peered through the window of the front door, searching the shadows. Tables and chairs were scattered. Puddles spotted the floor. Scorch marks streaked from the kitchen. I could smell soot, sulfur, brimstone. The Ouija board still lay there, abandoned.

I didn't want to think about it any more than that.

I walked around the building clockwise, because for some reason these things were always done clockwise, using a spoon to dribble out spots of Egyptian blood potion. If this didn't work, I'd look really silly. And if it did, how would I know? What if the thing didn't attack us here again? Would the potion have protected us, or would it be a coincidence? I could begin to see how superstitions like this got started. If you got a hot date the one day you happened to be carrying a rabbit's foot—well, why not?

But at least I was doing *something*.

Ben pulled up in his car just as I was finishing the bloody circle. He wore his "threw it on as I was leaving the house" look: rumpled trousers, rumpled shirt, brown jacket, hair brushed back from his face, obviously with his fingers. He smelled clean and showered.

"Hey!" I grinned at him as he came to meet me.

"Hey—oh, my God, what *is* that? Did you put that around the whole building?" His nose wrinkled, and he glared with disgust at the jar of bloody goo.

"It's the dust of a ruin mixed with blood. Odysseus

Grant's protection spell. It's supposed to keep nasty spirits away," I said.

"I can see why—it'll keep anything away. Gah!"

Sensitive werewolf noses. By this time, I'd gotten used to the reek.

"What brings you out here?" I said.

"I'm supposed to meet the investigator and insurance adjuster in half an hour. I have a feeling the insurance company is going to want to call it arson and fraud."

"Arson! Are they kidding?"

He shrugged. "We were there when the fire started. And in a way, 'weird-ass supernatural attack' might be classified as arson."

I groaned. "Great. That's just great."

"Don't worry, I think we have the investigator on our side. He's talking something about a gas leak igniting particulate matter in the air. A big *whoosh* with no outright *boom*. If the insurance company buys the explanation, we're set."

Another car, an old, small-size pickup, pulled up to the curb and parked behind Ben's. My poor little burned-out building sure had a lot of visitors.

"Is that your investigator?" I said, even as I knew I was wrong, because I recognized the truck. It was Mick's. Sure enough, Mick and Shaun got out. Both were frowning, walking with their shoulders bunched up, surly.

"Oh, this can't be good," I murmured. These were two of the pack's strongest wolves, apart from me and Ben. In fact, in a straight-up fight, they were probably stronger. We were the alphas because they let us be. Because they trusted us.

"Hi, Shaun," I said. "You're in time to walk through

with Ben and the investigator. You can see exactly what the damage is."

He pressed his lips, nodded. Peered in through the front door like I had, searching, and I hoped the fact that not much was visible from here made him feel better. Shaun loved the place as much as I did. He'd picked out the name.

Mick didn't stop staring at me. When Ben edged up to me, he stared at both of us. He had to know what that stare meant to our wolf sides.

"Is something wrong?" I said, my voice steady. I rounded my shoulders and stood straight. I didn't want to have to do something as gauche as growl at him.

He shrugged, offhand, like nothing was wrong. "I just want to find out what you're going to do to take care of this."

I held up the jar of blood goo. "Protective spell. I've got extras in the car. I'll give you some to take home with you."

He and Shaun regarded it with the same disgusted, puckered expressions Ben had. The stuff did smell pretty vile. But once it was spread around the place, it wasn't noticeable. Much.

"Are you kidding me?" Mick said, obviously not impressed. "I'm not smearing that crap anywhere near me."

"I'm open to other suggestions," I said.

Mick and Shaun glanced at each other, which made me even more nervous, because it meant they'd been talking about this beforehand. I was way too new at this alpha thing to be facing dissension in the ranks already. I wasn't sure it would work, but I'd have to handle this the way I handled most everything in my life: brazen it out and act like I knew what I was doing.

I crossed my arms and waited for an answer.

"We go to Vegas," Shaun said. He was fidgeting, just a little. Hands picking at the seams on his jeans, eyes darting, unable to look right at me. It made me think this was all Mick's idea. "Go to the source. Take care of that pack directly."

"Did you two come out here to tag-team me or what?" I said.

Shaun looked away at that, because I was right. Mick didn't. He said, "Well? How about it?"

"I thought of going back to Vegas. Did you consider that they may want us to do exactly that? That it's a trap? This is a cult that sacrifices werewolves. I don't want any of us going within a hundred miles of there."

Mick started in with more confidence, still staring at me like this was a challenge. "Then we hire someone to go there for us. Or we call the police."

"And prove to the cops what's happening, how?"

"I don't know—you think of something, you know so much."

"What, you don't like my icky blood spell?" I dipped my finger into the mixture and pointed it at him. Maybe I could obnoxious him into submission.

"I'm worried, Kitty. I'm worried that you can't handle this," Mick said.

"You think someone else could handle it better?"

"I think if it wasn't for you, this wouldn't be happening."

Ben, who had been standing behind my shoulder the whole time, studying the pair of them, sprang. Surprised the hell out of me. Out of all of us. Ben grabbed Mick's

T-shirt at the shoulders, wrapped it in his fists, spun him around, and shoved him to the brick wall of the building. Held them there. It was over before I could blink.

Ben's teeth were bared. Mick's eyes were wide, his feet working to try and scramble away. All his bravado vanished. Now he was scared. Ben was close enough—and seemed angry enough—to take a bite out of him.

I stared. "Wow. I didn't know you had it in you."

"Neither did I," Ben said, his voice hoarse. His expression was taut, his whole body tense, and his wolf glared out of his eyes. He gave Mick one last shove, then stepped away, rolling his shoulders back, shivering almost. His breathing slowed. Mick backed away to stand next to Shaun.

I moved to Ben and squeezed his hand. *Come back to me,* I thought at him. I wanted him to be human, not wolf, right now. I wanted to work this out as human beings.,

"I was really hoping we could have a pack where this sort of thing wouldn't happen," I said, sighing. New Moon was supposed to be the symbol of that. Peaceful cooperation. It was damaged, and look what happened.

"I'm sorry," Mick said, not meeting my gaze, only glancing warily at Ben. "I didn't mean for this to look like a challenge. But I'm worried."

"Yeah," I admitted, my voice soft. "But we're working on it. We'll figure this out. Tell everyone we'll figure this out."

Again, they glanced at each other. My hunch had been correct. They'd been talking to everyone in the pack. They, the toughest nonalpha males, had been appointed spokeswolves. And now they were backing down. Maybe I could do this job.

Shaun said, "How did you know we've been talking?"

"Female intuition," I said. "I have to go meet with some paranormal investigators about this whole brouhaha. Will you guys be okay if I leave you alone?"

"Paranormal investigators?" Shaun said. Finally, he was smiling, at least a little. "So you really are working on this."

"Yeah, I am."

"We'll be fine," Ben said. I was confident he was right.

Ben walked me to my car.

"You okay?" I asked. I didn't know how close we'd come to a fight back there. I didn't really want to know. Ben was still tense.

"Yeah. It just came out of nowhere. I just couldn't let them talk anymore. Or the wolf side couldn't. Hard to explain."

"Well, thanks," I said. "I'm sure they'll go back and tell everyone you're way tougher than you look. They'll be absolutely cringing around you from now on."

"Funny. I've come to rely on your fast-talking us out of these situations. Talk faster next time, okay?"

I grinned. "Sure."

We exchanged a kiss—a warm, comfortable, all's-well-with-the-world kiss—before I zoomed off to my next appointment.

As I was getting in my car, the grumble of a motorcycle engine revving caught my attention. The bike was at the end of the block. The rider looked around quickly, then set off with enough speed that his tires squealed. He took the corner at a steep angle and was gone. I caught only a glimpse; the rider wore a helmet, but I recognized the canvas army jacket.

Peter Gurney was tracking me.

After a moment of thought, I decided that didn't bother me. Maybe this was something he had to do, to feel he was learning as much about T.J. as he could. He could learn from me—I didn't have anything to hide. He was quite a ways down on the list of things I was worried about at the moment.

I called the Paradox crew to tell them I'd be late. Arriving at last, I found Jules and Tina waiting for me in the hospital cafeteria, sparsely populated after the lunchtime rush. They sat around a table, slumped forward, gazes vacant—still looking shell-shocked. Tina had a smoky cough. We'd been so worried about Gary, the rest of us had only sat still for cursory examinations by the paramedics. Smoke inhalation, minor burns. Get some rest was what we were told.

I felt fine, but I was a werewolf with super healing. I ought to tell them to get to bed to rest and heal. But I kept thinking, what if this happened again, and again? And now I'd dragged them into it.

"How's everyone this morning?" I greeted them, and they all grumbled. "How's Gary?"

When they didn't answer right away, I assumed the worst. I was all ready to run up to his room and check on him myself—assuming he was still there, but Tina said, "He's awake. He's okay. He's still a little groggy, but he'll be okay."

Relieved, I sank into a free chair and blew out a sigh. "That's really good to hear. Have you told him about your, um, talent yet?" I kind of wanted to be there for that conversation.

"Uh, no," Tina said. "I figured I'd wait until he was back on his feet."

I was going to say something about whether they'd be interested in doing the big reveal on my show, but Tina wrinkled her nose and peered hard at me. "What's wrong?" I said, wary.

"Are you okay? You've got something weird going on. This smell."

I wondered . . . I was carrying a jar of the blood-and-ruin potion in my bag, for the Paradox crew to use.

"Er," I said, chagrined. "I didn't think nonlycanthropes could smell it."

"Smell what?" Jules said.

"You can't smell that?" Tina said. "Oh, God, don't tell me—"

Tina didn't really smell it—she sensed it. Which gave me hope, because that meant there was something weird and magical about it. Maybe it would work.

I revealed the jar, half filled with viscous black goo. They twisted their faces up in expressions of disgust. "It's supposed to be a protection spell."

"What is it?" Jules said, already repulsed, though I hadn't even told him.

"Blood mixed with dust from a ruin."

They both went *Eww.*

"Got that out of a book, didn't you?" Jules said, cutting. "Something by Crowley, maybe?"

"As a matter of fact, no," I said. "I happen to have a consultant on the case. Like you guys. Have your contacts been able to turn up anything? Any ideas what we do next to track this thing down?"

Carrie Vaughn

Again, they answered with a long, hard silence. I blinked at them. "What's wrong?"

"It's really hard saying this, Kitty," Jules said.

"Because you're a coward," Tina muttered. Jules glared at him.

"What?" I said. "What's hard?"

They exchanged glances, frowning, slouching. If anything, they looked even more glum than they had when I arrived.

"We're leaving Denver," Jules said finally. "The producers yanked the plug when they found out what happened. What you've uncovered here, it's simply too dangerous."

"*I* think we should stay," Tina said, angry. This argument might have been going on all morning. "Gary wants to stay."

"Gary's in no state to be making these decisions," Jules said. "Besides, it's the producers' call, and they want out. It's back to ordinary haunted houses for us."

Looked like the werewolf pack wasn't the only group facing mutiny today.

Tina glared. "I'd rather listen to concussed Gary than the producers."

"Tina, it's too much. Voices in the attic are one thing. But this—we can't handle it."

The thing was, I couldn't blame them. Not even a little bit. This was my problem, not theirs. One of their people had been hurt, tens of thousands of dollars of equipment destroyed. Getting the hell out of town was the smartest thing to do.

I nodded, understanding. But I couldn't let them off that easy. "I thought you were investigators. I thought you wanted to study this sort of thing. Now you're telling me if it's not clean and pretty enough for TV you don't want anything to do with it?"

"Kitty, that's not fair," Jules said.

"No," I said. "It really isn't. None of this is. But you"—I nodded at Tina—"contacted this thing. You came closer to it than I ever could. And you"—at Jules this time—"have skills and knowledge to learn what it really is. You told me you got into this field because you were curious. Because you had to know. But I guess you don't have to know that badly."

They looked at me, and it was making me nervous. I wasn't going to change their minds by spouting platitudes at them, so I stood. Before I left, I put a jar of protection goo in the middle of the table.

"Just in case," I said and turned to stalk out. Maybe I hoped that they'd have a change of heart and call me back. They didn't.

chapter 9

My last stop had to wait until after nightfall, when I went to see Rick.

Rick occupied his predecessor's lair, which masqueraded as a high-end art and antique gallery called Obsidian. I'd never seen the place actually open for business, and no hours were posted in the window.

I didn't go in by the front door but passed right by the glass-fronted, stylish facade and went around back, where a concrete stairway led down to a utility door in the basement—the real vampire lair. I felt like an idiot knocking on the door. I should have had Girl Scout cookies or something.

I wasn't sure anyone would even answer; usually, we called each other and met someplace. Then the door opened in. A youngish-looking, annoyed guy stood there glaring at me—vampire, of course. He didn't look any different than anyone else, but the smell gave him away: cold. No warm blood moved under his skin. Rick had vampire minions, about the same number as I had wolves in my pack, some of whom had been Arturo's followers. I didn't know how smoothly the transition to the new leadership was going. Maybe I'd find out.

"Hi!" I said, and suppressed the "Avon calling" joke on the tip of my tongue. *We have some blush that would really do wonders for your pale complexion* . . . "Is Rick in?"

"Why are you here?" he said.

"I need to see Rick." My voice went lower, almost into a growl. My shoulders tightened. Wolf felt challenged, and I glared. But didn't meet his vampiric gaze.

His lip curled, like I'd said something funny. "You don't have the authority to beg an audience of the Master."

Oh, great. An old-school freak. I didn't have *any* patience for this bullshit.

"If you expect me to stand here and give you some line about how I *do* have the authority, as the alpha female of the werewolves beseeching his most exaltedness for a bare second of his infinite amount of time, yadda yadda and so on—no. Just no. You tell Rick I need to talk to him, and if he tells me to go away, fine, but I'm not going to argue about it with some flunky who has an inflated sense of his own importance. Being a vampire doesn't make you God or anything. Which leaves me baffled as to why you all feel the need to *act* like it."

His vampire hauteur slipped as he stared at me. Now he just seemed like a guy watching a car wreck.

"You have issues, don't you?" he said.

"You have no idea." As soon as I found a therapist who could even begin to deal with those issues, I might do something about it.

"I'm still not going to let you in to see Rick."

I took a deep breath for another round of arguing.

"Angelo." Rick appeared behind the gatekeeper, a shoulder to the wall, arms crossed, regarding the scene with amusement. Angelo started as much as I did; neither of us had sensed him approach.

On seeing him, Angelo ducked his head, cowering almost. He lowered his gaze and stepped back. The submissive gesture was almost wolfish.

"Let her through," Rick said. "I'll talk to her."

Without another word, Angelo stepped aside. He glared fiercely at me as I passed by him.

Side by side, Rick and I walked down the nondescript corridor to the inner sanctum.

"What's his problem?" I said.

"He was one of Arturo's, and he's decided he needs to work very hard to prove his loyalty to me. He doesn't seem to understand that I don't want to run things quite like Arturo did."

I was really glad that none of the wolves expected me to run the pack the way the old alphas did, which usually involved beating people up.

Inside the door to the back room, I had to stop and look around. I hadn't seen the place since Rick moved in. Mostly, it looked like a comfortable living room, or a library reading room. A couple of sofas and armchairs were grouped around a plain wood coffee table. Shelves on the wall were filled with books and boxes, almost cluttered. The walls were wood paneling, and area rugs softened the scuffed hardwood floor. A few lamps gave the whole room a warm glow.

"I like what you've done to the place."

"Thanks," he said.

Arturo, who'd acted like the king of his own little

world, had made the room a baroque fantasy, with tapestries on the walls, Persian rugs, and big red velvet and gilt chairs. Rick's decoration, practical and welcoming, almost made the place look like home. I might actually start to like spending time here.   •

On the far end, where Arturo had had what was essentially a throne on a dais, Rick had kept the dais but put a desk and big leather chair on it, turning it into an office. On top of the desk was a computer.

"Ooh!" I said, admiring it. "So vampires aren't allergic to technology."

He slid into the chair behind the desk and leaned back—very much like Arturo used to do in his plush and gilt monstrosity—and gave me a look.

I continued, "Now, what does a vampire do with a computer? Keep track of investments? Send e-mail to other vampires as you all plot to take over the world?"

"I spend a lot of time on Wikipedia making corrections to the entries of historical figures I've known."

I blinked at him. "Really?"

"No, Kitty. That was a joke."

"Oh. Because, you know, maybe you should."

"What's wrong? You wouldn't have come here to talk to me unless something's happened."

I pulled out yet another jar of Odysseus Grant's potion and set it on his desk.

He wrinkled his nose in disgust at it, even as he leaned forward for a closer look.

"What in the world is that?"

I shrugged. I was putting a lot of faith in this. "Ancient Egyptian protection spell. My attacker's been active the last couple of days."

"Yes. I heard about New Moon. Is everything going to be all right?"

"I think so. But I don't want anyone else to get hurt. I don't want to take any chances, so—here. If you want it."

He didn't seem any more enthusiastic about it, staring at the jar, vaguely repulsed. "We're resorting to witchcraft now?"

"You say it like you don't believe it'll work."

"It won't, against a vampire." Spoken with true vampire smugness.

I was starting to lose patience with him—it was like he wasn't listening to me. "I know you think this is part of some vampire plot. But it wasn't a vampire that tipped that van over or tried to burn down New Moon. This is something else entirely, and I could really use your help."

"Kitty, I promise, I'm doing everything I can."

"Like what? What are you doing? Pulling the Batman stunt on the tops of skyscrapers waiting for someone to walk along wearing a sign that says 'I'm the bad guy'? Do you have minions scouring the far corners of the globe for information? What are you doing?"

He studied me, calm and unflustered. Very little flustered Rick. When it did, he didn't panic. He just got angry. Calmly and pointedly angry.

"Here's what I know: This thing is invisible. It displays sentience and motivation. It's chosen the moments of its attacks carefully. The attacks are elemental, tied to fire. That makes it an old kind of magic—the kind of magic a vampire might use."

I tried to be calm like Rick. Calm like a vampire. "You're hunting for vampires. But what if this has nothing to do with vampire politics? This isn't about vampires, it's about revenge against *me*."

"A group led by a vampire is making attacks in my territory. This may not have begun with vampire politics, but I find it hard to ignore the implications. Magic like this doesn't come cheap. Is all this really a simple revenge plot?"

I had assumed it was pure revenge. We'd killed their head lycanthrope and several members of their cult and ruined their ritual. Revenge seemed like a good enough reason. "Now who's being paranoid?"

"When vampires are involved, the web is more tangled than you think," he said.

He had a point. Damn stupid vampires and their stupid sense of stupid superiority—

Rick turned aside to answer his cell phone. I hadn't even heard it ring.

"Yes?" A few moments of listening. I couldn't hear a thing, and I tried. "I'll be there in a minute. Stay out of sight."

He folded the phone away. "One of my people spotted a stranger nosing around New Moon. A vampire. We should go check it out. This might be what we've been waiting for."

He might as well have said "I told you so." Full of purpose now, Rick strode out the door, grabbing his black trench coat from a stand on the way out. I went with him, trying to be dignified and not scurry to keep up. A strange vampire lurking around New Moon? Of course I wanted to check it out; it made me territorial, and I wanted to growl.

I drove, with Rick in the passenger seat. New Moon

was only a few blocks away, but speed seemed important. "So how did vampires report in before cell phones?"

"Telepathy," he said.

"Wait a minute. That's a joke, right? Because if it was telepathy, you wouldn't need cell phones."

He just smiled. Sometimes I really hated vampires.

I pulled into the alley behind the restaurant. Yellow caution tape was stuck over the back door, waiting for the inspections and repairs that would get the place back on its feet. I hadn't noticed any strange figures lurking around. I climbed out of the car and took a deep breath.

I could still smell the fire, a tinge of wet soot coming from the building. But I didn't sense anything else. Rick, however, marched straight around the side of the building without hesitation. Again, I had to scurry to keep up.

At the front of the building we found a man standing at the door, regarding it like he was considering breaking it down. Frustration tightened his already sharp features. This, I decided, was a man who was used to getting his way. He wanted into New Moon, and he couldn't cross that threshold, and not because the door was locked. He acted like that wasn't what was stopping him.

He was a vampire. On a cool night like tonight, warm bodies made something like rivers through the air, trails of heat, living smells left behind. But a vampire was an island of cold. Almost, I couldn't sense him at all. Even the clean, dead smell I associated with vampires was muted on him, as if his scent had faded over the years.

I found that idea terrifying.

He turned to watch Rick and me approach. He was tall, thin, his face craggy. His whole body was probably lanky, but it was hidden under a long overcoat, turtleneck, slacks.

Expensive shoes. His dark hair was very closely shaved, giving him a severe, stern appearance. He frowned at us.

"You're Kitty Norville," he said, looking each of us over. Sizing us up. His expression revealed no conclusions. "What have you done to block the door?" His voice was nondescript. Steady, not particularly deep. Not particularly conversational.

Rick said, "May I ask: Who are you, and what are you doing here?"

He looked at Rick, taking him in in a glance, then gave me the same cursory look-over. Rick may have considered himself more laid-back than the average vampire Master, but he bristled at the perfunctory attention.

"I can help with your problem," the stranger said to us.

"How do you know we have one?" I said.

"The demon sent by the Band of Tiamat. Your problem." He turned his gray-eyed gaze on me. I avoided meeting that gaze.

How did he know this? My back went stiff, like hackles. This guy wasn't suave, blasé, bored, arrogant, or any of the other things I was used to seeing in vampires. Not even constantly, vaguely amused, which even the nice vampires were, like they'd seen it all and viewed the world as a humorous diversion. This guy was impatient, almost. On a mission.

"Demon?" Weird, having a name for it, an identification, whether or not he was right. "Are you some kind of demon hunter?"

"I suppose I'm an investigator. Of a sort."

"And I suppose you're trying to get inside to investigate?"

A single nod answered.

Rick said, "Who are you?"

"Roman," he said. He traced the door, running his hand along the hinges. "I noticed the blood around the outside, but that isn't what's blocking me. You haven't done anything specific to the entrance, have you? You've simply filled this place up with you and yours. Made it your own, keeping people like me out." He almost sounded admiring. Almost.

"There's really not much to see here. Not anymore. There was a fire," I said.

"You have no idea what you're dealing with, do you?" he said, sounding amazed, like he couldn't believe we really were that stupid.

"If you're trying to endear yourself to us, it's not working."

"And you might want to think about endearing yourself. At least to me," Rick said.

"Ah. Yes. You must be Rick. Or is it Ricardo?"

"I don't stand on ceremony. Rick is fine."

"Is there someplace we can talk? Since you don't seem inclined to invite me in."

"There's my place," Rick said. "A club, it's not far."

Rick wanted to get this guy on his home turf and thereby get some kind of advantage. I didn't argue.

The vampire Roman looked like he might want to try. When he gazed at Rick, eyes narrowed, he seemed to be calculating. Weighing the cost of refusing the request against his need to get what he wanted. I for one definitely wanted to find out why he was here, what he knew about demons, and what he knew about what the Band of Tiamat had released on me.

At last he said, "Fine. Shall we?"

He gestured sideways, across the street—in the direction of Rick's club, like he already knew where it was. He'd scoped the place out already. This guy was a real player.

Rick stepped off the curb and walked on. Roman fell into step beside him.

What could I do but follow?

chapter 10

I did *not* want to walk for six blocks with these two glaring at each other, sizing each other up, while I trailed behind like a stray dog. I *knew* that's what would happen, them marching together and posturing, and me prowling off to the side. I could holler at them and say that I was taking the car. Then again, I didn't want to miss anything good.

So, I skulked along, listening hard to catch everything they said. Except they didn't say a word. By nature and profession, I could not abide silence.

"So. Roman. Where's home for you?" Like I was trying to strike up a casual conversation with just anyone. But hey, that was my motto, wasn't it? Vampires and werewolves are people, too.

Too bad some of them didn't go along with my attempts at normality.

He didn't answer. Not a word. Silly me, I couldn't let it go. Had to keep poking until I got a reaction. "Come on, just a little hint?" I said. "You don't have to tell me where you're from originally. It took me years to get that out of Rick. I'm just asking where you hang your hat lately. Can

I guess? San Francisco? Miami? Although I can't imagine a vampire enjoying someplace like Miami."

Vampires didn't need to breathe, but I could almost hear Roman's exasperated sigh before he said, "I don't appreciate vapid attempts at conversation."

Now what did I say to that? "Huh. Vapid. That's a new one. I usually just rate irritating."

Rick chuckled.

We arrived at Psalm 23.

Along with Arturo's blood, control of the city, and a slew of vampire minions, Rick inherited God knew how much property around town in the form of corporations and holding companies, which formed the basis of his predecessor's wealth. Places like Obsidian. Another of those places was the trendy nightclub Psalm 23. It was dark, stylish, with a reputation as a hip young nightclub, a place to see and be seen. A meat market for the cool people. Maybe even a literal meat market. The place had a lot of shadowy corners and sheltered booths, and after dark, a few vampires could always be found lurking there, drawing in prey. Like spiders, as Rick had said.

I usually wasn't dressed well enough to get in without an argument. Or maybe it was the fact that some of the bouncers were vampires and didn't like me on principle. Not that I ever spent any time there for fun.

Tonight I was really not up to dress code in my jeans, T-shirt, and sneakers, but Rick waved us through and guided us to an alcove behind the bar, containing a small table and several chairs. This was his equivalent of my table in the back of New Moon. Impromptu office and vantage point. Rick offered me a drink; I took a soda. He did not offer Roman a drink.

While Rick and I sat, Roman remained standing a moment, surveying the main space of the club.

The place was surprisingly hopping for a Sunday night. Two bars, a large one in front and a small one in back, had people lined up, hip and well-dressed twenty-somethings in packs and in couples, most of them flirting. A DJ booth presided over a dance floor, which was empty now. Small tables here and there held another dozen people, nibbling on appetizers and sipping cocktails. Martini glasses glowed with a rainbow of concoctions smelling of alcohol. The air was heady with it. Some terrible hip-hop remix of an old eighties song thumped in the background.

We were quiet for a moment, watching Roman. He watched us in turn, and none of us twitched, none of us revealed a flicker of emotion.

Roman sat. "Hunting grounds for you and your people, I suppose?"

Rick didn't blink, didn't react. He regarded him with his thin, amused smile.

The stranger continued. "I suppose you even have your regulars, the ones who come here again and again, who've fallen under your spell and offer themselves to you. Your own herd. Like milk cows."

Vampires could draw blood from a person without killing, and I never asked too much about where Rick and his followers acquired the human blood that maintained their existence. They could even use a strange hypnosis to lull their prey and make them *want* to be bitten and fed on, which could be erotic for them both. They could also make their prey forget entirely what had happened. Clubs like this became prime feeding grounds. A suave, alluring vampire could come here, attract a young, vibrant creature who was also on the prowl for some kind of fulfillment, and if all the victims remembered was that they'd had a really good time, they'd probably come back for more. The parasitic circle of life—or undeath—was complete.

It was a pretty obvious setup when you knew what to look for. And the club made a hefty profit by overcharging for alcohol.

"Typical," Roman said, contemptuously. "Conventional. I'm sure you're aware, being conventional makes you predictable."

"That's not what we came here to discuss," Rick said.

"She called me a demon hunter. I suppose that's close enough. I've tracked one here."

"Demon," I said. Matter-of-fact, skeptical. "Horns, hooves, pitchfork. That kind of demon?"

"No," Roman said. "When it appears, you may not even see it, but it smells of fire, brimstone. You feel a sense of overwhelming dread. Of evil. The Band of Tiamat sent it to destroy you."

So, it was a demon. The thing had a label now. I almost felt better, like I was finally getting a grip on this. I could start searching the Internet.

It couldn't possibly be that easy.

"You know a lot about it," I said. "About the Band of Tiamat. About me."

He gave a wry smile. "You aren't exactly secretive about who you are and what you do. Five members of the Band were killed during your stay in Las Vegas, and soon after you are afflicted by . . . something. Obviously, they blame you for whatever happened."

"And you've arrived to do something about it," I said.

"For a price," Rick added. Roman inclined his head, a barest nod.

Of course for a price. Of course for an ulterior motive. He was a vampire. They didn't have any other kind of motive.

The way Rick was watching the guy—frowning, body straight and tense—I could tell he didn't trust Roman. He didn't like having this mysterious vampire of unknown power camping in his territory and dropping implications. Really, we had no reason to even believe him.

Once you started seeing the world in terms of conspiracy theories, such theories became darned easy to formulate. They were everywhere.

I said, "Here's the thing. There's a certain kind of con, where the con artist shows up someplace and conveniently he knows exactly what the problem is and how to solve it. This is because he created the problem for the express purpose of arriving in the nick of time to solve it. For a price."

"There's another alternative," Rick said. He glanced at me; I raised a questioning brow. Our silent conversation didn't exactly impart any information. "The priestess of the Tiamat cult—did you know she's a vampire?" Roman made a noncommittal gesture indicating that he should continue. No hint of yes or no. Rick continued. "Are you working with her?"

Ah, the great vampire conspiracy. I should have known Rick would take that route. I wanted to argue, because there was yet another alternative: Maybe Roman was telling the truth, and maybe he really could help.

"You're both right not to trust me, of course," Roman said. My alarm bells were still ringing because even that line was part of the con. Now he'd pull out a résumé and references from the mayor showing what a great demon hunter he was. He didn't, though. "You think I'm working for the priestess of Tiamat? Then why would I offer to end these attacks, when all she wants to do is destroy the werewolf and wreak havoc in your territory? Or you think that this doesn't involve the Band of Tiamat at all, and that I'm merely using them as an excuse to play my little trick on you? Did my research, found a likely rube with a likely story I could use to divert blame from myself . . . you're right. It's a very good con. I wish I'd thought of it. But you need my help. I'm here to remove that creature from the face of the earth, and I guarantee you don't have the skills or knowledge to do it yourself."

"You're not telling us everything," I said, and thought, well, duh, he's a vampire, they never tell everything.

"I tell you everything, you no longer need my help," he said. So much for altruism.

"And the price?" asked Rick.

"For banishing the demon, for preserving the sanctity of your territory, I want permanent free passage in Denver," he said. "Not so large a price, really."

This made his offer feel like even more of a setup. He'd been planning this. Now the question was: Would Rick allow a powerful demon-hunting vampire to set up shop in his territory?

Rick looked him over. They might as well have been a couple of guys playing poker, and for a moment I flashed on an imagined scene from Rick's Old West past: sitting across the table from Doc Holliday, sizing him up, wondering who was the fastest draw. Rick smiling just a little because he didn't need to be the fastest draw—a bullet wouldn't knock him down. Now that was the way I liked to gamble.

Rick traced an invisible line on the table. "No power? No territory? Just free passage. Live and let live. So to speak."

"That's right," Roman said. "I'm careful. I don't hunt to excess. I'm a good neighbor, as they say."

"You know, I made the same deal with the Master who preceded me."

"And he trusted you."

"Not quite. He just didn't think I was a threat."

"You think I'm a threat?"

Gah, another game of vampire chicken. I fidgeted.

"You're older than I am," Rick said. Casually. Like he didn't just make the bottom drop out of my stomach. I studied Roman, and of course he didn't look all that old, maybe a well-worn midthirties. But vampires could apparently smell the age rolling off each other—and they could mask their own power, hide their age, keep others from finding out. Not flaunt it, encourage others to underestimate them. Arturo had believed Rick was only two hundred years old.

So. Rick had just told Roman that he wasn't fooling him.

"Age is not the only criterion for power," Roman said.

"No. But it's a start."

"I could let you think about it. If you think you have that much time."

"There's always time," said Rick, the way only a vampire could.

"Of course. For some." Roman gave me a pitying glance.

He stood. Meeting over. "I'll confess, Ricardo. You aren't what I expected."

"I'm not sure I want to know, but what did you expect?"

"I'd have expected someone who snatched his territory from its former Master by wit and guile to show a little more fear."

Okay, this guy knew far too much about us and what had been going on here. I didn't need to know so much where he got such information; plenty of people knew about what had happened, but I wanted to know why he was so interested.

"You play much poker, Roman?" Rick said. Oh, I was so totally going to ask him about Doc Holliday.

"Some. Here and there."

"We should play sometime," Rick said.

Roman leaned forward. His smile was thin and wicked. "I thought that's what we were doing."

"Touché," Rick said, chuckling, and the tension faded. I hadn't realized I'd been holding my breath.

Roman's smile seemed a little more relaxed, a little more genuine. "You need time to think it over. I understand."

"I'd appreciate it," Rick said. "Come back in two nights."

"I look forward to it. Good night, both of you."

"Good night," Rick said. I waved weakly.

Roman walked straight to the front door, not even glancing at the slinkily dressed women who followed him with their gazes. He clearly had someplace more important to be than here.

I didn't like this. These two had taken the situation in

an entirely different direction, one I wasn't sure I could follow. When he was gone, I asked, "What are we going to do? We need his help."

"I can't let him in, Kitty. He isn't just here for the demon. That's an excuse."

"Can we worry about that later?"

"Not if you want there to *be* a later," he said.

I rolled my eyes. "When vampires get this pretentious, all I really want to do is make fun of them. Can't you give us little people a break? This thing, this demon or whatever it is, is trying to destroy my world piece by piece, and if this Roman guy knows how to stop it, we have to listen to him."

"There has to be another way," Rick said. "If he knows how to stop it, then we can find out how to do it without him. We just have to look for it."

"What do you think I've been doing?" I said, growling a little.

We glared at each other across the table. I almost never met Rick's gaze. I trusted him—but he was a vampire, and vampires could do things with their eyes. He could change my mind for me, and I wouldn't even know it. This time, I met his gaze anyway, just to show him how serious I was.

Glory be, he looked away first. The ghost of Wolf's tail waved like a banner in triumph.

"I'm sorry," he said. "I know you're taking the brunt of this."

"Damn straight."

"But Roman—we can't turn to him, Kitty. We have to find another way."

Wasn't a whole lot of *we* going on at the moment. Rick was so busy looking at the big picture he couldn't see the details, *my* details, like how we all could have died last night. Too bad Roman hadn't left a card so I could contact him behind Rick's back. I was only mildly shocked that I was considering going behind Rick's back on this.

"Remember, Kitty, we're supposed to have a partner-ship." I must have looked put-out, because he smirked at me. "I've had a lot of practice reading people. I may not know what you're thinking. But I can guess."

"I have a question for you: Did you ever meet Doc Holliday?"

"You're changing the subject."

I had little practice reading people in person. Listening to people, judging their voices, was another thing entirely, but Rick's voice was too calm. He was like a brick wall sitting in front of me.

"Why not? You've already made up your mind. Roman will come back, and you'll say no and let me burn."

He bowed his head. "It's not like that. But some prices are too high. If he's working with the priestess, and they get a foothold here—"

"But what if he *isn't* working with the priestess? What if he really can do what he says?"

Rick took a breath in preparation for speaking, then said, "We'll find a way through this, I promise."

I had to have faith that we would. We'd always managed before, somehow.

Before I left, Rick said, "Kitty. To answer your question—yes. I played a game of poker with Holliday once, in Central City. Interesting guy."

The bastard sat with his elbows on the table, fingers steepled, as nonchalant as if he'd just commented on the weather. I stared, my jaw hanging open, a million questions stopped up in my throat. He enjoyed that, dropping these bombshells, these epic stories waiting to be told. He always refused to elaborate.

So I didn't give him the satisfaction of having me beg him to tell me more. I walked out, but not before catching his amused grin.

Finally, far too late that night, I returned home. Ben was on the sofa, wearing sweats and a T-shirt, eating something straight out of a Chinese takeout box and watching a talking-heads news show on TV. That man was far too set in his bachelor ways for me to expect him to change his domestic habits. Actually, I thought it was kind of cute. I liked the idea that being with me hadn't disrupted his life too radically. I wanted us to be comfortable. To fit together without breaking.

As I closed the door, he sat up and set aside the food. Glared at me, just a little. "I was about to call."

"Things got busy," I said, tired. I wanted to curl up in bed with him and forget about the day. For now, I slumped onto the sofa next to him. He put his arm around my shoulders and we sat side by side, talking to the air in front of us.

"Productive busy?"

"Rick claimed that he once played poker with Doc Holliday." After all that had happened, that made the biggest impact.

"Huh. So, what does Rick knowing Doc Holliday have to do with whatever tried to burn down the restaurant?" Ben said.

"Nothing. It's just that he drives me crazy with all this stuff he isn't telling me."

"You expect him to tell you his life story? All five hundred years of it?"

Maybe he had a point. "Speaking of the Old West, a stranger rode into town this evening. A vampire claiming to be a demon hunter, says he knows all about the Band of Tiamat and how to stop the attacks."

"Really?" He glanced at me, brow creased like he didn't believe it. "What's the catch?"

"That's what I asked. He wants to settle in Denver, it sounds like. Rick doesn't want him here."

"Is it a real offer? Do you think he can really help?"

"I don't know."

"What's he like?"

"Vampire. Rick says he's older, but he's different than the old ones I've met. I was under the impression they tend to stay put, become Master of a city. Get pompous as hell. This guy seemed . . . I don't know. Driven. Like he was on a mission. I don't think I've ever met a vampire on a mission. Not like this. Maybe he's just a really dedicated demon hunter, like he says."

"But then he wouldn't be asking for something in return," Ben pointed out.

"This is why I'm glad I have a lawyer around," I said. "You don't trust anybody."

He shrugged. "I trust you."

He said it with such earnestness, I almost got teary-eyed. "Thanks."

We leaned into each other for a long, warm kiss that made the day's tension melt away. Eventually—about when the shirts came off and the groping started in earnest—we made our way to the bedroom.

"Can you do something for me?" he murmured between kisses and catches in his breath. My imagination rolled on for a moment, anticipating what he'd ask, wondering if it would be something I hadn't already thought of involving him, his body, my body, and the bed. I made an affirmative noise while nuzzling his neck.

"The next time you're gone all day, or you run into that vampire, or anything like that happens, will you call me?"

Well, that wasn't very sexy. I pulled back enough to see his face, which was tired and anxious-looking. "You sound worried."

"I guess I am. It was getting late, and I just kept thinking about what would happen if this thing attacked you and I wasn't there."

We hadn't spent much time apart since we hooked up, almost a year ago now. When we had been apart, either one or both of us had been in trouble. We were a pack, and we wanted to be together. Being alone wasn't safe.

"You want to watch my back for me?" I said.

"Don't you think it needs watching?" Watching, or feeling up, one or the other. His hands pressed into my skin, kneading my muscles, locking me close to him.

I pressed up to him and curled my legs around him. "You tell me."

With that, we returned energetically to the business at hand. I for one felt much better come morning.

chapter **11**

Researching demons went about the same as researching every other supernatural topic I'd ever delved into. Much of it was vague, paranoid, filled with warnings and hysteria. There seemed to be a higher degree of religious nuttery than usual. The most generally accepted way to repel demons was to find a priest to conduct an exorcism. In fact, the Catholic Church had an accepted, approved set of procedures for exorcising demons. It was usually for exorcising them from people. All too often, examples presented as demonic possession were in reality more mundane cases of severe mental illness. Those people needed medical help, not holy water and Latin chants.

Nearly any word for monster or supernatural creature in any language could be translated as "demon" in English, which still left a world of possibilities. I hadn't learned very much more than when I started.

This thing's attacks were getting worse, striking new targets, so I made a new, bigger batch of the protection potion. Then I went to my parents' house.

They weren't home, which was good. I was still hoping not to draw them directly into this, but I wanted the house—and them inside it—to be safe, so I made a circle around it with the potion. I hid it in the grass and shrubs, ran it through the gate in the fence around the backyard, then back up the other side. In front of the house, a concrete walk led to the front door. Wasn't any way I could hide the potion on the concrete, so I painted a sticky black line across it to finish the circle. Maybe they would think it was dirt, or the trail of a weird insect or something. Maybe they wouldn't notice it at all. I finished and left as quickly as I could, and no one called the police on me, which was even better.

At my sister Cheryl's, however, I got caught.

The problem was the golden retriever running loose in the fenced backyard. It was named Bucky or something. I didn't really remember, because I avoided the beast like the plague. He could sense what I was, had decided that I was a threat, and let his displeasure be known every time I appeared. When I came over to visit, Bucky was exiled to the backyard. Maybe he was just resentful.

I had spread the potion in the front of the house, then got to the gate in the fence. I opened it an inch and was met by the growling, slavering jaws of Bucky. Weren't golden retrievers supposed to be stupid and friendly? This thing was acting like a Doberman.

I slammed the gate shut and held it closed while Bucky threw himself against it. Oh, if I could just let Wolf loose to have a go at him, we'd shut him up real quick—

"Bucky, what the hell's the matter with you?" That was my sister, approaching from the backyard side of the fence. I heard a commotion, presumably her grabbing the dog by the collar, and the dog whining in frustration, trying to tell her what was wrong. *What is it, Lassie? There's a werewolf trying to break in?* She murmured admonitions at him, but he kept making noises like he was struggling to break free and have at me again.

So much for stealth.

"Hey, Cheryl?" I called. "It's me."

After a moment she said, "Kitty? What are you doing here?"

I winced. "Long story. Can you put the mutt inside? Then I'll tell you all about it." Well, I'd tell her some of it.

"Mutt?" she said, indignant. "He has papers!"

Whatever. But the commotion was moving away as she presumably hauled Bucky into the house.

Cheryl was my older sister. I'd idolized her when we were kids, even though we'd fought like heathens. Now she had settled into suburban bliss, with the nice house in a new subdivision, the swell husband, the two kids, and the dog, all with names out of a 1950s sitcom. But she still wore jeans and band T-shirts and listened to punk when the kids were napping. I loved my sister. We still occasionally fought like heathens.

When the backyard was quiet, I opened the gate and continued spreading the blood potion. Cheryl met me halfway across the backyard. Bucky was at the sliding glass door, barking at us, spitting dog slobber on the glass.

She wrinkled her nose when she saw what I was doing. "What is that?"

"It's a long story."

"Is that going to kill my lawn?"

That was something I hadn't considered. But blood was high in nutrients, right? A fertilizer? "No," I said, and hoped I was right.

"Okay," she drawled, hands on hips, glaring at me. "I may regret asking this, but *why* are you doing this?"

I tried to be as brief and clear as possible. "There's this demon attacking me—it's responsible for the fire at New Moon. This is a protection potion. It's supposed to keep you all safe."

She let me work in silence for a few more moments. Then, "Why is this demon attacking you?"

"I pissed some people off in Vegas. Long story."

Another long pause before she said, "Kitty, you're my sister and I love you, but have you ever considered another line of work?"

I had absolutely no response to that. I giggled. "I'm sorry. I try to be careful, honest. These things just *happen*."

"Are we really in danger? Is this like last time?"

"No, this is nothing like last time, and you're not in danger. This is just a precaution." This was like dealing with the pack—I had to sound confident.

Cheryl looked skeptical.

"So," I said. "How are Mark and the kids?"

"They're fine. You're changing the subject."

I stopped and faced her. "This'll work. And you have to promise not to tell Mom. I did their house already. They don't need to know."

I expected her to argue, but she didn't. Because she understood. We both wanted to protect our mother from anything that might upset her. This would probably upset her.

She walked with me as I finished the circle of protection. Mission accomplished.

"I guess I'd better get going," I said.

"How much trouble are you in, really?" she said, arms crossed.

"A lot, I think. But I'm working on it."

"Be careful." She sounded very serious.

"Yeah. Let me know if anything weird happens, okay?"

"Weirder than usual?"

"Yeah," I said, smiling. "That."

We hugged. I left another jar of the stuff with her, just in case. She waited to watch me drive away before going back inside.

My cell phone rang Tuesday morning when Ben and I were still in bed. I didn't want to answer it, but I couldn't pretend it wasn't my phone, because it played "I Wanna Be Sedated." It went almost all the way through the chorus before Ben grunted and poked me, forcing me to action.

Caller ID read Hardin. I groaned.

The very last thing I needed in the midst of all this was a call from Detective Jessi Hardin. She was the Denver PD's resident expert on what they called paranatural situations. If a body turned up in a back alley that looked like it had been mauled by a wolf or drained of blood, she headed the investigation. This was mostly through happenstance and Hardin's bullheaded determination to educate herself now that these things—these monsters—were in the open and publicly acknowledged. She was a believer, and the supernatural didn't scare her. No, it only pissed her off.

For some reason, she always called me when she

stumbled across something new and freaky. Like I knew any more than she did.

I didn't want to answer, but if I didn't, she'd show up in person. She usually brought along crime-scene photos of dead bodies. I wanted to avoid that if I could.

Just before the call would be shunted to voice mail, I answered. "You have a body, don't you?"

"I have a body," she answered, but without the peppy sarcasm I had come to expect from her. One of the things that made her good at her work was a sense of humor.

"I guarantee you it wasn't werewolves this time, I promise." If one of my pack attacked a person, I'd deal with the murderer myself.

"I know. This is something completely different. Kitty—"

"That doesn't make me feel any better. Why are you calling me? Are you going to show me gruesome crime-scene photos?"

"Kitty, be quiet for a minute, please."

I shut up, because she sounded serious, stone serious, like she wanted to be doing anything other than having this conversation.

She said, "Do you know a man named Mick Cabrerra?"

The name took a minute to click, because I'd heard his last name maybe twice in my life. But I knew only one Mick, and my mind turned worried circles wondering what my disgruntled werewolf minion could have gotten into. "Yes."

Hardin's voice was strained. "We found his body last night. I'm sorry."

"What?" I'm afraid I squeaked. "What? But how? I saw

him just a couple days ago, he was fine. What could kill him—he's a werewolf. Did you know he's a werewolf? He can't be dead."

"Yes. The blood test is standard autopsy procedure now. We haven't been able to reach any next of kin, and he had your name and number in his wallet as an emergency contact. Was he part of your pack?"

"Yes," I said quietly. "But how did he die?"

She sighed, which meant it was something odd, unusual, something she didn't want to talk about. "It's complicated. But there was a fire."

Somehow, strangely, that didn't surprise me. Fire had been hunting us, and now it had gotten one of us. I didn't want to picture Mick burned up like that, dying like that. I closed my eyes as the breath went out of me.

"Do you want to come down to the morgue? To see him? We can talk about it in person, if you'd like."

I wasn't sure I wanted to see him; I'd already seen enough bodies. But I thought that later on I might want the closure.

"Okay, yeah," I said. "I should do that."

"We're going to spend a little while longer looking for his family."

"I'm not sure he has any family, Detective."

"Then you may be it. But we can talk about that later. Do you need directions to get here?"

Ben was awake, sitting up, and looking at me as I listened to the directions and tried to memorize them. I'd probably have to look it up anyway. Or maybe Ben would know. I'm not sure what kind of desperate, forlorn expression I showed him. He touched my leg.

"Okay," I said when she'd finished. "I'll be there as soon as I can." I shut off the phone.

Ben waited for the explanation as I wiped tears away. This was stress, thinking of everything I needed to do, going to see his body, telling everyone else what had happened. I'd taken over this pack. I was the alpha. I was supposed to protect them.

I climbed out of bed and started dressing. "That was Detective Hardin. She says that Mick is dead."

For a moment, we paused and looked at each other. His expression was stark, disbelieving. "Oh. God," he said. "How?"

"Fire."

Then Ben was standing next to me and holding me, a tight, comforting embrace without words. Because what could we say, really? But I needed the hug.

chapter 12

What the police procedural TV shows can't get across is
the smell.

The morgue smelled overwhelmingly of alcohol and
death. More so even than a hospital, which at least had a
variety of odors of life and living overlaying the antiseptic
reek. This place was a war between sterility and decay.
A normal human would smell and maybe even be bothered by a sickly tang lodging in the back of the throat. But
for me and Ben, for any lycanthrope, the smell filled our
lungs and seeped in through our pores. My arms broke out
in gooseflesh. I should have been getting used to this, the
way these grotesque smells assaulted my sensitive werewolf nose.

I took shallow breaths and thought about escape.

Detective Hardin met us in the lobby. She was a brisk
woman, always moving like she was in a hurry and losing
her patience. Of average height, with dark hair tied in a
tail, she wore a functional pantsuit that might have been
on her for a couple of days now. The shadows under her
eyes suggested she'd worked through the night. Her smile

was grim, and she didn't have a quip, which added another layer of depression and unreality to the situation. I wanted Hardin back to her snide, not in the middle of a disaster self.

"Kitty. Mr. O'Farrell. Thanks for coming. It's this way." We walked with her through a set of double doors marked private, then down a chilly corridor of off-white walls and an institutional linoleum floor.

"Can you tell me what exactly killed him? You said it was a fire, but complicated. Did his building burn? Was it someplace else?"

Apparently, she couldn't tell me. "How long have you known Mr. Cabrerra?" she asked instead.

"A few years," I said. "I didn't know him well. We weren't best friends or anything."

"But you were both werewolves? Part of the same pack?"

"That doesn't mean we all walk around arm in arm singing 'We Are Family.' The pack here is pretty standoffish, to tell you the truth. I only ever see most of the others on full-moon nights."

She turned a quizzical expression to me. "Where exactly do you all go on full-moon nights?"

"I'm not going to tell you that, Detective."

Unsurprised, she shrugged and continued on. The question had been offhand and unimportant, but I wondered if maybe we needed to start driving out to Kansas or Wyoming, to make sure no one bothered us.

"Did Mr. Cabrerra smoke?" she asked.

"I don't think so," I said. I'd never seen him light up, and he didn't smell like someone who smoked. Now *there* was an interesting set of smells a werewolf could spot from a mile away. Detective Hardin smelled like that: sooty, musty, sharp.

"Did he work with fire at all? Was he a welder, a mechanic, anything that would have had him in contact with open flames, or with anything volatile?"

"I don't know. I don't think so. Why?"

"I'm just trying to rule out all the logical explanation, because the illogical one has everyone twitching."

Detective Hardin, as head of the Denver PD's newly established Paranatural Unit, got all the cases that made people twitch. She'd landed in the position by accident, but she seemed to be thriving in it. Fortunately or unfortunately, depending on your point of view.

We paused outside a room. So this was it. I braced. Ben curled his hand around mine.

She took a deep breath and said, "What do you know about spontaneous human combustion?"

I hadn't braced well enough, because I blinked at her, dumbstruck. "What?"

"I thought you knew about all this supernatural crap," she said. "Spontaneous human combustion, the idea that a human body can, for unknown reasons, suddenly generate enough heat to ignite."

"I know the definition," I said. "I can't say I've ever encountered it. Ever." I'd never even had a crazy person call in to the show wanting to talk about it, and that was saying something.

"Well. It's on the list of what might have happened to Mr. Cabrerra. It's on the bottom of the list—but frankly, it's about as likely as anything else, based on what I've been able to come up with. There's no reason he should have burned to death in the middle of his apartment, when nothing else caught fire."

Fire. Burning. The smell of sulfur and brimstone. The smell from last full-moon night, the van at Flint House, and the fire at New Moon.

I shook my head at the door we stood in front of. "Detective, I've changed my mind. I don't think I can do this." I didn't want to have to smell Mick burned and carry that memory with me forever.

"It's not that bad, Kitty." She touched my arm briefly. "Not as bad as you'd expect."

She opened the door. The room was small, sterile, with a linoleum floor and tiled walls. It seemed more like a doctor's office than what I'd pictured a morgue being like. A couple of plastic chairs stood against the wall, and a gurney rested in the middle. A body lay on it, a sheet drawn up to its bare shoulders.

He looked like Mick. I recognized him, short black hair, stocky frame, wide nose, and round cheeks. He hadn't been burned to a crisp, but he had been burned. His face was red, like a sunburn. Blackened scorch marks reached up from under the sheet, streaks climbing his neck to his chin. His hair looked singed, scorched. It was like he'd been caught in a flash explosion at the level of his heart.

Ben and I stared for a moment. I kept wondering what had happened. The protection spell, the potion Grant had given me—it didn't work. The thought almost pushed me to panic, because it meant none of us was safe. New Moon, my human family, everyone I'd given the jars to, all of it was for nothing.

But no, I'd given Mick a jar of the potion yesterday—and he'd scoffed at it. I'd have to find out if he had used it—he probably hadn't. Maybe this thing killed him simply because it could.

I should have done more. I should have protected him. Inside, Wolf howled.

"Do you need a minute, or are you ready to leave?" she said.

I closed my eyes and turned toward the door. "I'm ready."

Hardin led us to a nearby conference room, where we could talk. She offered coffee, but I wasn't thirsty.

"We got the call about ten last night," she said. "Someone in Mr. Cabrerra's apartment building smelled smoke coming from his unit. The building manager couldn't find the source, and Mr. Cabrerra's door was locked. The manager called the fire department; they broke in and found the body. Nothing else had burned. As I understand it, werewolves aren't indestructible, they're just really tough to kill without the magic silver bullet. Am I right?"

"You need to take the heart or cut off the head. Or do so much damage they can't heal before they die of blood loss," I said.

She nodded. "The medical examiner performed an autopsy last night. His heart was destroyed—we assume that's what killed him, that if it hadn't gotten to his heart he might have survived. But this is what has the ME wigged out. He burned from the inside out. It's like someone reached inside him and lit a blowtorch."

Numb and confused, I said, "This is why you brought up spontaneous human combustion?"

"Unless you know of some other weird, unlikely phenomenon that could cause something like this."

I looked at Ben, who shrugged and said, "Hey, you're the expert."

Why did people keep thinking that? I must have been doing a good job of fooling everyone. Werewolves were werewolves—that didn't make them any more prone to having unlikely things like this happen to them, did it?

As a matter of fact, it did. This thing had already proven it would go after the whole pack, not just me. A moment of dizziness made me hold my head to steady myself. I had to make this stop. There had to be a way to make this stop.

Ben put his hand on my leg, and the touch anchored me. Brought me back to the table, the conference room, Hardin, the horror of the situation. Didn't stop tears from falling.

Hardin watched me. "You do know something. What is it?"

Once again, I explained the trip to Vegas, the cult, the sacrifice, the attacks, Grant's potion, and my suspicion that Mick hadn't used it. If nothing else, there'd be no such thing as a secret Babylonian cult lurking in Sin City anymore. *Everybody* was going to know about it at this rate. Not that everyone believed me. I'd have thought that Hardin would be beyond disbelief after everything she'd seen and studied, but her expression was blank.

She said, "That doesn't get me any closer to figuring out what happened or who to arrest."

"Yeah, well, sorry about that."

"What's the likelihood of this happening again?" she asked.

Likely. Very likely. I didn't want to think about it, so I turned away, biting my lip.

"Do you want to talk about some kind of police protection?" she said. She was being as nice as she'd ever been to me, but her voice was still businesslike, almost harsh, when what I wanted was for someone to pat me on the head and say, "There, there."

Ben said, "Police protection isn't going to do a whole lot of good for people burning up from the inside."

"I can't sit around doing nothing," she said, scowling.

"Trust me, Detective, as soon as I find the magic spell that will make all this go away, I'll let you know," I said.

She made an offhand gesture that might have been saying, touché. "I'll keep digging on my end. But the usual request applies: If you find out anything, let me know, right?"

"You too, I hope."

"Will do. Thanks for stopping by."

She escorted us to the front door, said the farewells, then went back in. I almost said something to her about taking a break, getting some sleep, food, fresh clothes. I was worried about her and didn't want her to burn out—metaphorically or literally, given the circumstances. Every time I saw her she looked harried beyond all reason. But the door closed, she was gone, and I lost my chance.

Leaning against Ben, I prompted a hug. We clung to each other, squeezing comfort into each other.

I muttered into Ben's shoulder, "This isn't a coincidence, this can't be a coincidence. Spontaneous human combustion isn't spontaneous when you're being haunted by a heat-generating demon."

"That makes sense," Ben agreed.

"This is my fault. I'm the reason this is happening, and now I've put everyone in danger—"

"Kitty. You couldn't help it. You couldn't know. What

were you supposed to do, let those guys in Vegas kill you?" Ben said.

If I could go back, knowing what I knew now, knowing I could save Mick's life, maybe everyone's life . . . I might have let them kill me. I looked at him, despairing, my eyes large and shining.

"Let's go home," he said and kissed the top of my head.

"Even though we might burst into flames with no warning at any minute?"

"Kitty." He gave me a reprimanding look.

In the car and on the road, I slumped and looked out the window, watching the world go by. Wondering how to stop an enemy that we couldn't see, couldn't identify, couldn't anticipate.

I said, "I can't believe I'm the closest thing he has to next of kin." It wasn't fair that he didn't have anyone. I hadn't known him well enough to be the emergency contact in his wallet.

"You might not have noticed, but most people who get stuck as werewolves aren't the kind who have close ties to big families. Present company excepted, of course."

"I'd noticed," I said. "I am constantly reminded that this isn't the life I signed up for."

"Does that include me?" He quirked a wry smile.

Erp. I could see now how my statement could be taken the wrong way. Especially since a relationship with Ben had been about as unexpected as getting attacked by a werewolf in the first place.

I leaned my head on his shoulder. "I'm the last person to complain about the pleasant little surprises that happen along the way."

It was the unpleasant ones I was getting sick of.

Near home, I spotted a familiar motorcycle and rider in the rearview mirror. Same helmet, same jacket, following about three cars back. Peter, still at it. I wished I had gotten a phone number from him, so I could call him. Tell him to stop this. He wasn't going to learn anything I hadn't already told him, and I really didn't want him getting caught up in this demon business.

My first job was to tell the rest of the pack what had happened. We'd lost one of our own, and anybody could be next.

Ben took the notepad where I kept everyone's contact info away from me. "I'll make the calls," Ben said. "I'm a lawyer, I'm used to giving people bad news."

I let him. That left me to call Odysseus Grant.

His phone rang. And rang. He didn't answer. Either he was busy, or he had finally gotten sick of me and wasn't taking my calls anymore. I tried not to think the worst: Something had happened to him, he'd confronted the Band of Tiamat, or they'd confronted him, and it had ended badly. And I'd never know.

I turned on the computer and called up web sites for Las Vegas newspapers, looking for something spectacular and out of the ordinary: mass murder, fires, chaos in the streets. But I didn't find anything unusual, at least not by Las Vegas standards. A couple of crooked politicians were exposed, a tycoon announced plans for a new resort. If something had happened, it might have been so subtle it hadn't made the news.

Or maybe he was busy and not answering his phone.

By the time I'd finished, Ben set his phone down, blowing out a sigh. He pursed his lips.

"Well?" I said.

"I told Shaun and Becky. They'll spread the word. They want to talk. That's probably not a bad idea."

"Show some kind of leadership so the troops don't lose faith?"

"Something like that. They suggested meeting in the mountains. I told them we could be there in a couple of hours, for anyone who wants to talk."

The forest where we spent full moons would be heavy with the memory and smell of shifting, of turning wolf and running. Feelings would run high there. I wasn't sure everyone could handle it. I didn't want any more trouble than we already had. "I'm not sure that's such a good idea."

Ben ran a frustrated hand through his hair. "I would have told them New Moon, but so much for that."

We were running out of territory.

"Okay," I said. "But we'd better get going. I want to get there first."

"Occupy the high ground?"

"Something like that. I just think it'll go better if we're there already. It's a dominance thing."

"It usually is," he said.

The human side could be as sarcastic as it wanted about pack dynamics, but the pack still seemed to win out in the end.

chapter 13

We were too late. We arrived at the remote parcel of land where we parked on full-moon nights, and Shaun, Becky, and a half dozen others had already arrived. I bristled, because it meant they had the same thought I had and wanted to make a statement. It was almost a challenge.

They'd carpooled in a couple of cars, which were parked to the side. They lined up along the barbed-wire fence that marked the property: arrayed in a straight line, leaning on fence posts or standing in tough poses, arms crossed, glaring, frowning. Ben parked the car in front of them. We got out and leaned on the hood. Stared them down. I tried not to think about the OK Corral.

Most of these people knew me in the old days, when I was a new wolf, weak, bottom of the pecking order. Back then, being submissive was far easier than trying to stand up for myself. Being submissive meant the bigger, badder wolves looked out for me. Most of the time. When they weren't beating me up themselves. It had seemed like a fair trade at the time.

That meant some of these wolves remembered how

easy it used to be to knock me around. They had to be wondering, how tough was I *really*? How easy would it be to nudge me out of that top spot?

I got a lot of mileage out of the fact that me returning to Denver as a badass alpha had confused the hell out of some of them. It put them in "wait and see" mode. But I was running out of time to prove my worth. I had to convince them they were better off with me in charge than not.

What a mess. I wondered if this was the demon's main purpose all along: not to destroy me directly, but to undermine my position in the pack to the point where the other wolves did the job.

I thought about what a real badass alpha werewolf would do in a situation like this, and all I could think was drill sergeant, screaming at the troops to get them in line, punishing them for questioning my authority. I didn't want to do that. I wasn't very good at that sort of thing. I wasn't a drill sergeant, and we weren't in the army. We were supposed to be a family.

"Hi," I said, as neutrally as I could. Not cheerful, not angry, not scared. Definitely not scared. They had every right to be here asking questions. No need for me to get all defensive about it. Ben stood next to me, looking surly. The muscle of the operation. Good cop/bad cop. That made me want to smile. "Is everyone okay? Did anything unusual happen to anyone else last night?"

"Besides Mick dying?" said Dan. One of the tough guys, lanky and muscular. Not so tough that he liked to stick his neck out, usually.

"Yeah," I said softly. "Besides that."

I tried to read the body language. People were scared, trying to cover it up with anger. Bunched shoulders stood in for raised hackles. Eyes glared and lips were open, just a muscle twitch away from being bared. But they weren't threatening me, not yet. Nobody was glaring at *me*. They glared at the ground, or off to the side, or at my shoulder, but they didn't make eye contact to offer a direct challenge. I hoped my neutral tone put them off-balance. If I wasn't aggressive, maybe they'd be less likely to show aggression, and we could do this without fighting about it.

"He's really dead?" Shaun said. His arms were crossed, his dark eyes serious.

I nodded. "I saw his body at the morgue." Now I was glad I had done it, so I could say that with confidence.

"It was the thing. The same thing that went after us the other night?"

"I think so. He seemed to have burned to death." There were winces, a couple of hushed exclamations.

"Why him?" Becky—average height, sharp features, short auburn hair—asked.

Shaun said, "He didn't want to use that stuff you gave us. He didn't think it would work. I don't think he even opened the jar."

That didn't surprise me, but it made me sad. "He didn't trust me."

"I think he didn't believe there was a situation he couldn't fight his way out of."

My inner self diverged. I wanted to hang my head, shed tears, apologize. Because I was sorry. Maybe I couldn't have kept him alive in spite of his own stubbornness, but I was the one who brought this down on us all.

I couldn't react that way. Wolf couldn't. I couldn't let my back slouch an inch. I had to keep my gaze up. I had to be strong and not show a bit of weakness, or none of them would trust me.

Not that any of them ought to be trusting me, but I couldn't think that, either.

"What are you going to do about it?" Becky asked.

A death called for vengeance. Or at least justice. If nothing else, stopping the thing that did this meant it wouldn't happen again. That was all I really wanted. Now, if this had been a rival pack of werewolves attacking us, we'd have known what to do. But this demon was invisible, untrackable. My confidence sounded hollow.

"I'm in contact with someone who might be able to stop this thing," I said. "He seems to know exactly what to do. The bad news is he's a vampire."

"It always comes back to the vampires," Dan said.

"Yeah, that's exactly how they like it," Shaun answered. "What kind of deal are you going to have to make with this guy?"

"I don't know yet. I'm meeting with him and Rick tonight. I won't give up our autonomy, but I have to do what I can to keep us all safe."

"You could try keeping your head down," Dan said.

A few huffs of agreement answered, as well as a short laugh. Not keeping my head down had gotten me in trouble with the old alphas. And look where that had gotten me.

"Good advice to follow there," I said, glaring at him. He ducked his head and glanced away, like a good lupine subordinate. "You guys want the old management style back, I'll step aside and leave you to it." That came out more angry than I meant it to.

Nobody said anything. Score one for my side.

"The potion works," I said. "Use it. Know that I'm

doing something. I'm not going to let this slide. Any questions?"

"Let us know if there's anything we can do," Shaun said.

"Thank you."

Gaze down, Shaun came over, nodded at Ben, squeezed my hand, then continued on to the other cars. Then came Becky, Dan, and the five others, one by one, all with their gazes lowered, all giving me a brief touch to show that yes, we're still a pack. I tried to reflect comfort at them. Yes, this is our territory, and we're going to be all right. We watched as they drove away.

That left me and Ben, masters of the territory, leaning against the car, side by side, touching along the lengths of our bodies. We could lend each other our backbones. It was a beautiful day to spend in the woods, one of those fall days where the temperature spiked and drenched the world in golden sunlight. I breathed deep, taking in the rich forest air, chilled by the mountains around us. The air itself made me want to run. I let out the breath with a sigh.

"That went well," I said with false cheer.

Ben snorted. "If Shaun ever decides he doesn't like you, we're screwed."

"Yeah, well, that's why it's so important we get New Moon back up and running. Give him a stake in keeping us around."

"That almost sounds like a plan," he said.

I leaned my head on his shoulder. "Maybe I could call the Band of Tiamat and ask for terms of surrender." I could guess what they'd be: return to Vegas, allow myself to once again be tied to the altar of sacrifice for their insane little cult. Let them kill me.

Ben pulled away to look at me. He was frowning, worry creasing his brow, making his laugh lines deeper, making him look older. Hazel eyes studied me. And it was weird, because I'd have expected him to get angry, defiant, to say something cutting and sarcastic. But he just looked tired.

"No, you can't," he said without passion. Just clear statement of fact. "I won't let you."

"I can. You'd do it, too, if it meant making all this stop."

"It's not like you to just give up."

"How do you know? I used to give up all the time."

He smirked. "I'm glad I didn't know you back then. I like you stubborn."

Stubborn. Right. I had to keep being pigheaded. But being pigheaded was so much *work*.

"I'm going to remind you that you said that the next time we have an epic argument."

He looked heavenward and sighed like a martyr.

I said, "Maybe I could call the Band of Tiamat, offer to surrender, get them to call off the attack—then escape their clutches at the last minute and destroy them from the inside."

"That's more like it," Ben said. "But I'd still like to come up with a plan that doesn't involve the word 'surrender' at all."

Still working on that . . .

Rick and I had arranged to meet early at Psalm 23 so we could decide what to tell Roman. After what had happened today, I wasn't in the mood for talking to either one of them, but I had to. If Roman could stop this thing, stop anyone else from dying, I'd pay nearly any price. Rick could be damned. More damned than he already was, anyway.

I must have looked awful when I arrived at the club and made my way to the corner table where Rick was sitting, hands folded before him, waiting. His eyes widened when he saw me. Not a good sign, if I could startle Rick.

"What's wrong?"

The headache behind my eyes came in waves. The aspirin I'd taken an hour before hadn't helped.

"This thing raised the stakes," I said. "It killed one of my pack."

"Oh, no. When? How?"

"Last night. Burned to death, from the inside."

"I'm very sorry," he said, softly, sincerely. "Sit down. Can I get you something? A drink?"

The vast catalog of possibilities gleamed behind the bar, but I couldn't face that kind of escapism at the moment. "Just coffee. Thanks."

Rick called the order to the bartender, and a steaming mug arrived a moment later. I clung to the warmth and breathed in the fumes. The sensations anchored me.

"We can't tell Roman no," I said. I'd been practicing this speech. I couldn't let Rick turn Roman away. "I need his help. I don't have time anymore to figure this out on my own. I can't let it kill anyone else. It's my job to protect the pack—I took on that responsibility, and I'll do whatever I have to to keep them safe."

Rick turned away, and my stomach sank, because it meant he didn't agree with me. He was going to argue with me. He wasn't going to let Roman stay and help.

"Rick, please—"

"Anything. Even if it means giving up your freedom? The pack's freedom? *My* freedom?"

I glared. "What are you afraid of? Why does this guy scare you so much?"

"I'm not scared," he said, too quickly, too defensively. "Maybe paranoid, as you like to say. But Kitty, look at what's happening. It's too convenient. He knows too much. You said it yourself: What if this is a con game? What if he's working with the Band of Tiamat? What if all this is his doing, for the express purpose of coming here and gaining a foothold? Getting control over us? I won't let him take this city from me."

"This isn't about you. Why do you vampires always think it's about *you*?"

He arced a brow and glared back at me. "I'm going to tell Roman no. I'm going to tell him to leave town. We'll stop this thing on our own, Kitty."

"How? Do you have any ideas? Know anyone who can do a good exorcism? Because I don't think you do."

He had the grace to bow his head, because I was yelling now. A week's worth of stress had piled up and burst out. The bartender—human, normal, she may not even have known what Rick was—glanced our way, then went back to wiping down the bar.

"I'm sorry," he said.

I wiped away angry tears that had leaked out. Crying was the last thing I wanted to be doing right now. "You have to protect your own little empire, I understand that. But I keep wondering what that means to you. You're practically immortal. When you protect yourself and your people, you're protecting something that could last for centuries. I won't live for a fraction of your years. So do you look at the rest of us and think, well, we're all going to die in a few years anyway. Do we all seem expendable to you? Disposable?"

"Kitty, no. It's not like that."

My turn to look away.

He leaned forward, like he was going to say something else. Explain to me how vampires saw the world, once and for all. But he looked up.

Roman had arrived.

Tonight, along with his overcoat he wore a button-up shirt, black, something soft and rich, probably silk, and tailored slacks. Touchable clothing. He held his hands folded in front of him and quirked a wry smile.

"May I sit?" he said. We were both staring at him like idiots. Rick hadn't heard him approach. His vampiric sixth sense hadn't warned him that Roman was here—maybe because my blubbering had distracted him.

Quickly, I straightened and took a sip of coffee, pretending that nothing was wrong.

Rick gestured, offering Roman the empty chair opposite him. Roman sat.

"Have you had a chance to discuss my offer?" he said.

"I'm afraid we can't accept."

"*You* can't accept," I muttered. Unable to look at either one of them, I turned away and glared at a spot a foot out from my face, which I tried to keep a mask.

Roman acknowledged my addendum with a very slight tilt of his head.

"You don't trust me?" he said, to Rick.

"Of course not," Rick said. "Not unless you want to tell me how you're connected to the Band of Tiamat."

I rolled my eyes at the assumption Rick was making. Roman remained inscrutable.

"I understand," he said. "But you realize you have very few options here."

"So you say."

"What does our esteemed alpha werewolf say about this? She has a greater stake in this than you do."

"She might, but I don't trust—"

"I can speak for myself," I said, glaring at Rick. "To be honest, I think I'm up shit creek. But if Ricardo here says we can handle this without you, who am I to argue?" That came out snottier than it probably should have, but I was in no mood to be polite.

"You aren't very diplomatic, are you?" Roman said, sounding amused.

I agreed with a tight-lipped smile. "You know what the worst part is? We know this is revenge against me, but it's not just coming after me. It's about pain and chaos, so it's going to kill my pack one by one. It's going to destroy the places I love, and the people I love, until I have nothing left. And that's *evil*."

Roman glanced at Rick, as if to say that was all the explanation we needed. It was all the explanation I needed— I'd do anything to stop this thing in its tracks—but vampire politics trumped my own issues, apparently.

"I can't let you stay in my city," Rick said.

"Very well. If that's where you stand, I can't argue," Roman said. I wondered how I was going to chase after Roman and beg him to help me behind Rick's back. I wondered what I could give him that Rick couldn't.

Roman stood, businesslike, without hesitation. He wasn't going to waste his dignity by trying to talk Rick out of his decision. "It was good to meet you both. You have such interesting reputations."

I almost giggled at that. "That's what everyone says."

He held his hand out for Rick to shake, but Rick didn't. Instead, they held a minutelong staring match. I couldn't tell who broke contact first, because I was the one who blinked. One moment they were locked in a battle of wills. The next, Roman was holding his hand out to me.

"Kitty," he said.

I did shake his hand, because maybe Roman was only trying to be polite. The pressure of his hand was firm, steady. Not unpleasant. Not challenging. Just polite. Then he let go, gave us one last smile, and was gone.

I found a slip of paper palmed in my hand.

I curled the hand into a fist and pretended not to notice. Sitting there, my hands on the table in fists, Rick must have thought I was very angry.

"Kitty, I'm sorry," he said again, and would keep saying, as if that made everything better. "I'll do everything I can to help, you know I will."

"Everything except letting in the one person who claims to know how to stop it."

"If I let him in, if he gained a foothold in Denver, we'd never get him out again. You know that."

I did. Part of me, a big part, agreed with Rick. Roman was a stranger, therefore untrustworthy. Who knows what havoc he could wreak here in the long term?

"But you wouldn't even listen to him," I said.

Rick sat, not really looking at me, his jaw taut, body braced. This hadn't been easy for him. Him becoming Master vampire of the city hadn't been any easier than me becoming its alpha werewolf. We were floundering.

Which meant he couldn't, under any circumstances, give an inch to someone like Roman. Rationally, I understood, but I wasn't being particularly rational about this.

"Kitty—" he said, starting another round of apologies. I held up my hand to stop him.

"I understand, Rick. Really I do. I need to go check on my people. We both need to work on stopping this. Without outside help. So, I'm going to go."

He bowed his head, acquiescing.

I left the club, not knowing if we were still friends. Not knowing if we'd ever be able to talk to each other after what he'd done, and what I was about to do.

I walked to my car, about three blocks away, before daring to look at the scrap of paper in my hand. It had a number and street marked on it, about a mile away, toward Capitol Hill. Looking around, I took a deep breath of air, trying to catch the cold scent of vampire. To see if Rick had sent anyone to follow me. I didn't sense anything. I drove to the address Roman had given me.

It was on the corner of a block of run-down houses. Cars crammed the curb on both sides, making navigating the two-way street difficult. This late, though, no one else was out and about. I had to park a block away, slipping into a spot on the curb in front of a driveway. It was late, and I didn't plan to be here long. I hoped no one would mind.

Roman found me before I could backtrack to the location. The address was just a landmark, not a destination.

"I wasn't sure you'd meet me," he said, approaching me on the sidewalk.

"It's like you said, I don't have too many options."

"What will Rick do when he finds out you've gone behind his back?"

"I don't know," I said. I took a deep breath. "I don't really care. He's not in charge here—we're supposed to be partners."

"You assumed he'd say yes. That he'd do what was necessary to help you."

I looked away. I didn't want to go so far as to say I'd assumed, but I'd definitely hoped. Whatever my bravado, Rick wouldn't be happy about me talking to Roman like this.

Roman gestured for me to join him, and I fell into step beside him. We walked along, at midnight, in a part of town that really wasn't meant for walking late at night. But we were a couple of monsters, confident that anything that might try to bother us simply couldn't.

"The demon killed one of your wolves," he said. "The police are involved. What are they saying about it?"

"Spontaneous human combustion," I said, smirking.

"I'm constantly amazed by the explanations people will come up with to avoid the obvious, when they can't conceive of the obvious."

"Demon?" I said. Even me, with my experience, questioned it. I kept trying to draw a line around what I believed, what supernatural, legendary tales I was willing to buy. I kept having to shift that line outward. "Like, heaven-and-hell, fire-and-brimstone demon?"

"That word encompasses a wide variety of phenomena."

"So it could be anything," I grumbled. I crossed my arms tightly, frustrated. Roman had a brisk, no-nonsense stride, like he had someplace to be and wasn't about to dawdle. I had the feeling he took leisurely strolls through gardens the same way. I could keep up with him without too much trouble, letting my strides go long and wolflike.

I wanted to pace. Like going back and forth inside a cage, staring out.

"This one's very specific," he said. "I guarantee, even if you knew what it was, you don't have the ability to defeat it. I do."

"How very convenient for us both," I said flatly. He acknowledged the sarcasm with a smirk.

"Now that I'm dealing with you alone instead of Rick, I'll need other arrangements."

"Other payment," I said. "Since I can't give you vampiric permission to stay here. What do you want from me?"

He only glanced at me, not turning the focus of his attention from the path in front of him. A man with a mission. My senses were taking in everything, the hum of tires on the street the next block over, music coming from an upstairs window, the claws of a dog tapping on the sidewalk as it trotted away from us. The scents of garbage, a car leaking oil, grass and vegetation drying up in the autumn weather. The touch of a very faint wind changing direction. I was ready for anything, from any direction.

Roman only needed to know what was right in front of him. He was unconcerned.

He said, "Your loyalty. That's all."

His words were chilling. This was such a little thing, after all. So easy to say yes, since it didn't cost anything right now, but it was so open-ended. He could ask for *anything* later on. To vampires of certain ages, of certain sensibilities, who carried ancient values into the modern era, certain words—hospitality, honor, and loyalty—had weight and depth that they'd lost for someone like me, who had grown up in a rootless, disposable modern culture.

The old meaning of hospitality wasn't about napkin rings. It held that you were responsible for the total well-being of anyone you sheltered in your walls, that you were obligated to help someone who came to you and asked. Honor touched on the core of one's very identity, which when lost was nearly impossible to recover. And loyalty. Fealty. The word called to mind knights on bended knee before their kings. For someone of that mind-set, to break such a vow was to break the world.

That was what Roman was asking for, no matter how lightly he said the word. His gaze held an ancient gravity.

My steps slowed, then stopped. He continued a pace before stopping himself. I kept my gaze on his shoulder. Even if he hadn't been a vampire, with a vampire's hypnotic stare, I wouldn't have wanted to meet those hard, fierce eyes.

I swallowed and hoped my voice worked. "In my world, loyalty is earned. Not given away."

"And I will earn yours by protecting you and your people from this creature."

A lurch of déjà vu made me think, *I'm right back where I started.* Begging someone else to take care of me. To protect me. When I'd worked so hard to learn how to do it myself.

"You're asking me to submit."

He frowned. "Nothing so drastic as that. I'm not asking you to give up your authority."

He might not have picked up on the importance of that word—submit, submissive—and the shades of meaning that would be clear to anyone who'd been part of a werewolf pack. Or maybe he understood perfectly well what he was asking me to do. Maybe that was exactly what he wanted.

"I can't answer you right now," I said, hoping that no one else died, hoping that Mick would forgive me. "I need to talk to the others."

"You lead this pack. They trust you to decide for them."

"I don't lead my pack that way."

"Ah, one of these newfangled modern werewolves."

I managed a thin smile. "That's me."

"I'm baffled by this city's leaders' refusal to take decisive action," he said.

"Sorry," I said. "But not really. Is there some way I can get in touch with you when I've made a decision?"

"No need. I'll find you."

I didn't like that at all.

His face was angular, full of shadows in the odd nighttime lights from porches, from streetlights shrouded by bare trees. His eyes gleamed, and he frowned.

"You've seen what this thing can do. You don't have a lot of time to decide."

The hard sell, like this was buying a used car. But he almost had me cowed. I didn't want to argue with him anymore. "I know," I said.

He marched away, shoulders square, arms straight, tails of his coat rippling behind him. His steps were like drumbeats. Entranced by this image of determination, I watched. He never turned a corner. He was a small shadow, far ahead, when I went back to my car.

chapter **14**

I didn't have a lot of time to spare, so I didn't wait until morning to call Jules to get an update on the Paradox crew. For half a second, I worried about waking him up.

"Yeah?" he said curtly but not at all sleepily. These guys were used to keeping nocturnal hours.

"Are you guys still in town?" I said.

"What? Kitty? What's wrong?"

I hadn't considered how I must sound: desperate, angry, fierce. Panicked. "I really need you not to leave town. I need your help."

He let out a sigh. "We're still here. Gary's out of the hospital, but he's still resting. We're supposed to take a flight out tomorrow."

"I've gotten some information," I said, aware of how much I would have to leave out. But I didn't want to have to explain Roman to him. And I wasn't sure I was ready to talk about Mick. Or maybe I didn't want to scare Jules off. "I've been told it's a demon."

"Are you joking?" he said, half laughing.

"Oh, yeah, because I would totally joke about something like this," I said, spitting out the sarcasm.

"It's just that . . . demons. That's really getting into the lunatic fringe. But I think maybe your local Catholic priest can help you out. Do up a nice little exorcism for you."

"That's funny. I never really thought of Catholics as lunatic fringe. I thought that was you guys."

"You're not exactly middle-of-mainstream yourself."

And I *liked* it that way. "It's just that we've been trying to figure out what this thing is, and I got a lead that said demon. Thought you'd like to know."

"But what are we supposed to do about a *demon*?"

We scoff at what we don't understand. I had clearly stepped outside Jules's comfort zone. "Jules, let me talk to Tina."

"I'm sure she knows ever so much more about demons than I do."

"Maybe she doesn't, but I bet she doesn't talk at me like I'm an idiot." I smiled when I said it. Made me sound like a bitch. It was my radio-show voice.

The phone shifted, and then Tina said, "Yeah?"

"Here I was thinking Jules was starting to like me," I said.

"Don't worry about him. He's pretty invested in keeping up his front. What did you say to get him riled up?"

"Demon."

"Demon?" she said with a nervous chuckle.

"So. Do you know anything about repelling demons?"

"Don't demons usually possess people? Spinning heads, projectile vomiting, that sort of thing," she said.

"I don't know anything about it. That's why I'm calling you."

"I don't know anything about it, either."

"But you *talked* to it! Or it talked to you, through the board. Didn't that tell you *anything*?"

"It told me that this is way too big for me to deal with."

Deep breath. Keep it together. "Okay. You guys had your equipment monitoring the séance at New Moon, right? Have you looked over the recordings at all? Were you able to collect any data from the fire?"

"We gave copies of the video footage to the fire investigator," Tina said.

"But they're not looking for the things you'd be looking for. Didn't it occur to you to look for anything weird in the footage, anything to explain what happened?"

"Mostly we were worried about Gary," she said.

Fair enough. "There's got to be something, and we can cross-reference anything having to do with demons—"

"The chances are really slim we'll even find anything. They always are."

"I don't have a choice. It's getting worse."

"Did something else happen? What?"

I hesitated before saying, "It killed someone."

"Oh, my God. And after that you're asking us to help you?"

"I can't make you stay, but could you please review the video? Let me know if you find anything? I'm running out of ideas here."

"Kitty, it was just a fire. A normal kitchen fire—"

"You of all people can tell me that?" I said.

"I can convince myself of that. Kitty, I don't want to touch this thing again. It felt *wrong*."

"I need evidence, Tina. And I need a plan."

"I'll talk to the others," she said. She sounded tired, but I couldn't afford to feel any sympathy. I couldn't let them off the hook. "I'll let you know what we decide."

Reminding myself that screaming demands wouldn't get me what I wanted, I clamped my jaw shut and took a breath before I was ready to say, "Thank you. Just think about it. Please."

The next day, Ben and I made our weekly pilgrimage to Cañon City, about a hundred and fifty miles south of Denver. The timing was bad. I was afraid to leave town, in case something happened; on the other hand, it would be nice to get away. To *run* away. Ben wouldn't let any excuse short of lying in the hospital in a coma cancel this visit. I found I didn't want him to go alone, or I'd spend the whole day worrying about him.

Behind the glass at a visitors' booth of the Colorado Territorial Correctional Facility, Cormac Bennett rubbed his forehead in a long-suffering manner. "I don't know why you guys insist on telling me about a problem like this when there's nothing I can do about it."

Ben and I slumped in the chairs across from him, sharing an intercom phone, talking to a man serving time for manslaughter. Cormac—bounty hunter of the supernatural, Ben's cousin, and my friend—had saved our lives with that manslaughter. We'd sort of gotten used to him arriving in the nick of time, guns blazing, to save our asses. He couldn't do that much anymore.

Like we usually did on our visits, we asked how he was doing, and he said fine, as well as could be expected, and he asked how we were doing. I hadn't meant to tell him. We were supposed to be cheerful and keep up a good front so he wouldn't worry. He had enough to worry about. Then I'd said, "Oh, everything's great except for the demon."

Then I had to tell him the whole story, which left him rubbing his forehead like he suddenly had a headache.

"I'm not asking you to do anything. I'm just venting," I said.

"And fishing for advice, right? Just in case I know anything about hunting demons."

"Well, yeah, okay, if you know anything," I said, squirming. "So—you ever hunt down a demon before?"

Even Ben was looking amused.

Cormac glared at me. "Can't say that I have. I'd talk to a priest."

"People keep telling me that," I said.

"Interesting image," Ben said. "You've never even been inside a church, have you?"

He shrugged. "I've dodged a couple of vampires by going into churches."

Which was exactly the sort of answer I'd come to expect from him. That sufficiently changed the subject so that we didn't talk again about demons and how Cormac couldn't help us much from behind bars.

Before our hour was up, Cormac leaned forward. His expression was stonelike, unemotional. His voice was flat, but the words were fraught.

"I don't want to get too cheesy, but knowing you two are rooting for me is about the only thing that's getting me through this. So be careful. Don't get yourselves killed by whatever's going on out there."

It was a heavy responsibility. But it was also incentive.

When, I reflected absently, had I collected so much responsibility? Since when had this many people been depending on me? This time last year, I was all on my own.

Strangely, I didn't miss those days.

We answered him with thin, strained smiles.

Straightening again, Cormac said to Ben, "Can I talk to Kitty alone for a minute?"

Without a word, Ben stood to leave, giving Cormac a grim smile and touching me on the shoulder as he did.

Alone now, we spent a long moment looking at each other. Reading too much into each other's gazes. For as short a time as we'd known each other, we'd managed to work up a lot of history between us. A lot of missed chances. I couldn't make either one of us stop regretting them.

"What is it?" I said. "What can you say to me that you can't say to him?"

"You really want me to answer that?"

I ducked my gaze and shook my head.

"I don't want him to worry." He tipped his chair back, and his gaze turned slightly away from me, into space, into nothing. "Kitty, do you believe in ghosts?"

I wasn't in a good state of mind to answer that question rationally—I'd spent the last week hanging out with paranormal investigators and being hunted by a fire-breathing demon. My first reaction was emotional, maybe even screechy, with the thought, Oh, not him, too! Cormac wouldn't be asking this if something wasn't going on here.

I managed to answer calmly, "Of course I do." Didn't a werewolf have to believe in ghosts?

He leaned forward. "Can you do some of that research you're so good at?"

"Yeah, sure."

"I need to know the names of any women who were executed here. Let's say right around 1900, give or take a decade. And any history you can find on them."

I narrowed a suspicious gaze at him. I almost hated to ask, "Are you being haunted or something?"

Absently, he shook his head, his mind in a totally different place. "I don't know. It's a hunch. It may be nothing."

I hadn't considered the kind of trouble Cormac could get into in prison. Prison was supposed to keep him *out* of trouble.

"Is everything okay?"

The smile turned grim. "Hanging in there. Sometimes by my fingernails. But hanging in there."

I had a hunch, as well. "Would this make a good story for *Paradox PI*?"

"Just don't tell them it came from me."

"Wouldn't think of it."

" 'Til next time, then," he said. A uniformed guard loomed behind him to escort him back to the bowels of the place.

"Yeah. I'll see you," I answered.

Ben was waiting for me outside, in the grim parking lot outside the fences and coils of razor wire. "What did he say? If you can tell me. Not that I want to encourage my clients to keep secrets from me."

I joined him, and together we walked to the car. "He just wants me to look something up for him. He wouldn't tell me exactly why. He was worried that you'd freak out about it."

Ben didn't freak out. I didn't think he would. But Cormac had spent most of his life believing that he was looking out for Ben, protecting him. Funny how Ben thought the same about Cormac.

We walked on a few steps, silent. I let Ben ponder. Then he said, "This doesn't have anything to do with those Tiamat guys, does it?"

"No. This seems to be completely unrelated."

"Is he in trouble?"

I shrugged. How did you answer that question about someone in prison? "I don't think so. He didn't seem worried, just curious."

"Oh." A few more steps in silence. "Then I'm going to decide not to worry about this."

"You go right ahead," I said with a smile. Because of course we were both going to worry.

"This isn't anything he can't handle, right?" Ben said.

"Right."

We reached the car. He was driving today. In a few moments, we were back on the highway.

I said, "It's weird. I met Cormac before I met you, that time he tried to kill me. Remember?"

"Yeah, and if I recall he never actually fired at you."

"No. If he'd fired I probably wouldn't be here now." Ben grunted an agreement. We drove a few more miles, and I said, "Remember when we met?"

He smiled. "You needed a lawyer who wouldn't freak out when you told him you're a werewolf. So Cormac referred you to me. Now I have to ask, did you have any idea we'd end up like this?"

This was one of those heavy relationship questions that had no good answer. Just about anything I said would get me in trouble. "Not a clue. To tell you the truth, I thought you were kind of sleazy."

"Sleazy?" he said, indignant, but he was still smiling.

"Come on, anyone who'd be Cormac's lawyer?" I said. He laughed, because I definitely had a point. "Seems like a million years ago."

So much had happened. So much had changed. So many people just weren't here anymore.

"Yeah." He sounded sad. He'd been normal then. Human. Uninfected, with no hint that his life would swerve in this direction.

I squeezed his hand. More for my own comfort than his, if I was honest. But he squeezed back, smiled at me, and I felt better.

When the call from the Paradox crew came the next morning, it was Jules. That was the first surprise. The second was how pleased he sounded when he said, "We're staying. You've got to come over here."

"Why, what is it?"

"We found something," he said.

chapter 15

Ben and I arrived at their hotel suite within the hour.

The suite, in one of those modern, functional hotels that catered to business travelers, had a living-room area between bedrooms. The coffeemaker smelled like it had been going all night, and a half-empty box of donuts sat on the dresser.

The team had pulled chairs to a round table, where they huddled around a couple of humming laptops attached to heavy-duty speakers. Gary lay on a nearby sofa, resting. A gauze square was taped over his left temple. It actually made him look tough.

"Gary, it's good to see you conscious again," I said, smiling.

"Good to be conscious. I had no idea Denver would be this exciting," he said.

"It usually isn't. Most of our ghost stories are the garden-variety kind."

"Who wants garden variety when we've got this?" Jules said, nodding at one of the screens.

"What is it?"

"Here, watch," Jules said. We crowded around the laptop.

A video clip filled the screen. It had the grainy, filtered quality of a low-light, night-vision-type camera. Everything in the scene had a green tinge, but I recognized the view: looking along the bar at New Moon, across the back half of the restaurant, including the table where we'd worked and a partial view into the kitchen. A stainless-steel worktable and the industrial gas grill were visible, along with some shelves of pots, pans, utensils, and packages. It was one of a half dozen cameras the crew had set up before the séance.

The time stamp in the corner ticking off seconds was the only indication that time was passing. Nothing in the clip showed movement; we sat still around the table. And these guys watched film like this for *hours*. Even if you scanned through using the fast-forward button, it must have been tedious. But they'd also had a lot of practice. I certainly wouldn't have noticed the anomaly that Jules pointed out.

"There, there it is. You see it?"

He put his finger on the screen showing where, on the upper corner of the kitchen doorframe, a tongue of flame emerged. It looked white and glaring in the night-vision footage. It was like a fire had started on the inside of the wall, then burned through, licking outward and expanding like an explosion. One moment it was a hint of fire, emerging in one or two places. The next moment, a wall of fierce fire blew from the kitchen through the dining room, pushing air and heat—and the table, and us—before it. This was the fireball that had roared out to shock us. The rest of the film showed us reacting, panicking, the table knocking

Gary's head, me running for the fire extinguishers, Ben running after me, and so forth. Pandemonium.

The fire itself seemed to come out of nowhere.

"Spontaneous *building* combustion?" I said. If it could happen to people, why not structures?

"There's usually a reason a place catches fire like that," Jules said. "I talked to the investigators about this. They haven't finished their report, but they haven't found anything obvious like a gas leak or faulty wiring, or ignition of flammable materials, which is usually what happens. In an older building like this, there's any number of things that can go wrong, but there's something else. I didn't see it until I went through it frame by frame. The investigators wouldn't have caught it."

He proceeded to show us, backing up to the point where the fire started and clicking forward, a half second at a time. The flames moved almost like they were alive, dancing, swaying, each step and unexpected flicker captured on a split second of video. When the fireball burst, a brilliant sphere of light expanding out, searing my eyes, it was almost beautiful. Like some cosmic event rather than a destructive earthly force.

Jules hit pause and pointed, his excitement clear. "There, do you see it?"

I'd never have caught it. No one who didn't have the investigators' experience in looking for weird shadows, blips, and anomalies in video like this would have seen it.

A human figure stood outlined in the middle of the billowing flames.

It was off-color, a slightly more golden tinge than the fire surrounding it, a heat mirage within a heat mirage, shimmering at a different angle. But it had a head, body, legs, and arms, spread in something like ecstasy.

A frame later, it vanished, melting into the rest of the fire. The image only lasted for a split second. At full speed, the clip just looked like flames changing shapes.

Jules backed the clip up, so that we were all staring at that figure, unreal, undeniable.

"Is it someone in a suit?" I said. "Like one of those fireproof stunt-guy suits?"

"Except that it just disappears," Jules answered. "Granted, fire does strange things, it's unpredictable, but it's right there on the video."

I should have been happy to see a form, an actual enemy—the demon. We now had an image, a being that reveled in fire, maybe used it to destroy. But that also meant we were dealing with something sentient, with a mind, a will, and a mean streak. My gut felt cold.

Jules, at least, seemed happy at the discovery. "This is proof. It's *proof*."

"Proof of what?" Ben said.

"The impossible."

Ben pointed at the screen. "Just so you all know, the insurance company is buying that it was an accident. So I don't care if there's the slightest hint of supernatural nastiness going on with this. I don't care if you find Casper the Friendly Ghost playing with matches. If any of you talk to the insurance company, it was a gas leak due to the age of the building. That's what's going on the paperwork, that's the story, and we're all sticking to it. Got it?"

Full-on lawyer mode. That was my honey. "Got it," I said.

From the sofa, Gary shook his head. "A video like that is too easy to fake. It's not good enough for proof."

"That's the trouble," Tina said. "Everything we discover is too easy to fake."

For my part, I felt like I was finally looking my enemy in the eye. Not that I could tell whether this thing had eyes.

"But this gives us something," I said. "It's a thing. A being. It has a shape. Maybe it has a mind. That means we can lure it out. We can trick it. Trap it, maybe."

Tina huffed. "I can see us standing there with fire extinguishers blasting it. Why do I get the feeling that won't work?"

"Maybe we can talk to it," I said. "Maybe we can just *ask* it to stop."

"True to form," Ben said. "Always ready to talk it out." His voice was sarcastic, but his smile was sweet.

"I'm not sure I like that idea," Gary said. "This is out of our league."

I shrugged. "So change leagues. I want to try another séance. I want to talk to this thing."

Nobody said anything. If they didn't like the idea, they could have at least argued with me, but everyone stared, eyes kind of buggy, expressions taut. The anxiety was tangible. We all saw the monster, but nobody wanted to face up to it.

"Come on, we want to lure this thing out. Use me as bait! I'm the focus of all this anyway," I said.

"That's exactly why you shouldn't be acting like bait," Ben said. "Sure, maybe this thing wants you—so the last thing you should be doing is throwing yourself at it."

"Aw, honey, that's sweet. You trying to protect me and all." My smile was probably a little too sarcastic.

"*Somebody* has to," he said, curt.

We glared at each other a moment, a couple of not entirely happy wolves in people clothing.

"What does your contact say? The one who gave you the protective potion?" Jules said.

"I don't know. I haven't been able to get ahold of him. Give me a minute." I called Grant's number again. And again, no answer. I needed to find another way to get in touch with him. I had to know if he was okay, so I called the Diablo, the Vegas hotel that housed the theater where he performed. I keyed my way through the phone maze until I reached a real live person at the theater box office.

"Hi, I was wondering when Odysseus Grant's shows are today," I said to the clerk.

"Oh, I'm sorry, all his shows have been canceled for the next couple of days," she answered.

Damn. This couldn't be good. "Oh. Do you know why?"

"I think it's illness. I wasn't given any details."

Then Grant was in trouble, too. My hair prickled.

"What's wrong?" Ben said, after I put away my phone. I must have gone especially pale.

"I can't get ahold of him," I said. "His shows are canceled. He seems to have disappeared."

"So no help there," Tina sighed.

I was about ready to run back to Vegas to deal with this at the source, despite all the warnings. "What about you? Surely you have some kind of . . . I don't know, psychic hunch or something? 'Cause that would be really useful."

Another long and meaning-filled silence descended. Tina blushed, and Jules intently studied the laptop screen.

"I'm still waiting to hear about the psychic-hunches thing myself," Gary said. "Tina keeps telling me she'll explain how she's the only person I've ever seen get a Ouija board to act like that when I feel better. Tina—honest, I feel better."

"Huh. I assumed you all had already had that conversation," I said.

A loud, insistent pounding on the door started right about then. Good timing there, and I wondered how far Tina's psychic reach actually extended. Mind control of room service, maybe? Convenient.

Ben went to the door, checked the peephole, looked back. "I don't recognize him. Young guy, kind of scruffy. Anybody order a pizza?"

Nobody had. Ben called through the door, "Can I help you?"

"Tell Kitty to let me in," a voice answered. I recognized the voice and made a dash for the door.

"Why am I not surprised?" Ben grumbled.

"I'll talk to him. It'll only take a minute."

I cracked open the door to find Peter Gurney, young, intense, focused, slouching in his canvas army jacket, standing on the porch outside the room. This was such bad timing. I didn't know what he wanted—to accuse me of lying again or to demand more information that I didn't have—but there had to be a better time for it.

We regarded each other for a moment. "Peter. As much as I'd love to talk to you, this really isn't—"

"I want to talk to them," he said and pointed into the room behind me.

I looked at the PI team, who were now staring at us with interest, and back at Peter. I fought past the cognitive dissonance—what did Peter even know about them? "Oh? Why?"

"I'll tell them," he said, almost surly. He was nervous, his hands fidgeting with the hem of his jacket. He had to work to summon this bravado.

"What's happened?" I said. "What have you been up to, besides following me around?" He had the grace to look chagrined at that. That didn't stop him.

"I need to talk to you." He called this over my shoulder, toward the table where the Paradox team gathered. This couldn't have been great timing for them, either. I wondered: Was Peter a fan? Did they get accosted by fans a lot?

I said, "Peter, I'm sure you're upset, but this isn't a good time. Maybe you could come back—"

"I have a job for you," he said to the team, glaring at me as an afterthought. I blocked the doorway, or he might have shoved his way in.

"Sounds serious," Tina said.

"Maybe not to you," Peter said. "But it is to me. I want to hire you."

"Got a place that's haunted, then?" Jules said.

"No. Not really." He was still nervous, his gaze darting. I got the feeling he really didn't want to be here, but he was desperate. He said, "I need you to talk to my brother."

"What?" I said, disbelieving. Of all the ridiculous . . . Desperate didn't begin to cover it. My sympathy ran out, all at once. This wasn't grief—this was not being able to face reality. "Peter, what are you thinking?"

"I've been following you—"

"I know," I said.

His gaze was stone cold and dead serious. "If you were lying about Ted, I'd follow you and maybe you'd lead me to him."

"Except he's dead," I said, more harshly than I wanted. T.J. was dead, and I didn't want to keep dwelling on it.

He shut his eyes tight and marshaled words. "I know . . . I know that now. I believe you. But since I've been trailing you, I've been watching *her.*"

He gestured to Tina.

"I know about you. If there was another way to try this, I would, believe me. But I don't think there is. I want you to try to talk to him. Maybe . . . maybe he can tell you what happened. I just want to talk to him one more time."

God. He was a kid again. That was all he wanted, for his older brother to tell him he loved him. Some reassurance that he hadn't been abandoned. I understood the feeling. I kind of wanted to talk to T.J. right now myself. Maybe ask, Why didn't you tell me you had a brother? Why didn't you tell me you ran away from your family? Why didn't you tell me anything?

The Paradox crew watched him, silent.

Peter kept trying. "I can pay you. I'm not looking for a conversation, I just want . . . something. A sign. Some kind of proof."

"You and every other bloke in human history," Jules muttered.

"It's not that easy," Tina said, soft, serious, diverging from her bubbly on-screen persona. "It's not like making a phone call. So, no. I can't do it."

Peter grit his teeth. He was almost shaking. "But I know you can do it. Please, I don't want a séance, I just need . . ."

And he couldn't say it. Couldn't finish the thought, and none of us tried to finish it for him. He could have meant anything: closure, comfort, some assurance that his brother hadn't forgotten him, when all the evidence suggested that he had.

He turned away, hiding eyes that were shining with tears.

"I'm sorry," I murmured, and couldn't tell if he'd heard me. "But if you've been following us, you know what a really bad time this is."

Jules said, "Right. We're in the middle of something here. But later, maybe we can set up an experiment—"

"It doesn't work on command," Tina said. "I can't promise anything."

Peter had pulled himself together, but that only meant he was back to his surly, fidgeting self. "Thanks. Don't do me any favors or anything. I wouldn't want to put you out." He turned and stalked out.

I went after him. I wasn't letting him get away again.

"Peter, wait!" I said before he was halfway down the sidewalk, and I must have growled it, because he stopped in his tracks. I faced him. "I need something, too. I need to know about T.J."

He didn't answer—but then, he didn't leave, either, so I begged.

"Please," I said. "He was my best friend. I survived becoming a werewolf because of him, because he helped me. And now I don't even have a picture to remember him by. Please tell me about him." Watching him, face locked in a scowl, head bent, unwilling to stand tall and look at me, I thought this was what T.J. must have looked like at this age. Before he mellowed, before he grew comfortable in his skin. Before coming to grips with what he was. Peter hadn't acquired any of that confidence yet. But I wasn't going to let him walk away. I blocked his path to the parking lot.

He took a breath, steeling himself. "I've got some things I can show you. They're out in my bike."

Of course he rode a motorcycle, just like T.J. had. We walked to the parking lot, where he'd pulled his bike into the slot next to my car. It was an older model, not too big, not a muscle, speed, or status bike. Something tough and functional, with a helmet strapped to the back and saddlebags over the rear tire. T.J. hadn't worn a helmet. As a tougher-than-human werewolf, he hadn't thought he needed one.

Peter opened one of the saddlebags and removed a thick accordion file, setting it on the bike's seat like it was a desk. "It's been impossible getting a straight answer about him from anyone. I don't know why I thought the psychic would be willing to help."

"They're good people," I said. "They just don't want to treat it like a tool. It's not an exact science."

"It's like being a kid again. It's like everyone's keeping secrets, everyone knows something, but they won't tell you, because you're not old enough, or smart enough. I'm sick of it. I'm sick of not knowing anything."

"You seem to be a pretty good detective. You figured out their secret. You've figured out a lot of this." I nodded at the file.

"And if he were alive I could have just asked him. If I'd found him sooner—" He shook his head. His frown was deep. "He was eight years older than me, so we weren't real close. But it's like you said, he looked out for me. Helped me. He was good at that. Our parents weren't too involved, I guess you'd say. Kind of distant. We had two sisters, but I couldn't talk to them, so I always went to Ted. When he turned eighteen, he came out. Announced he was gay over the dinner table to the whole family. Mom and Dad didn't take it so well." He chuckled; the sound was bitter. "That's an understatement. They kicked him out. Wouldn't speak to him again. I think he expected it, because he already had his bag packed. He left, and that's the last time I ever saw him. But God, I would have gone with him. I wanted so badly to go with him.

"We weren't allowed to even say his name at home. I kept hoping he'd call, or maybe come back to take me with him. I left home last year. That's when I really started looking. Trying to track him down. I didn't think it would be this hard, but he didn't leave much of a trail. No credit card, no jobs—he only ever worked for cash under the table. I can't imagine him in a life like that. I don't think I ever really knew him." He did wipe a tear away, then.

"But you tracked him this far."

"By luck, mostly. The name isn't all that common." He pulled pages out of the file. T.J.'s life, all wrapped up in a neat little package. "He was in motocross racing for a while, working as a mechanic, fixing bikes, that sort of thing. I found some people who knew him then." He showed me sheets of paper with names and contact information typed out, a few pages with handwritten notes, probably from interviews, records of conversations. Grainy black-and-white photos—photocopies of photos. He set them aside to reveal a couple more pages, these ones typed forms. "I didn't start to worry about him until I found these. A couple years after he left home, he had an HIV test. It came back positive. A second one confirmed the positive."

I shook my head. This definitely wasn't the T.J. I knew. "T.J. wasn't HIV positive—I would have known that. Aren't these things supposed to be confidential?"

He turned a cocky smile, crinkling his eyes—and for a flash looked just like his brother, the way I remembered him. My breath caught.

"I got a job at the records department of the clinic. That's how crazy I've been over this. But here's the thing."

A few more pages down in the stack, he pulled out another sheet, an almost identical medical form. "About eight months later, another test came back negative. The odds are slim, but I'm guessing the first two were both false positives, or lab error. Something like that. So he wasn't really HIV positive. If he was, there'd be more medical files on him. Wouldn't there? But that third test is the last time he ever went to a doctor, I think."

Holding up the pages, I stared at them side by side, my mind tumbling. Lightbulbs of understanding flared to life. T.J.'s life, gathered together in a stack of papers. It shouldn't have been able to explain anything, but it did. It explained everything.

"The first two tests weren't wrong," I said softly.

"How can you tell?"

I pointed to the dates on the last two pages, the tests that showed the switch from positive to negative, from HIV infected to healthy. Eight years ago now. Just a few years before I met him. I explained, "Within this stretch of time, he was infected with lycanthropy. That's when he became a werewolf. Lycanthropy makes someone almost invulnerable. They're very hard to injure, they heal rapidly. They don't get diseases. He cured himself of HIV by infecting himself with lycanthropy." And how had he found out about werewolves? How had he found one who would bite him without killing him? The address on the letterhead of the test forms was in California. What had brought him to Denver? And what about the positive test in the first place—what kind of trouble had T.J.—a gay kid kicked out of the house, maybe living on the streets, doing who knew what—gotten into that led to getting HIV?

Peter probably wouldn't be able to answer any of those questions, but I now knew something about T.J. I'd never known before: He'd chosen lycanthropy. He'd gotten himself infected on purpose. And it had made him strong.

So, T.J., was it worth it? You might have lived longer with HIV.

No answer came from the beyond.

"Jesus," Peter murmured.

I gave the pages back to him. "I didn't choose this life. I always wonder why some people do. Why someone like T.J. would." Not that it made me feel any better.

"I think he must have been a different person than the one I remember. I just wish—" He shook the thought away. He hadn't seen his brother in ten years. He'd been a kid. If my memories of the man were idealized, what could his possibly be like?

We stood in silence, both of us wishing he was still alive.

"The thing is," Peter said after a moment, "I don't know what to do now. I had a plan. I'd find him, and he'd—he'd have a great life. I just knew he would. He'd own a bike shop somewhere, or be a mechanic for some big racer. He'd have his own place and a bunch of great friends. I wanted to be part of that. He'd get me a job, I'd meet his friends, I'd be his little brother again. He'd be happy to see me. I always imagined that he'd be happy to see me. He'd say, 'I knew you'd find me.' Like finding him was a test. I never thought that he'd be . . . that he wouldn't be here. And now I don't know what to do."

I spoke carefully. "I think he'd have wanted you to be your own person. He wouldn't want you trailing after him like this. Being in his shadow."

"Yeah," he said softly. "I'm sorry I was so rotten before. That I didn't believe you. It must have been a shock, me calling out of the blue. I didn't mean to stir up bad memories."

"It was a shock," I said, accepting his apology with a shrug. "But I'm glad you did. I'm glad I got to learn more about him."

"Were you really his best friend?"

That made me smile. "I don't know about that. But he was definitely my best friend for a while there."

Peter chuckled, like he understood the difference.

We both turned around at Ben's approach. "Is everything okay?" He gave Peter a sinister look. He was here checking up on me, and the statement was a warning.

"Everything's fine," I said, reassuring. "We're just going through our own little version of 'This Is Your Life.' Ben, this is Peter. T.J.'s younger brother."

Ben's eyes widened a little, and they shook hands.

Peter said, "Did you know him, too?"

"No, but he's kind of a legend around here. A lot of people miss him."

"I guess that's good," Peter said, shrugging deeper into

his jacket, looking younger. "Is it strange, that that makes me feel better?"

I patted his shoulder, because it didn't sound strange. He could be proud that T.J. had left a mark on the world. Not everyone did.

Ben pointed a thumb over his shoulder. "They're still talking. Tina wants to try again with the Ouija board, but they need to talk to you."

Back to it, then. I turned to Peter. "Are you going to be in town long? I can introduce you to more people who knew T.J., if you'd like."

He shrugged. "I don't know what I'm doing. I guess I'll be around a few more days at least, until I figure out what's next."

"Well. Okay, then."

"Kitty—" He stepped forward, looking boyish and nervous. "I don't know exactly what's going on here, but is there anything I can do to help?"

I started to say no, because I didn't want anyone else involved in this, but I hesitated. The thing we needed, more than almost anything else, was information. And Peter knew how to find information. Another set of eyes doing research had to help.

"You know anything about paranormal investigation?" I asked him.

He shook his head. "I'm more up on the mundane version."

I smiled. "That may be exactly what we need."

We went back to the suite. Ben leaned over to mutter at me, "Just what we need, another potential target."

"Yeah, I know," I admitted.

"So you invited him anyway?"

"I couldn't say no." It wasn't like I was hoping Peter might replace T.J. It just kind of looked that way from the outside.

"Everyone, this is Peter," I said, introducing him.

The sound of recorded laughter answered me, coming from Jules's laptop. Not eerie, sinister, Vincent Price laughter. Rather, it sounded like a grown man trying not to chuckle at a silly joke. It was sniggering. Then it vanished into crackling static.

"What was *that?*" I said, wincing. The noise grated in my sensitive werewolf ears.

"EVP. The timing matches it to the appearance of the figure in the fire," Jules said.

EVP. Electronic voice phenomenon. Another paranormal investigative mainstay, like EMF detectors. Great. Giving the creature a voice somehow made it even worse. "What's it mean?"

"I'm thinking of all the ways someone could claim the figure in that clip is a guy in a fireproof suit, like you said," he explained. "Even though we all know there was no one else in that building, and the cameras didn't pick up anything, no movement, nobody entering and leaving, nothing. Because I'm sorry, but that sounds like a guy in a suit laughing at us. Even though I *know* it isn't. But that's what the skeptics are going to call us on when we show this."

"But how do you prove a negative?" Peter said. "How do you prove it wasn't a guy in a suit?" The voice of the skeptic. The voice of reason, rather. If it weren't for everything else that had happened, I'd be there with him.

"Now you understand the problem with just about everything we do," Gary said.

"Maybe you've been going about this backward," Peter

said. "This isn't random, right? Someone put this in motion. So go to the source. Shut them down on their end."

"Kitty can't go to Vegas," Ben said. "They already tried to kill her once, I don't want to give them another chance."

"And Odysseus Grant, my contact there, is missing. I'm afraid something's happened to him."

Peter shrugged. "I could go look for him. Maybe dig up anything else on whoever's doing this."

"Would you?" I said.

"Can you front the money for a plane ticket?"

Straightforward guy. I liked him. Give him a few more years and a few more hard knocks he could do Humphrey Bogart's Sam Spade. "Sure."

"Maybe that's what we need," Jules said. "We work on the paranormal end of things, and you can figure out how they started this in the first place. Is that a plan?" With a look, he consulted everyone gathered in the room: me, Ben, Peter, his teammates.

Any plan that didn't involve Roman made me happy.

"When can you leave?" I asked Peter.

"As soon as we get a flight, I can leave. I'll need to park my bike somewhere," he said.

"You can use the carport at our place," Ben said. "I can drive you to the airport."

The plan, such as it was, came together. Using Jules's computer, we ordered tickets for an afternoon flight for Peter. Ben and Peter would drive to the condo to drop off Peter's motorcycle, then Ben would drive him to the airport. I'd stay and help with the research, even though I wasn't much good for anything beyond creative Internet searches. Sometimes, creative Internet searches could be incredibly useful.

The hope was we'd have more information by evening, so we wouldn't be going into the second séance quite so blind. Roman kept stressing how little time we had to solve this thing. I didn't know what that meant, but the sooner the eureka moment came, the better.

Peter and Ben headed out. On his way out, Ben took my wrist and pulled me to a private corner on the porch. It was about as domineering as he ever got with me, and I couldn't say that I liked it.

I pulled my arm away from him and glared. "What?"

He held my face in his hands and studied me, looking into my eyes like he could see through them, see to what I was thinking.

"Ben." He was starting to freak me out.

"I just know you're going to do something stupid and crazy as soon as I leave."

I smirked. "Don't have a whole lot of faith in me, do you?"

Glancing away, he brushed his fingers along my hair, then shoved his hands in his pockets. "We joke about being a pack. Like it's an excuse for every little neurotic twitch we have about each other. But it's real. It's there. It drives me crazy thinking you might be in trouble and I can't help you."

I knew that fear. There'd been times Ben was in trouble, when I'd believed I was too late to save him. Racing to him with a hole growing in my gut, draining everything but panic. I knew what Ben was feeling.

"Likewise," I murmured. "But do you think we could live never letting each other out of our sight?"

He chuckled. "We'd really drive each other crazy."

"We were both lone wolves for too long, weren't we? Not used to all this togetherness and sharing."

"Ah, more pop psychology."

By this time we'd pulled each other into a hug, belying my claim. "That's me," I said, tipping back my head so I could nuzzle his chin. He obliged me with a kiss. And another. We sort of kept going like that until someone cleared his throat. Loudly.

"Um, yeah," Peter said from halfway down the sidewalk, pointing a thumb over his shoulder. "Sorry, but we should get going."

Ben and I managed to pry ourselves apart. "Grr," I muttered.

He held my shoulders and planted one more kiss on my forehead. "Call me if something happens. Call me if you go anywhere. Okay?"

"I will, I promise."

"Be careful," he said. "Don't do anything stupid."

"I never do anything stupid," I said.

He gave me a very unconvinced glare.

"You be careful, too," I said.

He left with Peter and didn't look back.

Right. Time to get to work. No sense worrying about him yet.

chapter 16

Gary, still recovering, went to sleep. Jules had been making phone calls, about a dozen by my count, and the conversations ranged from merely odd to outright bizarre. He'd been saying things like, "Yeah, but this isn't localized like the Enfield Poltergeist. I'm talking about free-ranging activities linked to a specific person. You've never seen a similar case?" and "But EMF readings aren't a reliable indicator of psychic hostility." Finally, he said something that made sense to me: "Professor, I'm telling you, there was a fucking humanoid shape standing in the flames and laughing at us! No, it wasn't a guy in an asbestos suit!"

So. Jules's contacts weren't panning out so much.

Tina and I had been engrossed in Internet research on two different laptops. I'd been learning a lot about hauntings, demonic possession, hoaxes, and the people who talk about them. It was like a religion: No amount of proof seemed able to sway the absolute skeptics or the absolute believers.

Typing in a phrase like "demonic communication" got about a quarter of a million hits. After looking at a dozen sites, my eyes started to glaze over. The tones varied from wild belief to scientific skepticism. But a phrase kept jumping out at me, something that none of the Paradox crew had mentioned yet.

I leaned back, stared at the screen a good long time, and finally asked, "What do you guys think about trance mediums?"

Tina didn't say anything. Jules peered over the screen of his own laptop.

"Theory or practice?" he said.

I shrugged. "Both."

He leaned back in his chair. "The theory is that certain people have the ability to channel spirits directly. They go into a trance, and any presence at a haunted location can speak through them. In practice, it tends to be bollocks. It's too hard to verify and too easy to fake. The charlatans have built up this image of it being really dangerous, so they use it as a way to get a good scare out of people."

"So it's not real?" I said.

"It's real," Tina said. "Just very rare."

"Do you think it's something we could use to learn more about this thing?" I said.

"No, I don't think so," Tina said quickly.

Jules blinked at Tina. "Wait a minute. Tina. What do you know about trance mediums? It's not actually something . . . I mean *you* don't have any experience with it. Do you?"

She smiled. "It's almost gratifying that you're taking me seriously now."

"Can you really do it?" Jules said.

Her hesitation, and the way her gaze darted nervously

between us was enough of an answer. She couldn't come right out and say no.

"Oh, my God, Tina, this is incredible. We've got to get a tape of this. If we can show what the real thing looks like and maybe find a way to demonstrate how the fakes—"

"No," she shook her head. "I want to help, really I do, but this—the Ouija board is one thing, but actually channeling it directly . . . it *is* dangerous. I've never wanted to get that close. It's better having something like the board between me and the phenomenon."

A lead, any lead, was too good to give up. I said, "But Tina, if you could contact it directly—"

Tina said, "This thing has killed. If I let it inside me—could we even stop it?"

"Or maybe we could stop it from killing again," I said.

"If you could talk to it, directly, through me," Tina said. "What would you say?"

Good question. "I'd want to find out where it came from, what it wants, and what I need to do to convince it to go away. However it was sent here, there has to be a way to send it back again. If it's sentient, I have to be able to reason with it." That was my idealism talking again.

Tina took a deep breath. "The reason I've kept quiet all this time about what I can do is because in a way, even when this stuff works, it's still all parlor tricks. The only people who are really interested are the ones who want to exploit it, or desperate people messed up with grief, like Peter. They treat it like a psychic hotline they can call up whenever they want. When really, I don't understand what's going on most of the time."

"I'm just asking you to try."

"Gary wouldn't go for it," Tina said.

"We'll tell him it's an experiment," Jules said.

Tina leaned back and studied the ceiling. Communing with the beyond, maybe. I wondered for a moment what it would be like to be her. Did she hear voices all the time? Some of the time? Was it like listening to a faint radio, like she only tuned in to distant spirits, or did they speak to her directly, loudly? How did a person live with something like that?

How annoyed would she be if I asked her all these questions?

Rubbing her face, she leaned forward and let out a sigh. A weight seemed to settle on her, slumping her shoulders, pulling her lips into a frown. It made her look older, far different from her screen persona. It wasn't fear or trepidation, I didn't think. More like resignation.

"Here's what we do. I call the shots. If it doesn't feel right, we stop, no arguing. Got it?"

Jules and I nodded.

"Where are we going to do this?" I asked. "What can we burn down this time?"

She scowled at me. "Not here. We have to keep at least one place safe. Can we get into New Moon? It talked to us once, there."

I shook my head. "If we try to get in before the investigators are done with it, it'll screw up the insurance."

"Then we go to Flint House," she said.

"The house that kills people?" I might have shrieked a little.

"I figure the demon'll know where to find us, it's been there before."

A combined sense of curiosity and inevitability drove

us. We wanted to see what would happen. We also didn't have a whole lot of other options.

Well, there was always running away. Except we had no guarantee the thing wouldn't follow us. Which was also the problem with me letting it go ahead and get me. Self-sacrifice was all well and good if you could guarantee that it would actually stop the attacks. Wouldn't we all feel stupid if I let it kill me and it just kept attacking? Not that I'd be feeling much of anything at all. Or maybe I would, and that was another problem with this whole life-after-death concept.

I'd also kind of missed the moment when I stopped being able to run away. I had too much to protect now.

Being proactive was better than being morbid. So I helped Tina and the others set up another séance at Flint House. Jules summoned the *Paradox PI* camera crew, which arrived with the equipment van to set up the usual array of cameras, microphones, and gear.

"You guys really like getting your footage," I said. "You'll probably get a whole season's worth of episodes out of this."

"At this point, our production schedule is already screwed up beyond repair. We're doing this for science," Jules said. "Maybe we can get some hard, incontrovertible measurements. This is for posterity."

Almost made me feel like we were doing something noble.

"But it wouldn't hurt to get a good episode out of this," Tina called from the other room, where she was setting up another camera. "If I'm going to do this for science I want some good screen time out of it."

Noble and commercially viable. I could go for that.

I'd made up another batch of the blood-and-ruin potion. I should come up with a better name for it, like "Eau
de Ick."

"Don't put it around the house," Tina ordered when she
saw it.

"Why not? I don't want anything to burn down again."

"We want this thing to be able to get in so we can talk
to it. That can't happen if you use that crap. But you know,
keep it around. Just in case."

We also brought along extra fire extinguishers. Just in
case.

They set up a table like last time, but this time, Tina
filled it with equipment. She might have been showing off
an encyclopedia of medium and spiritualist tricks. There
was a Ouija board—a new one, since the previous one was
contaminated, she claimed; a pad of paper and a pen for
automatic writing; a couple of heavy wires, like straightened coat hangers—dowsing rods; a plumb weight on a
string; a bell.

"This must really be damaging your sensibilities," I
said to Jules. "All the table-rapping séance tricks, and here
they are, for real."

"I'm trying not to think about it," he said, distracted as
he tested yet another microphone, this one set up in the
kitchen in the back of the house.

Perfect haunted-house setting, and I wasn't sure anymore that this was a good idea. I'd felt safe at New Moon,
and look what happened there. I didn't at all feel safe here,
and we hadn't done anything yet.

The behind-the-camera techs left, and Jules, Tina, and I
gathered in the front room, what would have been a parlor,

now empty except for the round card table and filmy lace drapes over the front window.

"Right, Gary, I think that's it. We should be all ready to go now," Jules said into his headset microphone. Gary had woken up and demanded to come along. Jules and Tina argued, and Gary compromised by waiting in the van, observing via the monitors and speakers. I used the blood potion around the van, so at least they'd be protected.

Jules listened for an answer, gave a curt nod, and looked at us. "Ready?"

"What's going to happen?" I said. "What can we expect?"

He said, "When the fakes do it, there's a lot of swaying, moaning, convulsing, eyes rolling back in heads. That sort of thing. Their voices change, get really hoarse and deep and the like. Maybe that's really how it works. Tina, is that how—Tina?"

Tina went very, very still. She hadn't even sat down yet. She stood in the middle of the floor, arms straight at her side, fingers straight out, head canted to one side as if listening for something. Her eyes were closed, her back straight, like she'd just frozen there. And I knew something was happening, because her smell changed. It was subtle, like the difference in smell between the same perfume worn by two different people. She still smelled like Tina—hip twenty-something woman. But there was something *extra* now. A touch of brimstone. I tensed up and bit my lip to keep from growling.

Jules and I stood about five feet away from her, afraid to move.

"Guys, are you getting this?" Jules whispered into his

headset. I didn't hear the response, but I assumed it was affirmative.

"Tina?" Jules said. "Can you hear me, Tina?"

"No, no," she murmured. Her voice wasn't hoarse, deep, or scratchy like Jules warned it might be. It was her normal voice. Maybe a little sleepy, like she was hypnotized.

Then she tipped her head back and spoke a rapid stream of gibberish.

"Oh, my God," Jules said.

The speech cut out.

"Now," Jules hissed at me. "Kitty, talk to it."

"It?"

"Yeah—the demon, whatever it is. You're talking to it now."

Her eyes were closed, her face was blank. There was just the smell, and the hair on my neck standing on end.

"Hello? What do you want? What are you doing here?" I asked it.

She twitched a smile that made me flinch. I didn't want this demon to have a face, any face, much less Tina's. I didn't want to see the expression of malevolence.

She spoke a few more words. Her voice was rich with laughter. I still didn't understand her. Our demon didn't speak English, apparently. But I could tell it was teasing me. That it thought very little of me.

"How do I convince you to go away? I want you to go away."

Now she frowned and spoke a couple of terse words. A denial.

"Did the Band of Tiamat call you, or did the vampire Roman? Whoever it was—how did they do it? Are they paying you? Or do you just like mayhem?"

She laughed, rich, teasing laughter. It didn't sound like the voice Jules had recorded from New Moon, but it had the same tone, the same mocking emotion behind it.

I didn't think I could really talk this thing into confessing all its sins and leaving us alone. We were trying to learn more about it. Get some kind of clue to its identity that we could use to finally discover what it was and how to banish it. But I couldn't help venting some of my frustration at it.

"Mick didn't do anything to you. There was no reason to touch him. If this is about me, you should be coming after me, and I gotta tell you, you're a really lame demon if you can't get past a little blood on the ground and have to go after the guy who's undefended. You're a *coward*."

Maybe I shouldn't have resorted to name-calling. Oh well.

Grimacing now, with some kind of pent-up anger or righteousness of its own, it kept talking at me in its own clipped, musical language. It sounded superior, mocking. It had to know we couldn't understand it, right?

"Come on," I muttered at it. "Surely an all-powerful demon of the netherworld could set aside a few eons to learn English."

Tina—her body, at least—was sweating. A drop ran from her damp hairline down the side of her face, which was pink and flushed.

"Oh, my God," Jules said. "Kitty, she's burning up."

It was burning Tina up from the inside, just like it did to Mick.

chapter 17

We have to get her to wake up," I said, moving toward her, getting ready to shake her out of it.

"No!" Jules intercepted me. "It's supposed to be dangerous to touch someone in a trance like this."

"Then what do we do?" I said shrilly.

"I don't know. God, Tina, you didn't tell us what to do. Tina!" Her eyes flickered behind her eyelids, but she didn't wake up. Her lips were still moving in the demon's rant, but her voice was a whisper. She was breathing harder, and I could feel the heat coming off her. She was going to burn up in front of us.

I ran to my bag in the corner and grabbed the jar of blood goo, the one Tina wouldn't let me use on the house. I opened it, then I splashed it on her. Just threw the whole bottle of gunk right at her.

The sticky, blackened potion spattered over her like mud, over her clothes, her face, her hair. The voice cut out, and she fell, sprawling flat out like she'd lost her bones.

Jules and I crouched beside her. I touched her face; the skin was warm, damp, feverish, but not burning up.

It seemed to be cooling off, even. Jules went to one of his equipment bags and found a bottle of water, which he tipped to her lips. Most of it spilled out the side of her mouth, but her throat showed swallowing movements.

"Tina? Come on, wake up," I murmured, hoping that she would both wake up and still be herself. I didn't want to have her on my conscience, too.

"Tina," Jules said, more sternly but just as desperate.

Her eyes squeezed shut, then blinked open. She groaned. "Did I black out? Ow, my head."

She touched her forehead, and her hand came away sticky. Patting herself, her fingers landing in spots of blood goo, she grimaced in disgust. "Oh, gross! What happened? Don't tell me we're going to log the first verified case of genuine ectoplasm on top of everything else." Then she looked closer at it. "Oh God, I think I'm going to be sick."

We helped her sit up. She looked like she wanted to crawl out of her own skin.

"What do you remember?" Jules said. He touched his headset. "Are the recorders still running? Are we getting all this? Tina, do you remember anything at all?"

"I don't remember anything," she said, sniffing, trying to wipe off her face with hands covered in slime. Exhausted, she looked on the edge of tears.

"Maybe we could go over the video footage," I suggested. "Hey, there aren't any fires started anywhere, are there?"

We did a quick check of the house and didn't find anything burning, which was a huge relief. This was still just another haunted house. It felt like the only thing that had gone right in weeks. That, and the potion had worked and saved Tina from spontaneously combusting.

At Tina's insistence, we went back to the hotel suite so she could shower. She wasted no time and soon emerged with wet hair and fresh clothes, squeaky clean. Within a half an hour, we were gathered around the video playback screen on Jules's laptop.

"Here we go," Jules said, tapping keys.

The camera angle showed Tina in profile, frozen in her unnatural, possessed pose.

She frowned. "I don't remember any of this."

"Probably for the best," I said. "Can you imagine? That thing was *using* you. Like a puppet or something."

She paled, looking nauseated, her lips pursed. "Thank you for that image. I may never sleep again."

Oops. It only got worse when Jules started the audio portion. Tina's voice came out of the speakers, we all recognized it, but none of us understood a word she was saying. Not even Tina.

"What *is* that?" she said, her horror plain.

"Looks like a classic case of glossolalia," Jules said, almost happily.

Glossolalia. Speaking in tongues.

"That's it," Tina said, leaning back in her chair, holding her head in her hands. "I'm never, ever doing that again. It's all Ouija boards from here on out."

Nobody argued with her. We were all rather horrified. I had expected some kind of warning, but the possession of her had just *happened*. The demon had slipped into her presence without any sign. We'd had so little chance to react.

Tina was carrying a jar of blood goo with her at all times now.

"I don't think it's glossolalia," Gary said, looking even more quizzical with the gauze over his eye. "In classic glossolalia cases, the subject speaks an unknown or made-up language. I think this is a real language."

"But which one? Do you recognize it?" Jules said. "There are demonic languages. The medieval Cabbalistic writers talk about a language of demons, a language of hell—what if this is it?"

"No. There's got to be a more logical explanation," Gary said. "Don't go over the deep end on us now."

Jules said, "There are thousands of possible languages. We can't rule out ancient ones, either. How are we going to figure out which one this is?"

"Call it a hunch. Give me a sec." Gary turned the laptop toward him, closed the video screen and called up a Web browser. Within a minute, he'd found the site and played a video.

I couldn't make out individual words, but it had a clipped rhythm to it. And Gary was right—it was familiar.

"What is it?" Tina said.

Gary showed us the screen, which was a mass of squiggling script. A video streaming in the corner showed military Jeeps rumbling down a yellow, dusty landscape. If I had to guess, I'd say Gary had found an Arabic news site.

"Arabic?" Jules asked.

"That's only a demonic language if you're a warmongering Republican," I said, flippant. It was either laugh or cry in a situation like this.

"That's it, then. I'm done. I'm a complete and utter believer. At least in Tina," Jules said. "All those people who claim they're channeling medieval German milkmaids or Cleopatra—and then they speak English? Tina, you don't know Arabic, do you?"

She shook her head.

Jules laughed. "This is . . . it's *crazy*. Do demons even have nationality?"

"Maybe they do," Gary said. "If it really is Arabic it'll be easy enough to find a translator and find out what it said."

"So it's an Arabic demon," Tina said. "Now what?"

"Oh, my God, I know what it is," Jules said, dumbstruck by his own revelation, staring into space. "An Arabic demon—it's a genie."

I had to admit, I wasn't expecting that one. None of us were; we remained silent.

Jules kept on, pleading almost, like he needed us to tell him he was right. Or crazy.

"Like a genie in a bottle," he said. "Arabic folklore, all those stories in *One Thousand and One Nights*. Genies aren't supposed to have physical form. They're magical beings, but they have sentience and will—they're like people. Well?"

"Sorry," I said. "All I can think of are reruns of sixties TV shows."

"What if you're right?" Tina said. "We still have to figure how to stop it."

Gary said, "This is way outside my area of expertise."

"I could make another round of e-mails and phone calls," Jules said. "There's a guy at Oxford who's written about this. But he specializes in the folklore. I'm not sure what he'll say when I tell him this is for real."

"The worst he can do is say you're nuts," Tina said.

Jules smirked. "He's already said that."

I had an idea. Probably not a good idea, but I liked it anyway. "There's something else we can do. We can turn this one over to the group mind."

"Group mind?" Gary said.

"Friday night, my show. We throw this out to my listeners. See what happens. I've got a pretty diverse audience. Who knows? Maybe someone out there can help. We might be surprised." I blinked hopefully.

Jules chuckled. "Where you're concerned, I don't think I'll ever be surprised."

"Please don't say that," I said. "That's when the really weird shit starts happening."

Like a knock on the door. Not again, I thought. We looked at the door, but nobody moved. Nobody wanted to see who would come visiting at this hour. Like maybe the demon had found another body and wanted a rematch. The knock came again.

Jules went to the door and checked the peephole, then opened the door and let Ben in. My husband didn't look happy. My first thought was panic: What had happened? Who'd died now? But then, seeing him glare at me, the guilt landed in my stomach like a rock. I'd promised to call him, hadn't I?

"Ben. Hi," I said. I bit my lip.

"Would you believe I was just about ready to call the police?" he said.

I scrambled from my chair. "Would you all excuse us for a sec?"

As I passed Ben, I grabbed his sleeve and urged him outside. He was smirking.

There, in the dark under the porch light, we looked

at each other. He didn't look angry, just tired. Like he'd expected me to forget to call him. Like none of this surprised him. That made all this worse, and I didn't know what to say.

"I'm sorry," I said bleakly. It sounded lame.

"Have you checked your phone?"

My phone in my pocket. I'd turned it off before the experiment at Flint House and hadn't looked at it since. When I did, I found six missed calls. All from Ben.

"I forgot to turn my phone back on after the séance."

He blinked. "Wait a minute. You guys did another séance?"

"It never really got to the séance stage," I said, realizing I was just digging the hole deeper. "It was more a demonic possession, really, but we stopped it. And we think we know what's doing this now." Always end on a bright note.

Why did I feel like I was trying to explain to my parents why I'd broken curfew? Ben was my husband, not my father, and I hated feeling like this about him.

"You were supposed to stay out of trouble," he said, scowling, his voice tight, obviously trying not to yell. "You were supposed to call me if you got in trouble or did something that was likely to get you in trouble."

"I forgot. I'm sorry." I had an urge to look away, but I didn't. I didn't want to give ground.

He shut his eyes for a moment. "If it were any other time, it wouldn't be a big deal. But something out there is trying to kill you. When I got back to the condo and you weren't there, and you hadn't left a message—" He shook his head. "I could almost kill you myself."

I didn't believe it, but he spoke calmly, and there was

something in his eyes, amber and wolfish, and his shoulders were bunched up, tense, like hackles. His body language was edging toward ferocious.

"Tina and the others found something," I said. "Another clue. Maybe another step toward stopping this thing."

"That's good," he said flatly.

Then nothing, for five heartbeats. Six.

"We can't do anything else tonight. Maybe we should go home and get some sleep." Cue tail wagging. Imaginary tail wagging. I hoped the thought came through.

"Yeah. Okay."

Usually when Ben was angry at me, he yelled. We both yelled, and then it all went away. This tamped-down temper—it almost sounded like he'd given up. The problem of the demon almost faded from my attention.

I ducked inside long enough to tell the others to get some sleep and say good night.

We spent twenty minutes of dead silence on the ride home. I was so tense I wanted to scream. Howl. Something. I wanted to stick my tail between my legs and grovel. I'd have to turn Wolf to do that. It would almost be worth it; wolves were so much better at apologizing than people.

Finally, by the time we parked, I couldn't stand it anymore. I tried apologizing from the parking lot to the condo. Ben walked quickly, keeping a stride ahead of me. Making me beg until we were finally home. I shut the door behind us.

"I'm sorry. I'm sorry—how many times do I have to say it?"

"Until it sounds like you actually mean it," Ben said.

We both turned away at that one. Ben huffed a sigh, ran his hand through his already mussed hair. I crossed my arms and squeezed my eyes shut, trying to stop the stinging.

This was never going to get easier, was it? We were always going to fight like this. Being married to each other didn't change the fact that both of us were opinionated and stubborn to a fault. We both wanted to be in charge. We both thought we knew best.

I bowed my head. Took a deep breath. "I'm sorry," I said softly. "I'll call you next time." Be honest, now. "I'll try to remember."

I didn't dare look at him to see how he took this. I listened, took in his scent, tried to sense him, feel the heat of his body. When he spoke at last, there was almost a smile in his voice. "I *really* hope there isn't a next time. At least where the demon hunting is concerned."

Smiling weakly, I looked over my shoulder at him. Then I turned, sidling up to him. Tail low, ears flat—at least if I had them in this form, that was what they'd be doing. It was amazing, though, how much of that attitude the human body could emulate. Slouching, I looked up at him with big puppy-dog eyes.

"Can we go ahead and skip to the making-up part?" I said. Making up, making out . . .

He glared, resisting. Playing hard to get. Still a little angry. So, how much could I get away with? I took a breath through my nose, hoping to catch a scent, a clue.

He was focused on me. His body was saying yes.

I hooked my fingers over the waistband of his jeans, pulling myself toward him. He rocked a little but stood his ground, making me come to him. I was okay with that.

Body to body, I breathed out, brushing his throat, almost close enough to kiss him. Not quite. I watched movement under his skin as he swallowed. A quick kiss, a taste of salty skin with a flick of tongue at the V of his open collar.

My hands slid to the button of his jeans, unfastening it. Then I opened the zipper, slowly. He made a sound deep in his chest, like he didn't want to let it out, didn't want to admit I was getting to him. He was perfectly capable of running away if he wanted to. He didn't. Looking up, I could just see the smile touch his lips.

I slid my hand down the open access, maneuvered under his boxers to bare skin, and felt for him. Wasn't hard to find. Throbbing manhood, they called it. Ben had it. He shivered a little at my touch. Pressed into me. His hand—fingers spread, eager—found my hip, slid to my backside.

I kissed his chin—he turned his face and caught my lips with his.

Cradling him, melted against him, I urged him on. Pulled him to the sofa, pushed him down, climbed on top of him. I was hungry for him. And relieved that he hadn't walked away. Grateful and thrilled. It all wrapped together with heat and lust building in me. I pulled off my shirt, tossed it aside. Grabbed his jeans and yanked down. Rubbed my hands up his body and watched him flex under my touch. He closed his eyes, and his hand clenched on the sofa.

I considered: This had been a pretty big fight. I'd screwed up, I could admit that. That meant I was going to have to spend a good long time making it up to Ben, right?

I could do that.

*   *   *

I felt better in the morning. That might have been from anticipating the show, looking forward to taking the next step. Or it might have been from being curled up in bed with Ben, who was smiling vaguely in his sleep. The apology must have worked.

Despite everything, I was looking forward to talking about the demon on the show. Some people accused me of being a sensationalist, of fishing for controversy. Maybe even of inciting controversy. Really, I loved drawing back the curtain, dragging this stuff into the open, kicking and screaming sometimes, and shining a bright light on it. I thought of it as dispelling ignorance. Ignorance bred fear, and I didn't like being afraid.

I didn't want to have to wait through an entire day until it was time to do the show. On the other hand, vampires couldn't bother me during the day.

No, bothering me during the day was Detective Hardin's job. I would have loved another hour or two of sleep on a day when I had to be bright-eyed and bushy-tailed at midnight, but Hardin called my cell phone.

"What have you been doing?" said Hardin, and she wasn't happy.

"What do you mean, what have I been doing?"

"Are you near a TV? Can you turn on the news?"

"Just a sec."

The TV was in the next room. I pulled on a robe and went out to turn it on, then flipped channels until I found what Hardin was talking about: A local newscast showed a building on fire. Then another one. And another. A series of film clips showed five different buildings, in different parts of town, all on fire. The scenes were nighttime—

they must have happened last night. A caption read "Fire Department Stretched Thin."

Ben had been working at his desk. Drawn by the images, he leaned forward and stared at the TV.

"Oh my God," I said, sinking to the sofa. "What happened?"

"I was hoping you could tell me. Even apart from injuries from the fires, I have three more bodies just like Cabrerra."

A wave of dizziness hit me as the blood left my head. I sat down. "Who? Who are they?" Which of my pack members had paid for my curse this time?

"They're not werewolves. The victims are random, as far as we can tell. If these are all connected, and I dare you to tell me they aren't, this thing's gone on a rampage, and I need to know why."

Not werewolves. My pack was safe. But I didn't feel any better, since three random innocents had died because of this. No one was safe.

"I think we cornered it," I said. "Maybe even scared it."

"So you figured out what's doing this? You know how to stop it?" She sounded excited.

I winced. "What would you say if I said it was a genie?"

"Like in a bottle?"

"Yeah."

She paused for a long moment. "I don't know what I'd say. Aren't they supposed to grant wishes? Not go around burning people to death?"

"Well, there's the bedtime stories, and there's reality. We all know how that works, right?"

"This doesn't help me figure out what to do about it. I don't want anyone else to die, Kitty."

"And you think I do?" I said, shrill.

Taut with frustration, she said, "Why do these things always happen to you?"

I nearly screamed, but I swallowed it back. My voice sounded unnaturally calm. "If I knew that, I would make them stop."

We both simmered for a moment. Then she said, "How do I arrest a genie?"

That was always the first thing she asked. How do I arrest it? She'd managed lycanthropes so far and was gunning for vampires, and I had no doubt that if a way to arrest genies existed, she would find it.

"Some of us are working on the problem," I said, sighing.

"I want in on it," she said.

"What?"

"I'm not convinced you've ever really bought into this supernatural-and-law-enforcement-working-together philosophy, no matter how much you might talk about it on your show. I think you're still in this mind-set of working under the radar and making sure the supernatural takes care of its own problems. I don't know who you have working on this, and I don't really care. I just want in on it. Don't keep me in the dark."

Whoa. She not only listened to my show. She, like, paid attention. Read into it.

I changed my tone, leaned back against the sofa, and tried to sound nonchalant. Tried to relax so I could sound nonchalant. "Detective. You like my show?"

She huffed. "I consider it part of my job to listen to it. I don't know if there's any *like* involved."

Ouch. That wasn't exactly a vote of confidence. I avoided an urge to whine about it. "Listen tonight," I said. "Then you'll know everything I know."

I hung up before she could argue.

Leaning on the table, I covered my face with my hands. I wanted to run. Wanted to be wild, without responsibility. I didn't want to have to face this problem anymore.

We watched the news report run on. This was a special, not the regular newscast. Another fancy caption and graphic came on-screen: *Arsonist Loose in Denver?* They had no idea.

"That was Hardin, I take it," he said. "Calling about this?"

I nodded. "She says three people have died. No one from the pack, but still."

"Shit," he said again. "I hate to think what this thing is going to do next."

Him and me both. I shook my head, leaned back to stare at the ceiling with aching eyes, beyond tears and beyond words.

"There isn't enough blood and dust to protect the city," I said. Now it was all of Denver I felt responsible for, not just me and my pack. All I had to do was make enough of the potion to drench over the whole city. That would go over well.

"You know what this means?" Ben said. "If you bring this up on your show tonight, it'll strike again. Every time we've provoked it, it's struck back. Lashed out. It'll use your show as an excuse to attack again."

This had occurred to me. "Then you think I shouldn't do it. I shouldn't talk about it on the show."

He shook his head. "No. It just means you have to finish it tonight. You can't let it go on another night."

"What if we can't? What if we can't figure out how to stop it tonight? What then?"

"Then we'll deal with it tomorrow. One day at a time."

He was right. If we wanted to rile it up, it had to be because we knew how to finish it. No good just pissing it off for the hell of it.

That was it, then. One way or the other, tonight, we'd face the monster.

chapter 18

We had all day to prepare. That should have been enough time, right? I read everything I could get my hands on about genies, though most of what was out there was from the *One Thousand and One Nights* collection of stories, and I wasn't sure I bought most of that. They were mischievous and seemed most often trapped by clever tricks. The stories were like those of Celtic fairies, pixies, and leprechauns—over time, the truly scary, otherworldly creatures had turned into harmless, cute little beings who granted wishes. Time made the stories nicer. Grimm turned into Disney. Why couldn't I get a genie that granted wishes and sounded like Robin Williams?

Then again, this genie was granting wishes—just not mine, but my enemies'.

Peter called to check in from Las Vegas. "Hey, Kitty."

"Hey, have you found Grant?"

"There's something weird going on with that guy. I tried to get into his dressing room, but nothing worked, and I've picked dozens of locks before. I've never found a door I couldn't get into."

Was that even legal? "You know, if you ever want to do this sort of thing professionally, I think there are guidelines that say breaking and entering is bad."

"Yeah, okay, but there's still something weird going on."

"Agreed." He had no idea just how weird.

"I went to the police to see if a missing person report's been filed on him, and I think I found something. There's about a dozen people over the last five years who've gone missing at the Hanging Gardens. That's unusual, even for Vegas. If you need nonsupernatural proof that something's going on over there, this may be it."

"Enough to get the police involved?" I said.

"I need to get someone here interested enough to start an investigation and get a search warrant. I still don't know quite what I'm looking for—"

"Anything they might be using to cast spells or summon demons. Blood, daggers, arcane symbols, Arabic written on ancient parchment. Use your imagination. You'll probably be close."

"I still have to talk someone into serving a search warrant."

"I think I know someone who might be able to help you with that," I said and grinned over at Ben. I handed the phone to him at his desk.

They talked for a good long time, and I tried not to be antsy, sitting on the sofa with books and my laptop pretending to do research. I couldn't get a whole lot of meaning from only one side of the conversation, especially when Ben slipped into lawyer speak, but they sounded like they were making a plan.

"I'll fax you a copy of the paperwork," Ben said, and hung up.

"Well?" I said.

"You have a DVD of the show from Vegas?"

"Yeah. What for?"

"I'm going to use it as proof that your buddy Nick is psychologically harassing you and that the harassment is continuing, in violation of the restraining order. We convince the Vegas cops the harassment is dangerous and establish just cause for a search of their place for evidence linking them to the fires."

"Will that actually work?"

"It might. If it doesn't, we haven't really lost anything."

Nothing but time. "You're the lawyer," I said.

He started packing up his laptop and collecting a few papers from the file rack on his desk.

"I'm going to go try to get the police reports about Mick and New Moon. It may take me a few hours to get it all together, then get the files to Peter. Will you be okay?"

I smiled. "Yesterday you didn't want to leave me alone."

"But you don't need to go anywhere today, right? You'll head to the radio station this evening, but you'll be here the rest of the time, and the building's got all that blood gunk around it, right? So you'll be fine."

Truthfully, I wasn't sure, because I was worried about Ben out there by himself, unprotected, where the demon could get to him. And maybe I was nervous about being alone, too. But I nodded. "I'll be fine. Will you be fine?"

"Yeah, I think so. I hope so. I'll probably bring a jar of that gunk along, though."

"I'll go find one," I said and went to the kitchen, where I had a box of the stuff. I'd never get the smell of it out of my nose, would I?

When I returned, Ben was running his hands through his hair. "Do I look too ratty? I should probably comb my hair."

Aw. I touched his cheek. "Yeah, but you usually look like you need to comb your hair. You'll be fine." We kissed, and for that moment I really did think we'd be all right.

"I'll meet you at KNOB in time for the show."

We said our usual "be careful" version of goodbye.

Twilight fell, evening came. I grew more nervous, because the disasters always happened at night, like the world really was divided into light and dark, good and evil. I always tried to give the world the benefit of the doubt and pay attention to the shades of gray that seemed painted everywhere. Times like these, though, it was easy to feel an inexplicable black darkness rising against me. Easy to feel the monster that dwelled inside me and believe myself doomed.

Willpower. Had to keep going. In a world that seemed determined to turn us all into monsters, I had to keep making the list of reasons to keep fighting, to keep myself whole, to stay human, sane, and good—or at least the best I could. My family, my career, chocolate. Blazing Colorado sunsets, The Clash, Jimmy Stewart and Harrison Ford movies. My friends, which I counted more of every day. And Ben.

In that mood, I slung my bag over my shoulder and went outside to my car.

On the sidewalk, I stopped abruptly as I caught a scent. Smoke, smoldering, fire waiting to burst forth. Brimstone.

My skin flushed hot. Looking around, desperate to catch a sign of it, to see a figure outlined in flame or to hear ghostly laughter, I waited for fire to consume me. I'd caught the smell as soon as I left the protective barrier the blood and ruin potion formed around the building. It had been waiting for me. But the smell was everywhere, without source.

I'd had the feeling that someone was watching me for weeks now, and not just Peter. No matter where I looked, nothing presented itself. I couldn't spot anything. I swallowed back a whine.

"Stop stalking me!" I called, feeling like an idiot, but I could either yell at it or scream incoherently. "You want to come after me, then come after *me!* Face me! You could burn me to a crisp, so why don't you?"

A grating voice chuckled.

This was what I'd been reduced to: yelling at air in my parking lot. The demon was trying to drive me crazy, and it was succeeding.

"What are you?" I said, my voice low, like a growl. I'd attack it, I really would. If I had any idea how.

Something grabbed my wrist. I'd have sworn it was a hand, a strong, rough hand, four fingers and a thumb wrapping around me and squeezing hard, like it meant to drag me away. Gasping, I jerked away, scrambling back, cradling my hand to my chest. That chuckle sounded again, amused, mocking.

Red burn marks shone on my skin, like a sunburn, in the shape of fingers. Like a red-hot hand had grabbed me.

I managed not to scream, though I really wanted to. The only thing that kept me from running, as fast as I could without thought to direction, was my car sitting thirty feet

away. I really needed to get to my car, like someone in a
bad horror movie, fumbling with the keys, trembling. Except I had this feeling that a creature made of invisible fire
and the scent of ashes stood between me and it. To move
forward was to move toward doom.

I retreated until I pressed myself flat against the wall
of the building, behind the invisible barrier. Here, the air
smelled safe. I stared out. I couldn't see anything, but my
heart was racing.

I could stay here forever, lock myself inside the house
and never come out. But I wanted to get this thing. I tried
again, moving cautiously, paralleling the building as I set
out toward my car.

The feeling of heat and the oppressive scent of danger
confronted me immediately. I nearly dropped to my knees,
overwhelmed, convinced that I was going up in flames.
My breath came out in a sob. I clutched my chest.

What would it feel like to burn from the inside? Is this
what Mick felt?

Turning, I stumbled back to the building, back behind
the safe barrier, thinking, Yeah, okay, I could stay inside
for the rest of my life. No problem.

A strong voice called across the parking lot in a foreign
language. In a panic, I tried to think—was this the voice
that channeled itself through Tina? Was the language, the
words, the same? I didn't think so, but I couldn't tell—
the alien words slipped in my mind like water, I couldn't
recognize or hold them. But the meaning was clear: a
command, filled with authority and anger. Like a priest
performing an exorcism.

Maybe exactly like a priest performing an exorcism.

Roman marched across the parking lot. He almost

seemed to be marching toward me. But his approach veered—he was talking to a space in front of me. To a thing that wasn't there. He called to the space, his eyes blazing, his hands clenched into fists. I'd never seen a vampire so ready to do physical battle like this.

He repeated the words again, pointing this time, arms outstretched.

A roar like a flamethrower sounded, but without fire. Because it wasn't flame, it was this thing's voice, a scream of protest. The sound of a creature made of fire giving voice to rage.

I thought: What had I ever done to deserve this thing's anger?

At least it wasn't directed at me now. Roman had *really* pissed it off. The demon roared again, and Roman actually seemed affected, stepping back, turning his face aside, as if he had encountered a blast of fire. Fire was supposed to be one of the things that could kill a vampire. I wondered if that was true, if they burned as well as anything else organic.

Roman called out again, repeating the same forceful words. He commanded with the will and confidence of someone who was used to having his orders obeyed, who wasn't used to being questioned. No wonder he'd been annoyed with me.

This was a battle of wills. Roman stared ahead at his opponent, like he actually could see the demon's shape.

The sound of billowing flame answered him again, but weaker this time. I still couldn't see the form of the creature making this sound. I kept thinking if I squinted, I would see a shimmering outline, a wavering humanoid shape, like a heat mirage.

He repeated the phrase one more time, and the sound of flame vanished. Roman's head tilted back, his gaze flickering upward, as if he watched something fly away. Then he frowned, flexing his hands, massaging them together, like they were sore, aching.

I ventured outside the safety of the protective circle; the brimstone smell was gone.

Roman glanced at me. His cold, frowning gaze made me flinch. "I just saved your life," he said.

I took a deep breath before speaking, to keep my voice from shaking. Not sure if it worked. "Um . . . thanks?"

"This is temporary. It will kill you eventually if you don't do something."

"Do you know what it wants?" I said. "You can really tell what it wants? Then why don't you tell me?"

He scowled, his chiseled face turning hard with frown lines.

When he kept silent, I continued. "What was that you said? What language?"

Now the stone face shifted to a smile. *"Per vi mei, averte."*

I heard the words, but I'd never remember them to look them up. I wished I had a tape recorder. "You going to teach me that little trick?"

"Now that you've seen what I can do, will you let me help you?" he said.

That made me angry, the idea that he had the power to stop this thing, but he wouldn't do it without me promising a big chunk of my soul in return.

"This could all still be a show for my benefit," I said. "The con game again. You could have staged all this in a last-ditch effort to get me to agree to your terms."

He turned away, muttering, but my hearing was good and I picked up what he said: "Stupid wolf."

I so didn't have the time or patience for this. Setting my shoulders, I stalked forward, past him, not sparing him a glance.

"You're being foolish," he said.

I turned, scowled. Knew better than to launch myself at him, fingers curled like claws, as if I could really do him damage or even intimidate him. I'd seen a vampire drop a werewolf twice as large as I was without flinching. Roman might have been just waiting for me to lose my temper.

"Here's the thing," I said in my calm, careful DJ voice, like I might use to explain dirt to an idiot. It was the best way I knew to attack anyone. "You don't care what happens to me. This demon could shred me limb from limb right now and you wouldn't care." I refrained from glancing worriedly over my shoulder. That was just what I needed, to have the demon lurking nearby, waiting for an invitation of the Murphy's Law variety. "You could make this thing vanish anytime you want, and I believe you. I also believe you don't care about stopping it. You're using it as a stepping stone to something else, taking advantage of a difficult situation to get what you want. And that makes you a manipulative, amoral son of a bitch. Now tell me why I should put myself in the position of owing a manipulative, amoral son of a bitch a favor?"

I expected a retort, something along the lines of usual smug vampire haughtiness. Or more accusations and name-calling. Either way, I'd just turn around and walk away. I had nothing else to say.

But Roman didn't reply right away. He regarded me with that annoyed curl to his lips and studied me, like he could see through me. I turned and walked away because I couldn't take that stare for another second.

"Kitty," he said. I paused but didn't turn around. I shouldn't even have done that much. I should have kept walking to the car, then driven away. Not that it would have helped any when he said in that same commanding exorcist's voice, *"Lupus vincens."*

He spoke the words clearly and carefully, and this time I recognized the language. I could guess enough Latin to know what it meant.

"What?" I said, turning, and he said the words again, stronger this time, and a cramp ran from my gut to my skull, dropping me to my knees. Goose bumps broke out all over my skin, like needles pricking me. My bag fell off my shoulder as I hugged myself. Another wave of cramps wracked my whole body this time, every muscle clenching.

Another body inside me was bucking, fighting to break free. I knew this feeling, I recognized what was happening, but it had never happened like this before. Never so violent. Usually, shifting felt like Wolf was breaking out from the inside. Now she was being ripped free from the outside.

I screamed a rage-filled denial. Was this supposed to scare me? Was this supposed to prove how much power he really had? My muscles spasmed, teeth and claws trying to tear out of human skin. Hunched over, I tried to keep from hyperventilating. Looking up, I expected to see Roman standing over me, gloating, sneering. He kept his distance, though, and didn't smile. His frown seemed almost disgusted. I couldn't guess by what: this scene of torture he'd created? By the fact that I wouldn't agree to his terms? By the mere fact that I was an inferior, stupid wolf?

I could have fought it. I wasn't so far gone that I couldn't pull it back. I'd pulled back from farther than this before. But I decided not to. I decided I needed to fly. At *him*.

I ripped my shirt over my head and let *go*.

chapter 19

Not for defense, not to hunt, not to flee on faster legs. Now, and for the first time, this part of her is driven by rage. Vision is red. Kicking, writhing, saliva flying from bared teeth, she tears free of her tangled human skin. Thick claws scrape against a hard, flat earth. Not forest, not safe. The air smells of too many people, alien, oily scents of the human world.

And this thing, the being who attacked her. The figure smells of death.

Fur bristles, rising stiffly along her back. Head lowered, tail straight behind her, she bares her teeth and glares. Her opponent glares back, unmoving. Is it a challenge? Doesn't matter. He smells wrong, and she must fight. Claws scrabbling, she launches. She will pounce, put her jaws around his neck, topple him, and tear into his flesh.

The man of death merely steps aside. Grabs her foreleg at the shoulder. Wrenches. She slams against the ground, hits hard, yelps, but doesn't stop moving. Back on her feet, *she leaps away, braces, facing him. Deciding how best to flank him.*

"The alpha shows her colors," he says.

They circle each other. She can't—won't—turn her back to him. And he won't turn his to her. If he attacks, she'll be ready, but she won't strike him directly, not again. Her shoulder throbs with the impact of the last throw.

"A standoff. So. You're smart enough not to fling yourself against me again and again. That's something."

Her mouth is metallic with anger. With the need to tear flesh. Blood will soothe the bitterness on her tongue. But somehow she knows: This creature has little blood to spare. Still, she cannot turn away from him and stares her challenge.

The man of death smiles.

"You've made an error your human self would not have done," he says. "You've met my gaze. Look at me, wolf. Look deep, and do as I say."

Suddenly she hears nothing but his voice.

"I know what will hurt you worst of all. You think you're the first self-righteous werewolf in the world? You're not. Your kind always fears the same thing. So this is what I will make you do: Seek out people. Seek out crowds. They are your prey. Hunt them. Perhaps you'll even live long enough to wake and understand what you've done."

The voice inside her that always whispers, that urges her to one thing or another, is his voice now, and the metallic taste on her tongue, the hunger for blood, the need to hunt, rises uncontrollable. A brief smell of the air shows her how much prey is here. Too many people around, yes. Plenty of hunting.

She breathes out. Something in her whines. She wants to run, but her legs are stiff.

"Go," he says. "Go and hunt."

"No, Kitty. Don't listen."

Her name calls her back. She shakes her head, rubs her face on her paw. She feels like she's scented something awful.

There are two of them now. Two men of death. The first looks away, and she moves, trots back and forth, keeping them both in her vision. They stand on either side of her, as if they seek to trap her.

She can't fight them both. She needs her pack for that, but the wolves are far away right now. She is in a maze of concrete and steel. Growling low, daring them to follow her, she backs away. Then she turns and runs. Find her pack, find her mate, find a safe haven.

Even keeping to shadows, trotting along walls, out of sight, she feels exposed. Danger is everywhere. There are hunters hunting her. Her senses are so taut they hurt, smell and hearing stretched to breaking.

When he approaches, she smells him. The man of death. The second, not the first, who has left. The one who called her from the other's spell. How long has it been, how long has she been running, and how has he found her?

He moves from shadow to a circle of light, near a fence and a row of low shrubs where she tries to hide. He is calm, not challenging. Not staring, not bristling. It keeps her from running again.

"Kitty." His soft, murmuring voice is so different than the other's.

Part of her wants to flee, and part of her is drawn to him. Head low, she paces in a wary circle. He's a friend,

*part of her says. Trust him. Go to him. It's the part of her
that walks on two legs, like him, but she doesn't know if
she can trust that voice.*

But she's drawn to him.

*"I've never seen you like this," he says. "What a beau-
tiful creature. Not that I expected anything different."*

She growls low.

*"You can't hurt me. You know that, I think. Somewhere
in there you know I'm your friend." He crouches, offers
a hand. "Kitty. It's Friday. You have a show to do, don't
you? You need to come back."*

*His voice lulls her. But the anger that drew her into this
shape lingers. Who is he to tell her this?*

"Kitty. Shh. Shh."

*She glares and meets his gaze. "Go to sleep. I'll watch
over you. You'll be all right. Shh."*

*Pacing, she stumbles. Her body is succumbing to the
spell of his voice even as her mind panics. But her other
half agrees with him. Sleep. We have work to do. We have
to sleep.*

*He reaches to her, but she won't approach him. Nearby,
there's a shadow made by foliage, as close to a forest as
she'll find here. She curls up in this spot, folding her legs,
putting nose to tail. Tries to keep an eye on the man of
death who crouches nearby. But her eyes are heavy, and
they close.*

I awoke groaning, clenching my limbs, because nothing
smelled right. Nothing seemed right.

Vampires, there were vampires here, and I was all tangled up in the sheets, and . . .

Naked.

I was lying on dried grass, covered with an overcoat that smelled like Rick.

The whole episode played through my memory on fast-forward. The demon, Roman, Changing, Rick. He was sitting nearby, within arm's reach, hands holding his knees.

He glanced at me. "Hello."

I didn't have to get drunk and hungover anymore to wake up pissed off and groggy. I had this instead. I groaned again, rubbed my face, and decided against sitting up just yet.

"How much do you remember?" he said.

"Most of it, believe it or not. What did he do to me? He said those words, pushed me over the edge. I didn't know vampires could do that." But it wasn't just him. I remembered the rage that had spurred the final Change, and that rage had been all mine.

"That isn't part of a vampire's power. Roman has something else, some kind of spellcraft, maybe even a form of hypnotic suggestion. It was probably similar to what he used to repel the demon."

"You saw all that?" Now I did sit up, awkwardly keeping the coat around me. I was probably really lucky Rick had been around. I might have gone running off into traffic or something.

"Yes. I've been keeping an eye on Roman. On both of you," he said.

"Oh." He had probably seen us talking the other night, then. Right on the edge of plotting against him. "I guess I should say thanks. For the intervention."

"And I suppose I should apologize. For thinking you really would go along with him against me."

I sighed. "It's been very frustrating not feeling like I have a say in the matter. Feeling like I'm at the mercy of both of you."

"There's so much more to this than you know, Kitty. Who he really is, *what* he is—I've met vampires like him before, and they're dangerous. You have no idea how dangerous. Their manipulations have dozens of levels—I can't explain it all to you."

I smirked. "Spoken like a true vampire. 'You puny mortals couldn't possibly understand.'"

He ducked his gaze and chuckled. "You're right. I'm sorry. I thought I was protecting you. Sheltering you from people like him."

"Keeping me in the dark isn't protecting me," I said.

"Obviously," he said. "Still, his offer must be tempting, now that he's proven he can deal with this thing with a snap of his fingers."

"Yeah." I wondered who was going to die tonight, now that the demon was even more aggravated. "I'm not through yet. We've got a plan. Maybe it'll actually work."

"Can I help?"

"Just keep keeping an eye on Roman."

"I've only found him when I've followed you, but I'm working on it. I need to know where he came from and what he wants."

I huffed. "I can tell you that—he wants to get his greedy little paws into Denver."

"But why?"

We could keep asking that question, drilling further and further back for every answer we came up with.

Headlights appeared as a car turned the corner, driving slowly as it edged along the alley.

Rick stood. "Hold on a moment."

I looked around. I hadn't gotten far from the parking lot. Across the street and down the block, we sat against the row of shrubs and fence that divided the condo from the rest of the neighborhood. The car stopped nearby as Rick flagged it down. It was Ben's car. The lights went off, then Ben stepped out.

Relieved, because I felt a little safer now, I went to meet him.

"I called him," Rick said. "I hope you don't mind."

Ben looked relieved, too, his lips in a thin smile. "I found your clothes and bag by your car." He held them up to show me.

Ah, clothes. "Thanks," I said, leaning into him in an awkward hug—his hands were full, and I was busy holding Rick's coat around me.

"Are you okay?" Ben said.

"I think so. Just a little shook up."

Then came shock and panic—I didn't have my watch, I didn't know what time it was. It was Friday night and I was supposed to be working *right now,* not running around naked.

"What time is it?"

"You have an hour," Ben said. "Get in, I'll drive."

He handed me my clothes and got back in the car. I was left holding clothes in one hand, using the other to hold the coat closed, and contemplating how I was going to manage the next few minutes.

I looked at Rick. "You saw me naked, didn't you?"

"Maybe just a little." He quirked a smile. Sheesh.

With a long-suffering sigh, I decided to let it go. I handed him his coat and started pulling on my jeans and shirt. The vampire turned his gaze skyward and politely pretended not to notice.

Ben, however, leaned out the driver's-side window and watched.

"Okay," I said, finally ready to go. "I'm hoping this'll all be over tonight, one way or the other."

He nodded. "Good luck."

"Thanks." I flashed a smile, then jumped in the car, and we drove away.

Ben was smirking. No, he was positively leering.

"What?" I said, a little put out.

"You're awfully cute, you know that?"

"Is that supposed to be a compliment?"

He just kept grinning, all the way to the station.

chapter 20

I was exhausted, itchy, annoyed. My skin still felt like it should have fur. I couldn't have been asleep for more than an hour—not enough time to sleep off the Wolf. Part of me glared out, shoulders up, head low, like a pacing animal.

"Hey. Keep it together," Ben said outside the KNOB building.

I took a deep breath and tried to shake it off. Jules and Tina were already there. It was time to get to work.

I trailed Grant's blood potion around the station building, then left open jars of it inside, at the bottom of the stairs, the door to the elevator, and the entrance to the studio. I made Matt keep a jar near his console. The whole place stank with the sickly, rotting smell of it. The butcher who was supplying me had started to look at me funny.

However, this would keep us safe only here. The creature had made it clear that if it couldn't have me, it would create chaos elsewhere. Protecting myself seemed so futile.

"You're expecting trouble," Matt said. The smell was

so strong that even he, a normal human, was wrinkling his nose at it. "What kind of trouble?"

"It's under control. Don't worry about it," I said flatly. Like that was totally convincing. Ben, smirking from the chair he'd settled into near the door, seemed to agree.

Matt gestured at the *Paradox PI* crew, who were setting up in the back of the studio. "Have you all figured out what happened to your van last week?"

"Still working on it," I said blithely. "So, um, if anything really weird happens tonight, don't freak out or anything."

He scowled. "I *hate* when you say that."

"I don't think we're going to get any vans tipping over or anything. It should stay pretty low-key. Just . . . weird."

"Great. I feel so much better now." If that didn't sound sarcastic enough, his glare confirmed it.

At least, I was really hoping nothing happened here. I'd be heartbroken if anything happened to KNOB. More heartbroken than I already was.

Jules was tapping away at his laptop, with Tina looking over his shoulder. They were going to watch, listen, take notes, and cross-reference with their own research, and maybe add their own commentary off the air. The hope was we would come up with some information, then maybe we'd come up with some solutions. At least that was the plan. This was sort of an experiment.

As the start of the show neared, I put my hair back in a ponytail, settled before my microphone, adjusted my headset, and took a few deep, calming breaths. This was my world. I was in control. Nothing could touch me here.

The on-air sign lit. Creedence Clearwater Revival's "Bad Moon Rising" started, giving me a boost of energy and a sense of mayhem. Bad moon indeed. No matter what the disaster, you only had to face it head-on, with fortitude. Yeah, I could do that.

Matt pointed, and I talked. "Good evening, and welcome to *The Midnight Hour,* the show that isn't afraid of the dark or the creatures who live there. I'm your host, Kitty Norville, who keeps coming back for more.

"Tonight I want to do something a little different. I have a problem and I'm looking for information from the group mind. I've encountered a rather unusual supernatural creature, and it's been causing problems. Remember last week? Van tipping over, mayhem, and chaos? It didn't stop there, and a week later this thing is still out there, still after me. I need to figure out how to stop it, and maybe someone in radio land can help. Here's what I've got. It likes fire. It may actually be made of fire, but it looks like a person, it acts like a person, and has a really wicked laugh. It's been burning things down, burning people down, and I'm getting really sick of it. It seems to speak Arabic, and we think it might be a genie. Yes, I said genie. That's a new one for me, too. Let me play you a little something we picked up."

Matt cued up the recording we'd given him of possessed Tina speaking a language she didn't know. We'd gotten a quick translation. Most of the words had been variations of the same: *Stupid mortal, your ignorance is astonishing, I will burn you all, you're helpless before me.* Blah blah blah. The tone of the monologue had been clear: contempt.

"There it is. The language is Arabic, the words are chock-full of insult. Now I'm asking you. Animal, vegetable, mineral, or something from the great beyond? And

I do believe I've got my first call of the evening. Joel from Pittsburgh, hello."

A very serious-sounding man said, "Hi. Kitty. Clearly, Islamo-fascist terrorists are not just targeting us on the mortal plane. Obviously they've sent their netherworld demons after us, as well. We should have expected this. Those people will stop at *nothing* to destroy the American way of life."

I winced. I should have known, as soon as I broadcast someone speaking Arabic, the paranoid political loons would raise their freak flag. "Actually, I have it on pretty good authority that this is a personal attack directed at me in response to . . . well, in response to various things. Trust me, this isn't an ideological attack rooted in international terrorism. I'm not so egocentric or paranoid to think that I'd even be a target for international terrorism."

"That's exactly the sort of liberal head-in-the-sand attitude that is going to bring this great country to its knees! You'll never see reason because you're part of the biased left-wing media establishment." I swore the guy was slavering.

A sane talk radio host would cut the guy off right about there. Instead, I spoke calmly, baiting the guy. Because, you know, it was funny.

"Let's say for a minute you're right," I said, in the space where the caller paused to take a breath. "And this is a terrorist campaign waged by Islamic extremists. And, by the way, my research has indicated that the Koran does acknowledge the existence of genies. What would you do to counteract the attack? How would you stop it? Should I try throwing Republicans at it?"

He didn't get the sarcasm. They *never* get the sarcasm.

"Kitty," he said evenly, in all seriousness, "to rid yourself of this demon you must accept Jesus Christ as your personal savior."

"Actually, exorcism is pretty high on the list of recommendations. But if we're right about this thing, a Muslim cleric would probably be more helpful than yours. Moving on."

Some folks weren't convinced it was a genie.

"Hi, Kitty. Thanks for taking my call."

"It's my pleasure. You've got something for me?"

"It's not a genie. It's the Human Torch," Mike from Austin said.

"As in the superhero? From the movie?"

"No, I'm talking about the Golden Age Human Torch. He was a scientific experiment that got out of control, escaped the confines of his underground tomb, then became the archenemy of the Sub-Mariner, and—"

"So what you're saying is the Human Torch is fictional," I said, wincing.

"Yeah, but he could totally do everything you described."

"Except that he isn't real. And if he was, wasn't he a hero? Didn't he help people, not burn them down?"

The guy huffed. "The Wolf Man isn't real, either, but *you're* still sitting there, aren't you?"

"There are so many things wrong with that statement I don't know where to start. Next call, please. Hello."

I was definitely grasping at straws here. But at least it was entertaining.

"Hi—could it be a phoenix? Because I think of fire and I think phoenix. Maybe it's like a were-phoenix . . ."

". . . or a will-o'-the-wisp. Like they say happens with burning swamp gas . . ."

". . . a thunderbird spirit . . ."

"Pyrokinesis is a well-documented phenomenon, and I believe it's more widespread than anyone imagines . . ."

Most of what we got wasn't entirely helpful.

"You're supposed to put genies back in their bottles, right? So that's all you have to do."

"And how would you suggest I do that?" I said the fourth time someone made that recommendation.

"Uh, I don't know. You just kind of stuff it in?"

"Hard to do when you can't even see the darn thing," I said, frustrated, and hung up.

By the last half hour of the show, we hadn't gotten anything substantial. I was getting frustrated, and Wolf was pushing against the inside of my skin. Then one of the calls listed on my monitor said "Nick from Las Vegas." What were the odds? I punched up the call to find out.

"Hello, you're on the air."

"Kitty, baby, I expected to hear from you about this days ago." The voice was male, suave. So full of himself there was obviously little room in there for tact, or raw intelligence.

I recognized the voice. It called up a picture in my mind of a young man with a Chippendale physique, sun-baked blond hair, a sultry smile, and the strong scent of lycanthrope—were-tiger, specifically, sleek and feline. The new alpha of the Band of Tiamat.

"Nick," I said, speaking as brazenly as I could. I put a smile on my face and sugar in my voice, no matter how angry I felt. I curled my hands into fists and squeezed tight, because I could feel claws trying to break out. "What an unpleasant surprise. Listeners, I have here as my sudden unexpected guest Nick, a real genuine were-tiger and the star of the King of Beasts show at the Hanging Gardens Hotel and Resort in Las Vegas. Bet you didn't know the whole act is made up of lycanthropes, did you? Well, now you do." To think, when I'd first met them I'd been so sensitive about revealing their true natures. Keeping their secret. If only I'd known. I felt no compunction about blathering on about them now.

"If you think that kind of exposure bothers me, you're wrong," Nick said. "I always thought we should go public. I suppose I should thank you for getting rid of Balthasar. He was holding us back." Balthasar, their old leader, who was killed in the course of my escape from them.

"You may have called in to taunt me, but I don't actually have to let you talk at all."

"But you will, because you like talking. Tell me, how's life been for you? Getting a little hot?"

Ha, so it *was* the Band of Tiamat and not Roman who summoned the genie. Rick was wrong. Unless of course he wasn't, and the two were working together. No time to think about it now.

"Well, Nick, since I've got you on the line, maybe you could help me out with that. I'm really curious about where you dug up this thing. Do you have some kind of grimoire of evil demons? You flipped through and decided this one looked like more fun than a plague of locusts? Or is there a mail-order catalog that will deliver underworld creatures to an address of your choosing? I have to tell you, if that's the case I think you got ripped off, because their gift-card option sucks."

He laughed, which aggravated me. I refrained from growling. I tried not to growl on the air.

Tina and Jules were watching me, wide-eyed.

He said, "I thought you'd learned during your visit here that these are powers you don't understand, can never understand. You're dealing with the consequences of trying to interfere with them."

I groaned. "The consequences of saving my own life, you mean? And there is nothing more boring than the old 'dealing with powers you don't understand' shtick. I think that's a lame excuse used by people who don't have any better clue what's happening. Is that it? You and your priestess unleashed this thing, and that's all you could do with it? You don't understand it yourselves, and you can't control it. Once it's loose, you can't stop it."

That was a terrifying thought I hadn't considered until now. I had entertained the notion that if I figured out how to placate the Band of Tiamat and its priestess, they might call off their demon. But what if it wasn't theirs to control? Their cult was all about chaos. They might not *want* to control it.

He didn't answer right away. A couple seconds of dead air ticked over, and I started to switch to a new call.

Then he said, "I thought you of all people could appreciate anarchy."

"Anarchy only works when everyone's sane," I shot back. "I have another question for you: Where's Odysseus Grant?"

Nick hung up.

Shit.

Deep breath, had to keep going. I could panic over what

was happening to Grant in, oh—I checked the clock—about ten minutes.

"Well," I said at my microphone. "I don't know much about laying curses, but if any of you *do* know anything about laying curses, I know someone who needs cursing right about now. Next caller, hello."

The woman spoke with an accent, something clipped, refined, Middle Eastern.

"Kitty, this thing that haunts you. You're right. It is *djinn*." She pronounced the word with a different inflection, and I could hear the different spelling. She was pronouncing it correctly.

"Go on," I said, glancing at Jules and Tina. They were listening closely.

"The *djinn* are said to be fallen angels, or sometimes spoken of as a kind of person made up solely of spirit, where humans are made of matter. Among the *djinn* there is the *ifrit*. An *ifrit* is a spirit of fire, and it loves mischief. I think this is what has found you."

There it was, the chill up my spine, the gooseflesh on my arms. The ring of truth.

"I think you may be right," I said. "Now. How do I stop one of these *ifrit*?"

She hesitated. "This is a difficult thing. There is anger here, and vengeance. I risk drawing it on myself, if I help you more than this. He would know."

"Wait a minute," I begged, because my on-air sixth sense told me she was about to hang up. "If you know this much, you must know how to protect yourself. You know how to stop it."

"I have only listened to your show for a little while, Kitty, but I can tell you understand much. That in every tale there is a grain of truth. The trick is to separate truth from tale."

"You're right, I've found grains of truth in a lot of tales. But how do you separate them?"

"Wisdom. Intuition. We are not so far from the times when the tales ruled us. Our hearts remember."

"Maybe we can do this with twenty questions," I said. "The bottle part—stuffing it back in the bottle. Is that true?"

"Yes," she said.

"And how does one go about stuffing a *djinn* into a bottle?"

"You don't stuff," she said. "You coax. You lure."

"All right. Makes sense. How do we do that?"

"Aren't you a scholar of the arcane arts? Aren't you versed in the principles of spells and curses?" Her voice had turned playful. I recognized teasing when I heard it.

"Only the kind of curses I'm not allowed to say on the radio."

"Something had to call it to this world, to its current hunt. Learn what it was. Use that to banish him out of it. He will not be able to resist."

God, who *was* this? She talked like the old vampires did, or the real magicians. Who needed conspiracy theories when these guys were around?

"May I ask you a question? What are you?"

She put a smile into her answer, and for some reason, I imagined her winking. "Let's leave that another mystery, shall we?"

"Are you one of them?" I said, impulsively. "You're one of them, aren't you? A *djinn*? Can *djinn* even use the phone? What—"

But I was talking to air, because she finally did hang up.

From the corner, where they were stationed with their laptop, Jules and Tina were looking back at me. Their eyes gleamed, and they smiled. They'd found something, then. Maybe now we had everything we needed to stop this.

But first, the show. "All right, faithful listeners. I'm about at the end of my time with you tonight. I have to say, some days I finish off the show feeling more confused than I did when I started. Just when I think I've encountered everything there is to encounter, something like this comes along and smacks me upside the head. But that's a good thing. It keeps me on my toes. Until next week, be careful out there. Look under the bed one more time before you go to sleep. This is Kitty Norville, voice of the night."

And that was it. I was done.

With the credits still rolling in the background, Matt came out of the booth. Fuming, he pointed at me. "There's no way you can convince me that *I Dream of Jeannie* is after your ass."

I blinked. "I wouldn't do that. This thing's a little more with the flaming death and less with the cute blond nose wiggle."

"I think the nose wiggle was *Bewitched*," Ben said.

I rolled my eyes. "Details. So what is it? What have you got?"

Tina and Jules had been writing and making sketches on a pad of paper. Jules said, "Your caller was right. Some symbols, some basic principles, are the same in nearly every culture. The circle, for example, as a symbol of eternity and protection. She seemed to be suggesting that any sort of banishment spell ought to work on this thing."

"So we're back to exorcisms," I said.

"Sure," Tina said. "But we've seen this thing before, we've seen what it can do. Jules and I have a spell that ought to work."

"Custom banishment," I said. I almost said it wouldn't hurt to try, but it could. If we didn't succeed in trapping it this time, what would it do next when it lashed out? Why did I get the feeling the *djinn*—the *ifrit*—listened to the radio and knew we were up to something?

"We'll need some of your hair," Jules said with a perfectly straight face.

I stared.

"Just a strand or two," he said quickly. "Nothing terrible."

Using something personal like someone's hair was a common bit of spell lore from all over the world. I found the end of my ponytail and pulled out a few hairs, wincing. "Should I even ask?"

"The thing's after you—we're just going to make sure it knows you're around." He smiled as he stuffed the strands into a plastic bag.

Tina tapped a pencil against the table. "The thing I can't figure out is what kind of bottle we need to use. I mean, it seems kind of gauche to use just a plastic soda bottle or something. Like maybe we ought to use something all glass and fancy."

"Don't use plastic," Jules said. "It's not sturdy enough. Those oil lamps, like you see in the Aladdin story, are made of brass, right?"

"So what do we do?" I said. "You have a plan, right?"

Jules took a deep breath. A "here goes nothing" breath. "We'll go someplace we know the thing's been before— Flint House. We use components we know affect it—your potion. Something of yours because it has a connection to you—your hair. Build a trap, set the bait, and there you are."

"So it's a plan," I said hopefully.

"It's *something*," Tina said.

"Then let's get going." The sooner we got started, the sooner we'd find out if it worked. Or not. I didn't want to think about that.

"I swear, this job gets more surreal every week," Matt said, wandering back to the safety of his booth.

chapter 21

Tina and Jules rode in the *Paradox PI* van with Gary to pick up a few supplies. They were still debating about what kind of bottle to use: clear, opaque, plain, decorated, screw top, corked. Something without cracks, I told them jokingly before we parted ways. They didn't think that was funny. Ben and I drove together to Flint House.

Hardin called, not five minutes after the show ended.

"You've got a plan. I want in on it," she said.

I sighed and started to argue with her, because the last thing I wanted was another person in the line of fire. Trouble was, she'd keep pestering me until I told her, or she'd sic a patrol car on me. She'd probably already dug up the trail of accident reports from all our adventures this week and could check those locations as places we'd likely turn up again. The thought of arguing with Hardin made me tired.

Then again, another ally in the fight was always a good thing.

"Any chance you could get a fire truck on the scene?" I asked. "Just in case?"

She paused. "I do *not* like the sound of this."

"When do you ever?"

I told her where we were headed without going into too much detail about what we'd be doing there. Hardin promised me a fire truck.

"Hardin, right?" Ben said after I'd hung up. "Don't tell me the cops are going to be there."

"It looks like the cops are going to be there."

"I'm glad we're married so I don't have to be your official lawyer anymore. I don't envy whoever has to deal with it when you get charged with something."

Oh, God forbid, I didn't even want to think of it. "We're not breaking any laws. If anything, having the cops there makes it better, right?"

"If you say so."

Soon after talking to Hardin, I called Peter's phone. And got no answer, which meant he was probably in trouble along with Grant. I couldn't help them right now, though. Get through the next hour, then worry about them.

We all arrived at Flint House within a half an hour of each other. We each had a job and we set to work, anxious to get this over with. Gary and the PI production crew were at it again, setting up their cameras and monitors in a quest for elusive documentation. The hour was god-awful late at night, par for the course when doing battle with the supernatural. Typical creature-of-the-night bullshit. Didn't a standoff at high noon mean anything to these beings?

"I don't like this," Ben said, following me, not willing to let me out of his sight. I tried not to snap at him over it. He had a right to be worried, after everything that had happened. "I don't like going into this with a half-baked plan."

"It's not half-baked," I said. "It's *mostly* baked. Just a little soft in the middle." Actually, that was bravado.

"This'll work," Tina said, helping Gary with some of the remote cameras. Her nervous fidgeting belied her chipper demeanor.

I retrieved the latest batch of Grant's protection potion from the trunk of the car. I hoped this wasn't like antibiotics, that overusing it wouldn't encourage some sort of spell-resistant superdemon. I'd have to ask Grant about it. I felt a pang at that—I hoped Grant was okay, so that I could ask him about it. I dripped the potion in a circle around the house, like I'd done with every other building in my life. This time, though, I left an opening, a six-foot gap in the circle in front of the door, giving the *djinn* a way in. *Our* way.

Inside, Jules had more of the potion, which he used to mark out a path: from the front door, into the parlor, where more marks funneled the path to a circle in the middle of the floor.

"Are we sure we want to be doing this inside?" I said. Inside this very old house made of dry and flammable wood, I didn't need to add.

"We want it in a confined area," Jules said.

At least no one lived here.

Jules paused in his work. "Here's my problem. I'm a scientist. We're in the business of studying these phenomena. Investigating, collecting data, analyzing. We're not in the business of doing battle with them. We're not exorcists or crusaders."

"Maybe we should be," Tina said, leaning on the rickety banister near the foyer, regarding our handiwork rather than addressing anyone in particular. "You remember that house in Savannah? The two-hundred-year-old cottage that was supposed to be haunted by a murdered little girl? We recorded some sounds but didn't find anything definitive, like what usually happens. But I felt something. The place was old, and more than just one little girl had died there. The old woman who lived in the house was scared, really scared. She lived by herself on a tiny income, didn't have any family, and couldn't afford to move. She lived every day in fear that this spirit wanted to harm her. Maybe she was just paranoid, but if I could have done anything to convince her that the house wasn't haunted, or that we'd found a way to drive the spirit out, I would have. Who knows? If this works, maybe we'll discover there's a market for this sort of thing. We'll go from *Paradox PI* to *Paranormal Exterminators*."

I shook my head. "I so wish I was recording this. Are you guys recording this? The birth of a new show?"

Tina smiled. "If we start a new show, you'll be the first to know. I promise."

Hardin arrived with her fire truck, as well as a couple of patrol cars; her people had blocked off the street, to keep innocents from intruding, and to keep watch in case anything should happen. Like what? We all kept asking. If we knew, we'd be able to plan a little better.

The detective marched into the house, lit cigarette in one hand, cup of steaming Starbucks in the other, and announced, "I can't decide if I want something to happen to prove I'm not nuts, or if I don't want anything to happen because of the mess it would make," she grumbled. "But if I hear my boss humming the *I Dream of Jeannie* theme one more time, I'll kill him."

Daaaaa-dum, da dum da dum dum . . .

"Great, now you've got it stuck in my head," I said. The music was way too jolly for this situation.

"American television," Jules hmphed derisively.

Everyone took their places. Hardin, Gary, and their people waited outside. Ben was stationed near the door of the parlor with a fire extinguisher. Jules was waiting outside the circle in the parlor. Tina and I were by the front door. Playing bait. That was the plan: Announce our presence, summon it, like had happened the other times, then piss it off enough that it would stumble into the trap.

"I still don't like this," Ben muttered for the umpteenth time. "I don't like you putting yourself in the way of this thing." His expression had gone taut and snarly. He was pacing back and forth along the wall like a wolf in a cage. I didn't point this out to him, since I was doing the same thing.

"I'm not putting myself in the way of anything, yet. Besides, I'm beginning to think it's way too smart for us," I said. "It's probably not going to come anywhere near here and is off killing people somewhere." Hardin had one of her people in touch with the 911 dispatchers. If there was any emergency in the city that had anything to do with fire, we'd hear about it when they did.

We really needed to come up with a *djinn* detector. Something that would tell us exactly where it was, so we could go after it. Because *that* sounded like a good idea.

Jules shook his head. "All the evidence suggests that this thing is tied to you and has been watching you. It won't stop now."

"Since when did you know so much about it? I thought you were the rationalist in the bunch," I grumbled, unfairly. He was only trying to help.

"Even magic follows rules," he said.

This was true. Vampires burned in sunlight, silver was poison to lycanthropes, and the right spells controlled a demon like this *djinn*. All that was fact. Rational. Just a whole different kind of rational.

"Right," Tina said, brushing her hands on her jeans. "Let's get started."

She retrieved a box from a bag shoved in the corner: the Ouija board again. I wasn't sure I was ready to call this part of the plan rational. She set it up on the floor inside the open front door, within sight of the gap in the protective circle. Sitting cross-legged before it, she gestured me to join her. We sat with the board between us.

Ben stalked menacingly behind us, fire extinguisher in hand.

Tina rubbed her hands before setting her fingers on the planchette. I didn't want to touch it. I knew I'd feel some kind of spark, an electric shock, and I wasn't sure I could handle it.

She didn't look like a medium performing a séance. She had none of the closed eyes, relaxed breathing, and meditative stance that were supposed to happen. Hunched over, braced and glaring, she looked like someone preparing to do battle.

"Come on, come on," she murmured but wouldn't say what she was thinking, what she was doing to call this thing besides sitting there, glaring at the board. I figured it was more likely to burst into flames than talk to her.

Nothing happened.

We waited. The house creaked, a normal sound of old, settling wood, something shifting in a breeze that rattled outside, shushing through vegetation. To tell the truth, I had almost forgotten that the house was supposed to be haunted. This might have been spooky if I wasn't so worried about the *djinn*.

"What's happening, Tina?" Jules asked in a hushed voice.

"*Nothing* is happening," she answered around gritted teeth.

I started pacing. "It's too smart for this. It's not going to walk into our trap." But if it wasn't here, where was it? What part of the city was it burning down this time?

Frustrated, I went to the front door. My pacing carried me right through it. Ben called after me, a warning. I didn't stop. I went to the end of the walk and looked up and down the street.

The breeze picked up, and I caught a scent.

That scent was now so deeply buried in my memory that I'd never associate it with anything else. Years from now, the barest hint of it would bring all this to the front of my mind: fire, fresh ash, smoke-tinged air, sulfur, brimstone.

The shrubs around me—overgrown, climbing, tangled, and dried out from a hot summer—ignited. Towering flames appeared with no warning, no opening spark or ember, and roared into the sky. I was caught in the inferno.

Strangely, my fear was an undercurrent, buried. Because what I was mostly thinking then was *gotcha*.

The quiet, late-night world erupted with noise. Sirens from down the street came to life, and behind me Tina was yelling, "Kitty, get in here, get behind the line!"

The fires weren't stopping here. Flames leapt from shrubs to trees along the street, to trees at the next house. It was only a matter of moments before the houses would ignite. I was glad Hardin had brought along the fire department.

I turned and ran to the front door of the house. Then I stumbled, falling to my hands and knees when my heart clenched. Like something reached in and squeezed, and it was hot, burning, like a fever. Sweat broke out over my skin. I felt heat from the fire around me, from the burning within. I groaned—it was Wolf squealing through a human throat.

Tina and Ben were at the front door, yelling at me. Five steps. I could do this.

I hauled myself to my feet and stumbled up the house's porch. The flames behind me seemed to growl, but I didn't have time to stop and growl back. I ran, over the threshold and across the line of potion we'd drawn on the floor. Ben's and Tina's hands were on me, helping me.

A flare, like an explosion of fireworks, burst in through the front door with me, singeing my hair and clothing. Instinctively, we screamed, raising our arms to shield our heads, falling back, scrambling out of the way—

I felt no heat. The searing flames around me, the fire gripping my heart, all of it was gone now. I was safe, behind the stripe of blackish goo painted on the floor. On the other side of that barrier, hand-sized tongues of flame danced on century-old floorboards.

Ben leapt forward. I grabbed him, calling, "No, stay back!" But he didn't cross that magical line. He fired the spray from the fire extinguisher over it. The flames vanished, leaving behind blackened streaks and the smell of scorched hardwood.

Something made a growling sound. It might have been a natural creaking in the house, or a distant rumble of thunder. Except the sky outside was clear. This sounded like a voice, very close by, muttering low, too soft to make out the words, assuming it even spoke in a language I could understand.

Outside, people were shouting, water was spraying from fire hoses into front yards and against houses, and the sirens were still wailing. Inside Flint House, though, was oddly still.

We braced, waiting for the flames to overtake us. My heart hurt, it raced so hard, bruising my ribs from the inside. My skin prickled, my shoulders bunched, fur and hackles. Wolf snarled from my hindbrain. Adrenaline kicked the need to Change into overdrive.

Ben gripped my shoulder, his fingers like claws. I touched his hand.

"What's happening?" Jules said, low and urgent, from the next room.

"It's here," Tina said. "It's looking right at us." We stared at the doorway, where the fire had followed me, but saw nothing.

I squared my shoulders, took a breath, and wondered if this was what bungee jumping felt like. You couldn't think of all the things that could go wrong as you stood on the edge of the precipice and looked over; you just had to take that step and trust.

"Kitty," Ben said, his voice low, almost a growl. His hand twitched on my shoulder.

Squeezing it, I pushed it away. "Just be ready with that fire extinguisher."

I stepped over the dark line on the floor.

All remained still. I could look through the front door and see fires still burning outside, but the fire department had those under control. By all appearances, the thing had fled, but Tina said it was still here, and I believed her.

"Hey!" I called out, venting my anger at the flames for lack of a better target. "You son of a bitch, where the *hell* do you get off setting fire to my city? Not to mention killing people. I'd have thought some ancient fire demon like you would have better things to do than harass me. Don't you have a lamp somewhere that needs redecorating?"

A voice spoke words I didn't understand, and a furnace engulfed me. Like leaving an air-conditioned house and entering a summer desert. It was supposed to be autumn, but I'd never felt so hot. The heat rumbled like a furnace pumping full-force. I heard words in the noise, but I couldn't understand them.

This was what was supposed to happen. This was what I wanted. I ran.

My clothes might have been on fire, but I couldn't stop. Ben and the others might have been shouting at me, but I couldn't concentrate to hear what they might have said. Any moment, I expected to fall, to be engulfed by the thing that chased me, to be smothered in foam from the fire extinguisher, or any other of a thousand things that could happen. But none of that did. I trusted that the thing followed me, keeping to the path we'd put in place. It had to be following me, because the air was so hot I couldn't breathe. Or maybe I was burning up, like Mick had.

Ahead of me, Jules shouted, his eyes wide with panic, urging me on like I was running a race. I sprinted into the next room, crossed the dark line drawn on the floor, and slammed shoulder first into the opposite wall, because I didn't bother slowing down. My clothes were smoking, my skin was red.

Jules leapt forward with a jar of the blood potion, splashing it across the floor in a messy arc that managed to close off the circle painted in the room.

Inside the circle drawn in blood, the floor caught fire, exploding up in a column of flame that reached the ceiling. No little flickering campfire, this. This was the inferno of a forest fire, right in front of us.

Jules and I fell back, curling up for protection while the fire merrily burned on the hardwood. Tina and Ben appeared at the doorway. Ben had his fire extinguisher in hand and sprayed the conflagration. The foam streamed, then sputtered, then died. Empty. He went to grab for another one.

Tina stared at the fire with an expression of awe. Shielding my eyes, I looked into the light.

A figure stood in the midst of the fire, wavering, like a distant shape lost in a heat mirage. Far from harming it, the flames seemed to give it form: indistinct limbs, definite torso, and a strange face that kept changing. Its body hunched over, arms bent and fists clenched, ready to launch into a fight. It hovered, snarling. This was the figure we'd seen in the video footage from the New Moon séance. The *ifrit,* manifesting to confront us properly.

The room filled with the scent of flaming disaster, we were surrounded with searing heat, but the floor, though scorched black, was no longer burning. We all just stood there looking at each other.

"Er, now what?" Ben said. He had a new extinguisher, but like the rest of us, when confronted with the humanoid figure, he could only stare.

The thing spoke, in Arabic I assumed, the same clipped language from the video. Though I couldn't understand the words, I understood the emotion behind it: anger. The *djinn* raised a fist, gestured, its whole body lurching with the motion of its tirade. It ranted at all of us, looking back and forth between us. Like we'd kicked its dog or walked on its lawn.

The stories, the lore, said that *djinn* were like people in all ways but what they were made of. They had families, jobs, their own societies, all invisible to us. They felt all human emotions, love, grief, joy, anger. They prayed. This was a person standing before us. I may not have understood that until now, when it was yelling at me in rage.

I couldn't go soft on it. This thing had killed Mick.

My job wasn't over yet. This barrier wouldn't hold it forever. If it didn't burn down through the floor, it might go up through the ceiling. The whole house might burn down around us. We had to finish this, which meant I had to distract it while Tina and Jules worked.

I called, "Hey, shut up a minute! I'm not finished telling you off! God, what a jerk." I didn't know if it understood English. But the same way I recognized its anger, I was pretty sure it recognized mine. Sure enough, it turned. Were those yellow shadows within the orange flames its eyes? The spots flickered at me, as if blinking.

It may not have understood me. I was guessing not, since it fired back a stream of Arabic, probably with as much rudeness as I'd flung at it. We should have brought along a translator. I was a little sad that we couldn't talk this out. Not that we ever had a chance of that.

I didn't wait for it to finish before continuing. "I don't understand why something as powerful as you would let yourself be controlled by a bunch of idiots like the Band of Tiamat. Even if they are run by a vampire."

It chuckled. The light sound, like sparks crackling in a piece of wood, couldn't be anything else. It was a condescending laugh, clearly suggesting I didn't know what I was talking about. True enough.

I focused on it. To even let my gaze flicker to the others to check their progress would be to draw attention to them. But it wasn't like I'd ever had a problem running my mouth off at someone before.

"I think you can't possibly be such hot shit if you let yourself get trapped with a little bit of paint."

It roared, starting softly and letting the sound grow. The sound turned into a word.

"Bitch."

Note to self: Never assume a person speaking a foreign language can't understand what you're saying.

Tina started yelling, "Thus by a spark the power that binds you is destroyed. Be banished now and never bother us henceforth!"

It was a formal, archaic, and definitely mystical speech, exactly the sort of thing found in a magical grimoire, and I had no idea if Tina had found the chant in such a place, or if she made it up, or if she was channeling some other spirit, some other power that she'd called on to help us here.

She held a bottle—she'd finally decided on the kind used to hold powerful acids in a chemistry lab, pint-sized, made of thick brown glass with a heavy rubber cork—over the edge of the boundary, its mouth pointed toward the *djinn.* Jules put a lighter to a small bundle of hemp tied up with my hair, which he held over the mouth of the bottle with a pair of tongs. The fibers lit immediately, glowing hot red and sending up a tendril of black smoke.

Tina repeated the chant, with variations but with the same meaning, commands of banishment, of release. The *djinn* turned to look, the flames surrounding it swaying in another direction, sparks licking out behind it. Jules blew on the smoke from the burning hair, so it drifted forward and mingled with the flames writhing around the *djinn*.

An odd thing happened.

The line of smoke from the burning hair shifted direction and began to move into the jar, as if sucked in by a tiny vacuum or draft of air. The flowing smoke began pulling the *djinn* with it.

Realizing what was happening, the figure inside the flames flinched back, flailing its arms, like a swimmer fighting against a riptide. It shouted with its furnace-and-flamethrower voice, begging while it gasped.

A burst of light threw me to the floor. I curled up, covered my face with my arms, convinced something had exploded and the house would now fall down around us, killing me, Ben, everyone. Our rapid healing wouldn't help us if our whole bodies fried first. My nose was dead, unable to smell anything, unable to tell me where Ben had fallen. I thought I had seen him for a split second, holding the fire extinguisher up as a shield, flung away from the circle as I was, a silhouette against the atomic flare. The sound—this must be what the inside of a star sounded like, a constant nuclear explosion times a thousand.

At least, that was what it felt like to my senses. Like the world had ended, like the *djinn* was ending it with his final scream, with blasts of fire.

Then it all went away, and I sat up and looked.

I had a feeling the room had been still for some time, it was so quiet. No fires burned anywhere, not even on the floor, which had been roaring with flames. The acrid stench of soot and sulfur, which should have been overwhelming, had faded. I could almost taste a hint of freshness, as if someone had opened a window.

The circle drawn in blood on the floor was gone. The *djinn* was gone.

Jules and Ben were picking themselves up off the floor, brushing off their clothes, shaking their heads as if dazed. Tina, however, knelt at the edge of where the circle had been, one hand clutching the bottle, the other hand clamped tightly over the cork, locking it shut. Far from being dazed, she held the bottle straight-armed, tense before her, staring at it in a panic.

"You got it?" Jules asked finally. "It's in there?"

She nodded quickly. She had it and was obviously afraid to let it go, in case it escaped.

"I can't believe that actually worked," Ben said.

We looked at each other across the room and didn't need words. A month's worth of anxiety, and an equal amount of relief, filled the silence. He pursed his lips, and I smiled, and cried a little, tears slipping free. We crossed to each other in a couple of steps, and I nestled in his arms. We rested like that a moment, heads bent together, taking in each other's scent, reassuring ourselves that our pack, our mates, were safe now. We were safe.

He touched my hair, stroking lightly, and let out a sigh. So did I. He smelled like Ben. Maybe a little scorched, but still Ben.

"You look awful," he said, and I suspected he was right. My arms stung like a bad sunburn, my face felt scorched and sooty. But none of that mattered. I'd heal soon enough.

"Funny," I said. "'Cause I feel pretty good."

Gary and Detective Hardin burst in and pounded into the parlor, looking flustered.

"Is everyone okay?" Gary demanded. Hardin had her hand on her belt, where she kept her gun holstered.

"Yeah. Yeah, I think so," Jules said, his voice shaky. He rubbed a hand over his short-cropped hair. The hand was shaky, too. Soot smudged his glasses.

"The video cut out—everything went to static when you lit the hair," Gary said. "What happened?"

None of us spoke. None of us could explain it.

"Tina, you got that cork in?" Jules asked, kneeling next to the woman.

The shocky look still gleamed in her eyes. Jules put his hands around hers and eased the jar to the floor. Together, they tested the lid. It was tight. Then they let it go. The jar sat by itself on the floor, inert, harmless. Opaque. I imagined the *djinn* inside, screaming in anger, beating fiery fists against the interior wall, trying to get out, sealed by magic, against all reason and the laws of physics. Or maybe it had been sucked into another dimension, a pocket universe, that the ritual had somehow opened. Maybe the ancients had understood the crazier notions of theoretical physics better than we did. I'd have to file that away to think about later.

Tina heaved a sigh—she'd been holding her breath—and slumped into Jules's arms. They hugged each other.

"How am I supposed to charge a thing in a bottle with murder? How am I supposed to write this up?" Hardin said, looking lost. She said this sort of thing a lot.

"Can't you close a case without actually arresting anyone?" I said.

"Say the suspect was killed in the course of arrest," Ben said helpfully.

"No and hell no. The paperwork for that sort of thing is even worse than the paperwork for . . . this." She gestured vaguely at the aftermath of our trap. The whole place was covered with soot, scorched like it had been flash fried.

"Besides, it's not dead," Tina said, still staring at the bottle.

Well. Wasn't that a cheerful thought?

"Let's get out of here," I muttered and led the way out the door. It was still dark. Maybe I could get a few hours of sleep. The first sleep in weeks where I wouldn't be worried about some creature of flames waiting to pounce on me.

The fires in the yards up and down the street were out. The sirens were off, but lights were still flashing, red, blue, and white flickering merrily, reflecting off pools of water in the street. Some people had wandered out in bathrobes to gawk at the commotion, and the police herded them safely out of the way. The yard at Flint House was blackened, and the air smelled of wet soot, thick ash, and puddles of dirty water. However, I didn't smell any fresh flames or brimstone. Nothing that reminded me of the *djinn*.

I spotted the figure on the sidewalk only because he was so pale, stark against the flashing police lights. He emerged from shadow, stepping toward me up the walk, regarding the scene with an appraising, military look. Like he was trying to figure out how to take it all apart.

It was the vampire, Roman.

chapter 22

A frown creased Roman's face as he studied the house. He seemed to glance at me only as an afterthought, then said, "Usually, a house that stands empty as long as this one has, there's nothing to keep me out. I ought to be able to walk right in. But there's something here."

I stopped on the porch and stared, causing a bottleneck behind me. Just as well. I wanted to turn and tell them all to run, get out, get away from him. This couldn't be good. But he couldn't enter the house, the home. *Something's* home. A ghost's home? If the place really was haunted, did the ghost call it home? It made a weird kind of sense. It meant as long as we all stayed on the porch, or behind the door, the threshold, Roman couldn't hurt us.

"Upset because the ghosts won't invite you in?" I said. He didn't credit that with a response. He only smirked at me. Softly, I said, "What are you doing here?"

"I've been following you. You know that. For longer than you think."

I took a breath and prepared for a battle of wills. "Oh, really?"

"You saw me, even. In Dom's penthouse. In the foyer outside the elevator. Do you remember?"

I remembered . . . vampires standing guard. Part of Dom's entourage. The one that looked like a linebacker, and . . . the other, quiet one, with the short-cropped hair, the cold gaze. He'd looked like a bodyguard. He'd blended in.

When he came to Denver with his mission burning in his manner, I hadn't recognized him.

"Oh, my God," Ben whispered behind me.

I let anger cover up how off-balance Roman had put me. "You're more than Dom's bodyguard . . ."

He chuckled. "Of course I am. I hold Dom's leash."

"And the Tiamat cult?"

His smile fell. "That is a tool that has outlived its usefulness, I think."

My mind tumbled over itself, and I started thinking out loud. "Dom's a front, so no one will know who's really running Vegas, and you gave the priestess—"

"Her name is Farida," he said.

I didn't break stride. "—a place to run her cult in exchange for . . . for her power? Her magic? What?"

"She's one of my soldiers. Or, she was," he said, scowling at the burnt vegetation around him. "I'm impressed. You shouldn't have been able to banish that spirit."

"I had a lot of help."

"Trust me, I've taken note of it."

I'd just put all my friends on Roman's radar. What would he do to us? Rick was right all along, this was a conspiracy. I didn't want this guy in Denver. But how to get rid of him?

I felt Ben at my shoulder, Tina, Jules, and Gary behind

me. Hardin edged around me, her gun drawn. Roman gave her a dismissive glance. His frown held contempt.

"What now?" I said.

"I suppose getting control of this city will have to wait, for the time being." Now he turned a smile, a smugness born of supreme, unassailable confidence, earned not just by decades of experience, but by centuries.

I swallowed against a tightness in my throat. Inside, Wolf was screaming, howling. Ben touched my back, his hand stiff. He touched for comfort, but it only accentuated our anxiety. His wolf was nearing panic, as well. We both recognized this man's power.

"Who are you?" I said, my voice hoarse.

"Gaius Albinus, isn't it?" a newcomer called. "A centurion with the Tenth Legion stationed in Judea. First century, Common Era."

And there was Rick, standing on the sidewalk, relaxed, hands in his coat pockets, as close to Roman as Roman was to me.

"Roman," I murmured, understanding dropping like a weight.

"It's not his name," Rick said. "It's his nationality. A very calculating people. They kept good records."

The elder vampire's smile turned wry. "The provincial cultures that came after the empire left a lot to be desired. Spain, for example."

Rick laughed. "I was never very patriotic, I'm afraid. I've always been happy with my own little piece of ground, wherever it happens to be. Unlike some people."

"You've come to face me. Do you really think that's a good idea?" Roman said. But he didn't face Rick. He kept his back to him, like he didn't consider the other man a threat. Roman never looked away from me. He studied me, trying to see through me. His gaze made me itch, made me fidget. I clutched the seams of my jeans. He was waiting for my guard to drop, so he could catch my gaze by accident. But I kept looking at Rick. Concentrated on Rick.

"No, it isn't. I'm just going to ask you to leave Denver."

"All by yourself? You're *just* going to ask me?"

"No. Not all by myself."

Others appeared. They might have been standing ready the whole time and I just didn't notice. Like every Master of every city, Rick had his followers. I didn't know much about the vampires in his Family. There were men and women among them, some slick and fashionable, some a little more rough and tumble. But all were serious. Moving toward us along the street, from around the house, from behind trees, they converged on the yard of Flint House. Rick by himself didn't have the age and strength to confront Roman. But a dozen vampires together? They might.

Rick said, "While I stand, this city is protected. You have no power here." The words had power. I didn't know if it was real magic, like what we'd used to trap the *djinn* in the bottle, or if it was the power of words spoken by a talented orator. But the weight of them fell over us.

And he was right. Roman had no power here. A vampire of his age ought to have been able to cow us all with a glare, but this wasn't his city.

I met his gaze. Just for a moment. Cold gray eyes, pale skin crinkled at the corners. A two-thousand-year-old gaze. Eyes that might have seen Christ walk the earth. If I thought there was any chance in hell he'd let me interview him on the air, I'd have groveled for it, but I didn't even try to ask.

"Wolf," he said, and my skin prickled with the ghost of fur. "He's right. Roman isn't my name. But neither is Gaius Albinus. Everyone who called me that has been dead for two millennia. After all this, though, you've earned something. A true name: Dux Bellorum. And know this: You will see me again. Remember me, next time."

He turned away, and my breath caught. Ben clutched my hand.

Roman—Gaius, or Dux Bellorum, or Dom's Master, or whoever he really was—walked away, down the street. Staying out of the narrow rings of streetlamps, he vanished from sight quickly. Or maybe he just vanished. Nobody followed him. Like me, Rick watched him silently, and continued watching the space where he disappeared.

"Rick?"

"Dux Bellorum. Leader of wars. The general."

My mouth went too dry to even swallow. The general, commanding his army. When he'd asked me for my loyalty, had he hoped to add me to those ranks?

"Holy *shit*. I hate those guys," Hardin said, letting her arm with the gun drop finally. "How did you people get past my patrol? Never mind, I don't want to know."

"Are we in trouble?" Tina asked, her voice small.

"No," Rick said. "As pawns go, you're too small to bother with. Most of you." And he looked at me.

I jumped off the porch to face him. All I could do was stare. His followers, a small horde of vampires, surrounded us, all of them glaring like they wanted to take a piece out of me. Ben stood at the end of the porch, reaching after me but hesitating. We all froze in tableau. And I couldn't think of a damn thing to say.

"I told you I'd learn who he was. It just took a little time," Rick said, far too calmly. He raised a brow when I didn't answer. "Speechless?"

"The Long Game," I said.

He nodded. "The Long Game. The game of empire. Some people never lose the taste for it."

"What does he want with me?"

"You've ruined a couple of his plans, which in his eyes means you've thrown in as a player. He'll be keeping an eye on you. Not like that isn't hard to do, celebrity that you are."

I rubbed my face. "Is it too late to quit?"

"What, after all this work you've done to make yourself notorious?"

I lost it. Not totally. However much Wolf wanted to Change and run howling to the hills, I kept that part of me together. But I lost the ability to think straight.

"How can you just stand there? How can you be so calm? Two thousand years! Ancient Rome? What is somebody from ancient Rome doing in Denver? Doesn't he have better things to do? Doesn't it freak you out that he wanted to waltz in here and take over? And you just stood there and faced him down. Dude, you totally scared him off!"

In the course of my rant, my panic had turned to awe. I suddenly understood why some werewolf packs would put themselves in the control of a strong Master vampire, if it protected them from the attention of vampires like Roman. I could feel myself blinking up at him with huge, gleaming eyes. I imagined it looked pretty ridiculous.

"I wouldn't go that far," he said, ducking his gaze, almost bashfully. "There's a lot to be said for safety in numbers." His Family, his own pack, were still gathered. Lips pressed thin, he glanced around at them, nodded once. The vampires left, fading into the dark like Roman had.

"I guess this is when I admit that you were right and I was wrong," I said.

He smiled. "If you'd like. I won't hold it against you."

"Gee. Thanks."

Rick tipped back his head, for all the world like a wolf scenting the air. "I'd better get going. It'll be morning soon. I want to make sure Roman's really leaving town."

"Even if he doesn't have a place to bed down for the day?"

"He's lasted this long, he'll find a way. I used to dig myself a hole and wrap up in a blanket when I was caught in the open. Not very dignified, but it works."

I shook my head, trying to wrap my mind around the image. Urbane Rick, wrapped in a blanket in a hole in the ground? That was another story I'd have to dig out of him.

I looked back to where Roman had walked away, as if expecting him to return with an army of centurions.

"I'm not important enough for a vampire like that to pay attention to," I murmured. My skin was chilled, and I hugged myself to try to get warm.

"Kitty," Rick said, a smile hiding in his voice. "There's a pattern here, and in the middle of it all is you. You draw people to you. Things happen around you."

"I'm danger prone, you mean."

"You're just one of those people."

"What people? What are you talking about?"

He just shook his head, his smile lingering. "Take care, Kitty."

He offered his hand. After a moment of hesitation, I decided to accept, and we shook. Partners. He walked off in the opposite direction Roman had gone.

Reality slowly crept back, we started to get on with our lives. Gary went to the van to consult with his camera crew. Hardin, with her cops and fire fighters, continued cleaning up the aftermath. Jules walked around the outside of the house, studying details, looking for who knew what in his quest for science. Tina sat on the steps, cradling the bottled *djinn,* refusing to let it out of her sight.

Ben put his arm around my shoulders. "I need to sleep," he said. And yes, he sounded sleep deprived and grouchy. His eyes were shadowed, his skin pale. "Are we done here?"

"I don't know." We all had a posttraumatic dazed look. But none of us, even Ben, despite what he'd said, looked like we were ready for sleep. "I'm kind of antsy." But not to run. It wasn't anywhere near the full moon, and I didn't want to Change, however much Wolf nagged me. But I wanted to do *something.*

Ben raised a brow and looked at me. "Really?"

"Yeah. We just saved the city, you know."

He rolled his eyes. Not impressed, apparently.

I called to the others, "Anyone want to go grab a cup of coffee?"

"Are there any all-night diners around here?" Jules said.

"Hell, yeah. Detective? You up for it?" I said.

"Only if you tell me what the hell's been going on."

"Deal."

Ben, still skeptical, said, "You think this is what the Justice League does after saving the city? They go out for coffee?"

"I don't care what the Justice League does," I said, hooking my arm around his. "This is what werewolves and paranormal investigators and police detectives do."

"Whatever you say, dear."

"I need to call Shaun and everyone," I said. "Tell them they can stop using that gunk."

"How well does that stuff clean up, anyway?"

I was afraid the answer to that wouldn't be good.

Then my phone rang. A call at this hour of night couldn't be good. I pulled it out of my pocket, answered it, and started pacing. "Yeah?"

"Kitty, it's Peter," he said breathlessly, like he'd been running. I heard the electronic jangle and mayhem of a Las Vegas casino in the background. "We found it, we figured it out."

I clutched the phone tighter. "Peter! Oh my God, are you okay? What's going on? What's happening? Where's Grant?"

"Grant's with me, I found him, he's got the solution!"

"The solution—" But we'd already caught the *djinn*. I almost didn't have the heart to tell him. "Peter, a lot's happened here since you left. Can I talk to Grant?"

"Sure, here he is." I heard shifting noises as he passed the phone over.

"Kitty," said a cool, unflappable voice. "I've discovered how they did it. How the Band of Tiamat summoned what's been attacking you."

"Grant, where have you been? I've been trying to call you, the box office said you canceled your show—"

"I ran into a bit of trouble."

And I wouldn't get anything more out of him than that.

"That vampire priestess, I put her at about twelve hundred, tops." Which still made her damn scary—but not as scary as Roman. "She really did start as the priestess of a remnant of a Babylonian cult dedicated to Tiamat, but her real knowledge is in another area of magic entirely, drawn from Arabic lore. The demon she sent after you is a *djinn*."

He sounded so enthusiastic and pleased with himself—rather, as enthusiastic as he ever got, which meant his voice had a little more of a lilt to it. "Grant, I know—"

"She used several strands of your hair to work the spell and bind the demon to you. Like setting a dog on a scent. I imagine she acquired stray strands of your hair from when you were tied to her altar."

Or when I was sprawled out in the decadent, pillow-strewn lair of the Band of Tiamat's hotel suite, practically in their leader Balthasar's arms. All they'd have had to do was pick my blond hairs off the upholstery. But nobody had to know about that part, did they?

"It wasn't easy, but I destroyed the amulet of your hair."

This might explain the little adventure he'd been having the last couple of days. The priestess probably kept that amulet very well protected, deep in her lair. Grant would have needed all his talents to accomplish the task and get out of any resulting trouble. He may even have needed Peter's help. "The *djinn* is no longer bound to you. It should return to its own realm now," he finished.

Oops. I winced. Was he saying we hadn't needed to go

through all that ritual? Surely his solution couldn't be that simple. I'd have to work out the timing—surely he didn't *just* destroy the amulet, at the same time we were working our spell. Surely he'd done it a while—an hour or more—before. Which meant the *djinn* was still coming after me. Which meant we really had needed to trap it.

"Grant?" I began apologetically. "We know. We bottled the thing, actually. We went ahead and worked out this plan to trap it. And, well, it worked."

He hesitated, then said, "Did you say you bottled the *djinn*?"

"Yeah. That protection spell you gave me worked really well, and we were able to use it to trap the *djinn*. And Tina—did Peter tell you about *Paradox PI*? Anyway, Tina and Jules figured out this spell. They did it by burning my hair—I guess it's the same principle, they just used some that was a little fresher. We've got it sitting here in a bottle right now. I think. It's hard to tell. If we shake it or something, will it rattle?"

"We're so not shaking this thing," Tina said. She was still on the porch, cradling the bottle, like she was afraid to move.

I waited through another long pause. He said, "Hmm. I see. Interesting."

"Are you angry?" I said.

"Of course not. I think I'm impressed. I'll want to talk to your *Paradox PI* friends, find out exactly what they did."

"I think they'll be fine with that," I said.

"And Kitty? Take very, very good care of that bottle. It's secured? Sealed tightly?"

"I think so."

"This isn't over yet—the vampire priestess is still at large, and as long as the cult remains intact, they're a danger, but I have an idea. Can you bring the *djinn* here to Vegas? We can dispose of it and its mistress at the same time."

I'd fly to Vegas on a red-eye for a chance to see that.

"I'll get there as soon as I can. And Grant—thank you. Thanks for sticking your neck out."

He said, "I'm duty bound to help. And we're not finished yet."

"Yeah. I'll call you when I'm in Vegas. Don't get in any trouble until I get there!"

We clicked off.

Ben gave me a dark, suspicious look. "For a minute there, it sounded like you're going back to Vegas to face down the cult."

I winced. "Yeah. I'm going to take that thing to Grant. He has a plan to get rid of it for good." Ben wasn't going to like the idea. I *knew* he wasn't going to like it. We were going to have another fight, weren't we?

He took his phone from his pocket and made a call. I stared, confused, wondering who he was calling—divorce lawyer? I couldn't get the question out.

He twitched a smile at my expression, which must have been dumbstruck. "I'm seeing how early we can get a flight."

"We?"

"I'm coming with you," he said.

So, we were headed back to Vegas.

chapter 23

Within a couple of hours, we stood in line at security at Denver International Airport, waiting to catch the morning's first flight to Vegas. We didn't even pack. I had a backpack, Ben didn't have anything. I carried the bottled *djinn* in my arms. Tina and I had packed it in a box, padded the hell out of it, wrapped the box with duct tape, packed the box in another box, padded it some more, wrapped more duct tape around it. We weren't taking any chances.

I didn't want to let the box go to put it on the conveyor belt. What if the X-ray machine supercharged it and let it escape? But I also couldn't see myself explaining any of this to the nice TSA folks. So I let it go and held my breath. I passed through the metal detector without incident. So did Ben.

Then the guy at the X-ray machine said, "Ma'am? Does this box belong to you?"

Oh, no. Of all the obstacles we'd overcome, of all the world's wickedness we'd faced, I hadn't expected this.

I looked at the guy, round-faced and mustached, sagging

in his early-shift fatigue. I smiled, cheerful and feigning ignorance. "Yes?"

The X-ray operator inched the conveyor forward, and the guy who'd addressed me picked up the box.

"Ma'am, I'm going to need to take a look in this box."

No no no. I must have looked stricken. Ben leaned forward and whispered—without looking like he was leaning forward and whispering—"If you argue, they'll get suspicious and put you in a holding room. Say 'All right.'"

"Um . . . okay?" I said. My smile froze.

The TSA agent led us over to a stainless-steel table and took out a box cutter, no doubt confiscated from some other hapless traveler. And what was I going to do if he confiscated the *ifrit*? Did the TSA manual even cover something like this?

With great precision, he sliced through the duct tape around the box. Watching, I bounced in place a little. Ben was a picture of aggravating serenity. Maybe he had some lawyer-fu he could pull out at the last minute to avert disaster.

The TSA agent dug through the wadded-up newspaper and drew out the next box. Holding it, he eyed us, as if inviting us to share the great secret we were hiding. We didn't oblige him.

"Fragile?" he said.

"Very," I said.

He cut through the tape on the second box. I winced, thinking maybe it would explode. It didn't. Ben wasn't quite the picture of calm anymore; he clenched his hands behind his back. His courtroom face didn't reveal anything. I would have to learn from his example, because I was fidgeting. I was *this close* to grabbing the box from the guy and running. But that would be so very bad. *Down, girl.*

Finally, the agent drew out the brown bottle. My hands were reaching for it.

"Is it liquid?" he asked. Holding up to the light, he peered at it.

"No," I said quickly. "Nothing liquid, nothing dangerous at all. Just a perfectly harmless bottle." Corked, sealed with wax, with another layer of duct tape wrapped over the wax for good measure. The agent studied the elaborate corking material with great suspicion. Not that I could blame him. But I so didn't have time for this.

"Mind if I have a look inside this?"

I winced. Truth-or-consequences time. "Actually, I'd really rather you didn't. I'll never be able to get it closed up just right again." And wasn't that the truth? This guy had no idea. If I said there was an evil *djinn* locked inside, he'd probably call the police.

He gave me the talking-to-crazy-people look. "There doesn't seem to be anything in here." To make his point, he gave the bottle a shake. I wanted to scream at him not to do that. What if it pissed the *djinn* off? Pissed him off more, anyway.

"Please. It shouldn't be opened. It's sealed like that for a reason."

"Why? It's not radioactive, is it?"

"It, uh, has the breath of Elvis inside?"

The expression on his face changed, subtly. The lines around his eyes grew softer, the hard edges of his frown vanished. It was a shift from a "dealing with crazy people" look to a "dealing with crazy but harmless people" look.

I'd take that.

He put the bottle in the little box, the little box in the big box, not bothering to arrange the packing or reseal the tape. He handed the box back to me, with crushed newspaper spilling out the top. "You folks have a nice flight."

"Thank you," I said around gritted teeth. Quickly, we retreated. I didn't even pause to rearrange the packing. Time enough to do that while we waited to board—which was in about ten minutes, thanks to Mr. Vigilant.

"So," Ben said. "That went well."

I glared at him.

It was near dawn when Peter met us at Las Vegas's Mc-Carran Airport in Grant's car. He seemed to be in a rush. Excited, at least. Positively gleeful, like a plan was coming together. We climbed into the car's backseat.

"Is that it?" He nodded at the box.

"Yeah," I said. "So what's the plan? What's Grant cooking up?"

Grinning, he shook his head. "I think Odysseus Grant is the freakiest guy I've ever met. He's so cool."

I glared. "You're having way too much fun, Peter. What's going on?"

"Grant said to tell you to just be ready with the jar."

I hated all this man-of-mystery crap.

Even at this hour, Las Vegas was overstimulating. The Strip, the main street, home to all the mega hotel resorts and most of the crowds, was all lights, bleached slightly by the first hint of the rising sun. I had to squint against the glare. It was like a giant parade that had stalled out in the desert.

We turned a corner, crossed the Strip, and continued toward a great concrete ziggurat.

Ben groaned. "We're not going where I think we're going."

But yes, we were. The Hanging Gardens Hotel and Resort, home of the Balthasar, King of Beasts Show, now fronted by Nick, since were-lion Balthasar died in a blaze of silver-bulleted gunfire. Right before he tried to sacrifice me on his unholy fake altar. We were heading toward where this whole sleigh ride started.

Peter pulled into the drive and handed the keys to the valet parking guy. He barely broke stride while collecting his ticket, turning to us, and saying, "We need to hurry."

"But what are we doing?"

"You'll see."

I held the box under one arm, and held Ben's arm with the other, as we followed Peter. He walked briskly, almost jogging through the lobby and past the tourists and gamblers and noise. I was so focused I barely registered the area. I was in hunting mode, and the prey was in sight.

Peter led us to the King of Beasts theater, then to a side door. It was unlocked. We went in, and before us was the stage, just as it looked at the end of the show: torches, palm trees, vegetation dripping off the backdrop of a giant fake ziggurat, like we'd landed in some lost jungle temple. I'd seen the show—way up close. It was on this stage and setting that the cult of Tiamat had tried to kill me.

Now Odysseus Grant stood downstage center, next to a six-and-a-half-foot-high coffinlike box, painted black and covered with faded decorations, vines and flowers, arcane symbols. Part of his magic show, he put people inside and made them disappear. He always brought them back—during the show, at least.

I knew better than to ask how he'd managed to get the box here from his own theater at the Diablo Hotel, at least a mile away. Grant just *did* things.

Ben hadn't seen any of this. He'd just heard the aftermath stories. He stopped halfway down the aisle and stared at the setting, agog.

"When I said this was fucked up, that was an understatement," he said.

"Is that it?" Grant said to me, marching to the edge of the stage, reaching toward me. I fished the jar out of the box and handed it to him.

He held it up to the light, turning it, as if he could see through the mostly opaque glass. As if he could see anything inside. For all I knew, the *ifrit* had simply vanished and the jar was empty. Except for the way Tina had stared at it, and how carefully she handled it.

"Extraordinary," Grant said softly. When he glanced at us, he was actually smiling. "Do you know what you've done here?"

I shrugged. "We weren't trying to do anything fancy. I just wanted to keep my city safe."

Peter had lingered by the theater door, and now slammed it shut. "They're coming."

"Get out of sight," Grant said to us. We didn't argue. Not that it would help; we were facing a vampire and a pack of lycanthropes. They'd be able to smell us. Peter waved us over to the far edge of the stage, where we could hide in the wings, at least for a little while. This was going to come down to the face-to-face battle I'd been hoping to avoid.

I whispered to Peter, "This is going to get ugly. You should get out of here, okay? I don't want you to get tossed around or bitten."

"Shh." He didn't promise. I decided that my first priority was going to have to be looking after him. Might not be the best policy. But I owed it to him—and his brother.

Downstage, Grant had opened the door to the box of vanishing and placed the *ifrit's* jar inside.

A breath of cold passed through the theater, like an air conditioner had just come on. Then she was standing before the stage, looking up at him. I'd seen the woman only twice, once as part of Balthasar's show, the dark priestess of a mock ceremony, and once as the real priestess, wielding a silver dagger over my heart. That time, I'd gotten a good look at her, a good smell of her, and knew she was a vampire. Now she was dressed in a black flowing gown, a robe wrapped around her, belted with gold. Her hair was long and loose down her back. She was like a statue, unbreathing, solid as stone. I swallowed back a growl. Ben squeezed my hand.

Her entourage accompanied her, a half-dozen young men who walked with graceful, easy strides and spread out around the theater, blocking the exits. They were handsome, decorative, and smug; they knew how gorgeous they were and knew how to show it off. The fur and wild smell of lycanthrope was thick around them. Their leader, Nick, stood at the top of the center aisle, gazing over the stage as if they'd already won.

I wasn't sure Grant would be able to hold his own against the group.

"This is a trap," the vampire, Farida, said, in a rich, clipped accent I couldn't identify.

Flat on his palm, facing her, Grant held a cross. It wouldn't stop her in an attack, but maybe it would make her hesitate. She stepped forward, moving to the side of the stage and a set of steps hidden there. Though she seemed to move slowly, she was on the stage in moments, approaching him. I blinked, sure I'd missed something.

Grant stood his ground and spoke as if placating a wild animal. "I'm only returning what belongs to you."

She glanced at the jar with a look of distaste. "I do not want it. It has failed. As you will."

"I should have done this a long time ago," Odysseus Grant murmured.

I had to keep my breathing slow. I didn't want to panic. Grant looked nervous, which made my heart sink. His lips were thin, his breathing was deep—I could see his chest moving. That cross wasn't going to protect him if the vampire made a move.

He was drawing her in, waiting for her to get closer. I could almost see him counting, ticking off seconds as she stepped forward. She moved like she didn't think his magic could hurt her, and I wondered if it was true, if there was a reason Grant had hidden himself away all this time rather than confronting her and stopping the cult earlier. For all his air of power, he was mortal.

She paid no attention to the box or the *ifrit*'s jar. Her gaze focused on him. A vampire's gaze had power—all she had to do was make Grant look into her eyes, and she could immobilize him.

I crouched, getting ready to spring. I couldn't defeat her, but I had to try. I couldn't let her take down Grant.

Ben put his hand on my shoulder, squeezed, holding me back like he knew what I was going to do.

Grant threw something to the floor at the base of the box, at the jar. A puff of smoke and sparks exploded around it. Special effects, I thought—a smoke bomb or explosive squib of some kind, a distraction. But the smoke spread, rose up, and from it emerged the outline of a figure, broad and hunched, licked all around with tongues of flame, rising from the broken jar.

I almost screamed, jumping forward and shouting a denial. All that work—we'd set a neighborhood on fire to capture that thing—and he just let it go. Ben held me back.

The *ifrit* clenched blurred, fiery fists, tipped its head back, and screamed, a sound like that of a flamethrower. Grant had vanished—probably not literally vanished, but had gotten well out of the way and out of sight. The demon hovering before the box had turned its rage toward the vampire—who took a step back.

We hadn't been the first ones to capture the *ifrit*. Farida had trapped it first, then set it on us. The vampire priestess had used it as a tool, and now that it was free, it went for the closest target at hand. Blasting fire from its limbs, it reached for her, enveloped her—

Then something else reached for both of them.

I didn't see what. What I did see: Enveloped together, wrapped in a struggle, they leaned toward the inside of the box, then they fell in. They both gave short cries, not of anger, but of surprise. Terror. The vampire was burning, struggling in the cage of fire that the *ifrit* had wrapped around her. The *ifrit* wasn't looking at anything but her.

Then it was like they'd been yanked off their feet, and they disappeared.

Grant stepped around the box, closed the door quietly, and held it shut, leaning against it for a long moment. The theater was quiet. I smelled burning fabric and brimstone.

The magician finally stepped away from the box and brushed his hands.

From the back of the theater, Nick might have shouted, "No!" but the word was lost in a full-throated feline roar. He must not have believed his vampire mistress could lose. I had to admit, I hadn't quite believed it, either.

He ran, straight for the stage and Odysseus Grant.

I sprang to intercept him. Ben couldn't hold me this time.

Nick was fast, with a feline grace that gave him a powerful sprint, bent low, head down, strides long, muscles working. I could see the tiger in him, all that instinct and power coming through. He made an inhuman leap and reached the stage easily, his next stride ready to take him to Grant and tackle him.

My own jump across the stage, aiming for Nick, wasn't nearly as graceful, but it worked. My legs went wild, but my arms got him, wrapped around him, tackled him. Our combined momentums sent us rolling, limbs tangled, bodies hitting the stage and each other. I was going to be seriously bruised after this. And I wasn't quite sure what the move had gotten me.

Nick didn't waste time. He kept the roll going until he landed on top of me, wrenched me facedown, and bent back my arm. His breath blew on my cheek, and his teeth closed around my throat, going for blood, with nothing sexy about him at all. Growling, I bucked, looking for the leverage to throw him off me.

Then he was just gone. I scrambled to all fours, bracing for the next attack, sure that Nick had let me go so he could play with me like a cat with a struggling mouse. But no— my pack had come to save me—or at least Ben had. He'd grabbed Nick from behind, arm across his throat, weight bracing him off-balance. Nick kicked and struggled, hissing, spitting around sharp, half-transformed teeth.

This was exactly why wolves traveled in packs. We weren't meant to hunt by ourselves.

Nick was thrashing, and Ben's grip was slipping. The struggle showed in his grimace.

Grant opened the door to the box and nodded at me.

I grabbed Nick's flailing feet and dragged him toward the box. Ben followed my lead. With Nick howling, we managed to wrestle him into place, half throw and half drop him through the doorway. If it had been just a box, Nick's struggles would have knocked the thing over, but when he fell in, he fell all the way in. I smelled something dank, and a draft came in through the shadowed interior.

Clinging to Ben, I lunged away from the box, lest the thing inside make a grab for us, too. Grant slammed the door shut again.

Ben and I crouched on the stage, gasping for breath, not letting go of each other. My fingers were knotted in his shirt, which was damp with sweat. He'd wrapped his arms around me and stared at the box.

"What the hell is that thing?" he said to Grant.

"Stage prop," Grant said. "Among other things."

"Shit," Ben said, then buried his face in my hair and took a long, comforting breath. I giggled, a tad hysterically.

The rest of the Band of Tiamat approached, stalking like cats but not attacking, fearful maybe, as if unsure of what they'd seen. Grant moved to the end of the stage and addressed them, his voice calm but tired.

"The show's over. Leave. Scatter. Or follow your masters into that place."

The half dozen lycanthropes who were left looked at us, looked at each other. Without their show, their alpha, their context, they just looked like young men in jeans and T-shirts. Good-looking, but maybe a bit lost. Would they be able to make it on their own, without their pack? Without their show and their cult? Were they thinking the same thing?

The answer must have been yes, at least to the first one who turned and walked away. One by one, the others did likewise, glancing over their shoulders, resignation settling over their features.

The show was over, and maybe, just maybe some of them were relieved. Maybe this was for the best.

Eyes wide and shocky, Peter emerged from backstage. The theater was quiet now, as if nothing had happened. The box was still, and the scent of fire had faded. The only clues that there'd been a fight were Ben and me, hugging tightly, and Grant, who sat down on the edge of the stage, his shoulders slumping as he ran a hand through his hair.

"It's over?" Peter said.

Grant looked up at him; his smile was tired, but he was smiling. "It's over. Though I think it may be time to retire that particular prop."

It wasn't over. This battle was over, but Roman—Dux Bellorum—was still out there, scheming and plotting, a major player in the Long Game. This cult had been one of his pawns. He'd tried to use it to get a wedge into Denver, and he'd failed. He didn't seem like the kind of guy who'd let a defeat like that pass.

For me and my city, this wasn't over by a long shot.

Epilogue

This time, I was excited about going to visit Cormac in prison.

This wasn't to say I usually hated going. Hate wasn't the right word. Seeing how Cormac was doing, live and in person, on a regular basis, was reassuring. But the situation was uncomfortable. The prison, even the visitors' room, smelled like being trapped to the Wolf side. I hated to think of Cormac being trapped, and he looked terrible in orange.

I brought a file folder with me and, along with Ben, grinned at Cormac through the glass.

"You found something," he said.

"I did," I said.

"Which means, I assume, that the demon problem is all fixed and everything's okay."

"Would I be smiling if it weren't?" I said.

"Sorry," Ben said. "We forgot to tell you. The genie is bottled and everything's okay."

Cormac pointed. "See, I know when the problems are

solved even when you don't tell me, because you just stop talking about them. And did you say *genie*?"

"Can I tell you about your executions now?" I said quickly, opening the folder. He leaned forward, interested. "If you take in the twenty or so years before and after 1900, there were about half a dozen women executed. There was only one woman executed in 1900."

"What was her name?" Cormac said.

"Amelia Parker. Her story's a little different." I even managed to dig up a few scraps of information here and there, a footnote in an old history book, a couple of hundred-year-old newspaper articles copied off microfiche. I talked like I was delivering a lecture. "Lady Amelia Parker. British, born 1877, the daughter of a minor nobleman. By all accounts, she was a bit of a firebrand. Traveled the world by herself, which just wasn't done in those days. She was a self-taught archeologist, linguist, folklorist. She collected knowledge, everything from local folk cures to lost languages. She has her own page in a book about Victorian women adventurers."

Something lit Cormac's eyes, some recognition, familiarity. He knew something. I stopped myself from calling him on it and demanding that he tell me, because I wasn't finished with Amelia's story yet.

"She came to Colorado to follow an interest in Native American culture and lore but was convicted of murdering a young woman in Manitou Springs. The newspaper report was pretty sensationalist, even for 1900. Said something about blood sacrifice. There were patterns on the floor, candles, incense, the works. Like something out of *Faust*. The newspaper's words, not mine. She was convicted of murder and hanged. Right here, in fact. Or at least, in this area, at the prison that was standing here at the time."

Cormac leaned forward. "The victim. How did she die? Did it say what happened to her?"

"Her throat was cut."

He chewed his lip and stared off into space.

"What is it?" He didn't say anything, and I pressed. "You know something. This all makes sense to you. Why? How?"

Finally, he shook his head. "I'm not sure. May be nothing. But she's got a name. It's not all in my head."

"What isn't?"

He looked at me, square on. "She didn't kill that girl. She was trying to find out who did. *What* did."

I blinked. "What do you mean *what*?"

"Never mind," he said, leaning back and looking away. "I'll tell you when I know more."

"Why is she important?" I said. "She's been dead for over a hundred years."

His smile quirked. "And you really think that's the end of it? You've been telling ghost stories for years. Are you going to sit here now and tell me it isn't possible?"

For once, I kept my mouth shut.

Ben leaned forward and smirked. "She just doesn't like the idea that someone else is having adventures without her."

"I'll have you know I'm looking forward to a good long adventure-free streak from here out," I said.

They chuckled. No, actually, they were doubled over and turning red in the face with laughter. At me.

"A month," Cormac said finally, wheezing. "I bet you don't go a month without getting into trouble."

"How are we defining trouble?" I whined, irate. "Are we talking life-or-death trouble or pissing-off-the-boss trouble? Hey, stop laughing at me!"

Which only made them laugh harder, of course. I growled.

Ben straightened and got serious. "I'm not taking that bet." Cormac shrugged as if to say, oh, well.

I closed the folder. "I could try to mail this to you, but I'm not sure it would get past the censors."

"Just hang on to it for me," he said.

"Right," I said.

We had a whole box of stuff waiting for when he got out. A whole world waiting.

A couple of months later, *Paradox PI* broadcast an entire episode on the Band of Tiamat and its aftermath. Peter dug up all kinds of dirt on the Band of Tiamat and their King of Beasts cover operation, including evidence that the group had been quietly murdering werewolves for almost a decade. They did a class job on the episode, bringing in experts with opinions on all sides of the debate. What could have been an exploitative show featuring fire and mayhem ended up being a fairly reasoned documentary on spells, *djinn,* and what happens when magic goes awry. Which wasn't to say they didn't air plenty of footage of flaming chaos.

Some skeptics still claimed that we'd staged the whole thing. I didn't care, because the *djinn* was gone and Denver was safe. And we got in a big old plug for *The Midnight Hour.*

I also forwarded all the data to my contacts at the NIH's Center for the Study of Paranatural Biology. Let those guys see if they could figure it out. Did a being made of fire even have biology?

We had a party at the refurbished and open-for-business New Moon when the episode broadcast. Rented a couple of big-screen TVs, served up lots of beer and pizza. Even my parents and Cheryl and her family came. I kind of wished they hadn't, since I'd have to suffer my mother's appalled expression when she realized what was really going on during those weeks. Maybe I could convince her that we'd staged the whole thing and hadn't really been in danger. Enough skeptics out there were already claiming it.

A bunch of people from KNOB were there, as well as a good chunk of my pack. The *Paradox PI* team—Gary, Jules, and Tina—also came back for the party. The place was filled.

Shaun had plenty of staff on hand, but I still found myself carrying pitchers of beer and bouncing from table to table trying to be social with everyone at the same time. I was getting flustered playing hostess for so many people. So many disparate parts of my life had come together. Part of me wanted to run, but I clamped down on that side of my psyche.

Another part of me felt a thrill at being in charge, being on top of it all, being at the center. Rick had said that—being at the center of the pattern. Bringing people together. I felt pride in what was happening here, and that was new. I liked it.

Ben grabbed my hand when I happened to drift close enough to our table in the corner. "Hey," he said. "You okay?"

I was flustered, and he'd noticed, which made the world a little sunnier. Squeezing his hand, I sank into the chair next to him. "I've decided it's my job to make sure everyone has a good time."

He chuckled. "How's that working out for you?"

"I think it's really good that we hired Shaun to run the place," I said.

"Hey, Kitty," Gary called. He, Tina, and Jules were sitting at a table halfway across the room. It pleased me that I now had a few more people I could hit up for information the next time something bizarre happened. Cormac was right. There would probably be a next time, and sooner than I liked.

Ben and I squeezed hands again, and I flitted off to be social with them.

"You guys okay? Need any more drinks? Any more food?" I asked.

"Maybe you should take a break for a minute." Gary pulled an empty chair out from the table and nodded at it, encouraging me to sit.

"Of course, it's nice to be worrying about not enough beer instead of demonic death," I said, sitting with a sigh.

Gary had turned away to pull a manila folder out of an attaché case. He handed it to me. All three of them looked expectant.

"What's this?" I said.

"We finally got a translation of the Arabic from the last séance. That's the transcript. Thought you might be interested." The video feed of us capturing the *djinn* had cut out, but one of the microphones inside the house had recorded the creature's last ravings.

Of course I was interested. I started reading, and it was

what I expected: curses, threats, some of them pretty creative. My favorite was the one that went, "You pathetic creatures of flesh and dirt, animals of crude matter." And so on.

"Look at the end," Tina said.

The last line. What it was ranting when it realized we had trapped it, when it was being drawn into the bottle. The transcript read, "No, please. I have a wife, a family. I had to do these things, the priestess forced me, she would not release me until I did these things. I am not evil, have pity on me, please."

For a moment, I felt sick. We had condemned a sentient being to supernatural imprisonment, without trial and without recourse. The priestess had controlled it. In some ways, it had been as much a victim as the rest of us.

But it had killed Mick, and others. I kept coming back to that.

I set my expression and looked back at them, keeping any pity at bay. "It's a manipulation. It wanted us to feel pity. To feel guilty. It's still a murderer and deserved what it got."

This was supposed to be a celebration, and now I was getting depressed. I needed another drink. I'd set my last beer somewhere and couldn't find it now.

"Hey, Kitty!"

I turned and saw Peter Gurney standing by the door. His appearance was the same as always, kind of scruffy in his army jacket and biker apparel. But he looked better now: stood a little straighter, smiled a little more. He wasn't so angry anymore.

After the confrontation with the Tiamat cult, I'd asked him what he'd planned on doing. Turned out *Paradox PI* made him an offer—they could use another person on the team, and Peter passed the audition. He brought his investigative skills to the show and played the part of their junior member in training.

"You made it!" I said, standing to meet him as he came over to join us. We hugged briefly, and he waved at the others, who all waved back. "Come on, sit down."

He did, then pulled something from his coat pocket. "I brought this for you. Just to say thanks."

"Thanks for what?"

"For filling in the blanks about Ted. For being his friend."

He handed over a snapshot. It was T.J. A younger, cockier one than the guy I'd known. He was thin, with rough-and-tumble hair, looking very James Dean in a white T-shirt, tight jeans, and biker boots. Arms crossed, he was leaning against a motorcycle with lots of black and chrome, an older model I didn't recognize, not the finicky Yamaha he'd had when I knew him.

"This was right before he left home," Peter said. "He was eighteen. Just got his first bike. Looking back, I think he planned it all out. He worked, bought the bike himself. Bought himself a way to escape when Mom and Dad kicked him out. He expected them to kick him out. I know he never could have taken me with him. But I still wish . . . I don't know. I wish he'd stayed safe."

I had to smile, and I had to cry a little at the same time. I had a little piece of T.J. outside my memory now.

"Thank you very much for this," I said.

"It's the least I could do. It means a lot to know there's someone else who feels the same way about him."

"That your brother?" Tina said, craning her neck to look over the table.

"Yeah," Peter said, and I handed Tina the picture, which she studied.

"Hm. Cute," she said. "We could use more like him batting for our side."

I almost laughed at the joke, but I had to stop and think: Had any of us mentioned to her that T.J. was gay? Had she overheard Peter and I talking about it? Before I could ask, Peter was talking.

"I know it was stupid of me to think you could talk to him on cue," Peter said, shrugging inside his canvas coat. "I was assuming he'd have something to say to me."

A thoughtful expression pursing her features, Tina slipped the photo back to me. Then she reached in her purse.

She said, "Peter, what do you know about automatic writing?"

"Nothing, I guess."

But Gary raised his eyebrows, and Jules dropped his jaw.

"You're not serious," Jules said. "Are you serious?"

"What?" Peter said. "What is it?"

"Just open it," Tina said, handing him an envelope.

We watched him intently as he tore open the envelope. He pulled out a sheet of paper, slowly unfolded it, and went a bit ashen. Looking over his shoulder, I could see mostly white, with just a line of handwritten text. He must have read it a dozen times, his eyes flicking back and forth.

Then he dropped the page, covered his eyes, and took two or three deep, shuddering breaths.

"I'm sorry. This probably wasn't the time or place for this," Tina said.

The page was lying there on the table. I couldn't help but read it. It said: "Petey. Let it go."

My eyes instantly teared up. It was like a Pavlovian reaction. I couldn't control it, the tears just happened, in response to the implication of the note. If Tina could do what she said she could, these were his words. This was as close and as real as he'd been in over a year.

And he was telling us to move on. To let *him* go.

When Peter straightened and raised his head, his eyes were dry. "No. That's okay. Thank you, I guess. I can almost hear him," he said, chuckling. "Like a voice over my shoulder. I haven't seen him in ten years, and it's still hard to think he's gone."

I touched his arm. Like that would do any good. I could almost hear T.J.'s voice, too. I'd also had a voice whispering over my shoulder.

"It's funny," Tina said. "We try so hard to hold on to them. I think every ghost story, even the scary ones, is about the fear of dying. We don't want people to just end. So we tell stories where they don't. We try our damnedest to talk to them. We'll believe anything. But I think if we asked them, the ones who are gone, they'd tell us to get on with our lives."

Funny. I didn't imagine Mick saying that. I imagined him saying, *You were supposed to protect us.*

Let it go, Kitty.

With an obvious flourish to break the mood, she drew out another sealed envelope. "I have something for you guys, too." She put it on the table between Gary and Jules.

"What's this?" Jules said.

"Remember the episode we did on Harry Houdini?

About how he vowed that if there was a way to communicate from the great beyond, he'd do it?"

It took us all a minute to register the implications of that. Of that and *her.* My eyes got real big. "No *way.*"

In a near-frenzy, Jules tore open the envelope.

"Why didn't you say anything before?" Gary said.

Tina said, "I couldn't say anything about it without blowing my cover or coming off sounding like a quack. We'd just debunked three fake examples of automatic writing. I couldn't exactly say, 'Yeah, here's the real thing' and not say where it came from. But. Well. I thought you'd be interested."

Gary and Jules leaned in to read the sheet.

"What's it say?" I was nearly out of my seat.

The note read, "Everyone who knew my codes is dead, this will not work, no one will believe you. But thank you for trying."

"You're having one over on us," Jules said.

Tina said, "Here's the thing. Most of the psychics are trying to contact Harry Houdini. How many of them ever try to contact Ehrich Weiss?"

Ehrich Weiss was Houdini's given name. The *really* funky thing about it? The handwriting was different than the writing on Peter's note. Wildly different. More different than someone could fake, unless they were really good.

I asked Tina, "You wrote these both?"

"I held the pen," she said.

"Peter," I said. "Does that look anything like T.J.'s handwriting?"

"I don't really know. I could check, though."

Then we'd have to compare the other note to samples of Houdini's writing. God, this was *weird*.

"It's like the channeling Arabic, isn't it?" Jules said.

"I don't understand it," Tina said. "That's why I hooked up with you guys, remember? Somebody's got to figure out a way to explain stuff like this."

In the end, maybe that was what separated the real paranormal investigators from the charlatans. The charlatans kept up the aura of mystery and obfuscation. The real investigators kept asking why and how.

"Hey, it's starting!" Shaun announced, punching at the remote to turn up the volume on the TV. The show's intro came up, and there was a cheer. Everyone turned to look at the Paradox crew's table. I beamed at them proudly.

"Have fun, guys. Let me know if you need anything."

I'd meant to sit down with Ben again, and not get up for the rest of the evening, but I saw Rick standing in the doorway. I went to meet him.

"I invited you in once already, isn't it supposed to keep working?"

"The invitation stands. I just can't stay long," he said. "I only wanted to say congratulations on the publicity." He nodded at the screen, which now showed my grinning face talking to Tina. I might actually get used to this TV thing someday. I seemed to be showing up on it more and more often.

"Thanks. But I think you owe me some stories, after everything I went through. Doc Holliday and Central City stories. And Coronado. And Spain."

He twitched the sly smile that meant I wasn't going to get any stories this time. "You never give up, do you?"

"Nope," I said. "Not anymore. Not ever."

"Good," he said softly.

My smile fell. "I guess you haven't heard anything about Roman. Where he ended up, what he's doing now?"

"No. But I'm counting that a blessing at the moment. The usual request still stands. If you hear anything—"

"Same with you. Don't treat me like I'm an ignorant underling. No more of this you-puny-mortals-wouldn't-understand garbage."

"All right. I promise."

With a guy like Rick, that promise really meant something.

I glanced over at Ben, intending to see if there was space at our table where we could invite Rick to sit. But when I turned back to Rick, he was gone. Back to being all inscrutably vampiric and vanishing in plain sight.

So it was just me who returned to the table and sat next to Ben. "How are you doing?"

He donned a vague smile. "This feels like the first time in weeks I've been able to sit and catch my breath."

"Amen," I said.

We leaned back, our chairs against the shelter of the wall behind us, and gazed out over our realm. He squeezed my hand.

"I'm thinking of something else," he said.

"Yeah? What?"

"You want to go out?"

Wolf perked up her ears. She knew what "out" meant, like any canine wanting to go for a run. I played obtuse. "Like on a date?"

"Sort of. Maybe out to that open space west of 93."

"Full moon's a week away," I said.

"I know. But I keep thinking about waking up in the

cold air curled up with you. No one around, just the two of us. Leave the kids at home."

You know, it actually sounded romantic.

"I don't like to make a habit of that sort of thing."

He put his arm around my shoulders and pulled me close until he was whispering in my ear, his lips tickling against me, almost but not quite kissing me. I wanted to lean into him until he had to kiss me.

"Here's the thing," Ben said. "Who says we have to shape-shift in order to go out in the woods, get naked, and make out under the stars?"

Oh my. That flush reached all the way to my toes. My face felt like it had caught fire. Metaphorically speaking. There was something to be said for having one's inhibitions lowered. I never would have done anything like this before becoming a werewolf.

I turned my head, leaning my forehead against his. "I think you just got yourself a date," I whispered back.

Paradox PI had just gotten to the part where New Moon was on fire. The audience was riveted, staring ahead, completely enthralled. Good thing Ben and I were sitting in the back. Moving quietly along the wall, we slipped to the door, then crept outside. If anyone noticed, they didn't complain.

Ben and I drove away, to wilderness and star-filled skies.

About the Author

Carrie Vaughn had a happy and relatively uneventful childhood, which means she had to turn to science fiction and fantasy for material to write about. An Air Force brat, she grew up all over the U.S. and managed to put down roots in Colorado, though she still has ambitions of being a world traveler. Learn more about Carrie's novels, her short stories, her dog Lily, and her fascination with costumes and stick figure cartoons at www.carrievaughn.com.

MORE KITTY!

**Here is a special sneak preview
of Carrie Vaughn's
next novel featuring Kitty Norville!**

~

Coming in 2010

~

I knew if I stayed in this business long enough, sooner or later I'd get an offer like this. It just didn't quite take the form I'd been expecting.

The group of us sat in a conference room at KNOB, the radio station where I base my syndicated talk show. Someone had tried to spruce up the place, mostly by cleaning old coffee cups and take-out wrappers off the table. Not much could be done, with the worn gray carpeting, off-white walls filled with bulletin boards, thumbtack holes where people hadn't bothered with the bulletin boards, and both of those covered with photocopied concert notices and posters for CD releases. The tables were fake-wood-grain-colored plastic, refugees from the '70s. We'd only just replaced the chalkboard with a dry erase board a couple of years ago. That was KNOB, on the cutting edge.

I loved the room, but it didn't exactly scream high-powered style. Which made it all the funnier to see a couple of Hollywood guys sitting at the table in their Armani suits and metrosexual savoir faire. They seemed to be young hotshots on the way up—interchangeable. I had to remember that Joey Provost was the one with slicked-back light brown hair and the weak chin, and Ron Valenti was the one with dark brown hair who hadn't smiled yet. They worked for a production company called SuperByte Entertainment that specialized in reality television. I'd looked up some of their shows, such sparkling gems as *Jailbird Moms* and *Stripper Idol*.

They were here to invite me onto their next show and eagerly explained the concept to me.

"The public is *fascinated* with the supernatural. The popularity of your show is clearly evidence of that. Over the last couple of years, as more information has come out, as more people who are part of this world come forward, that fascination is only going to increase. We're not just trying to tap into a market here—we hope to provide a platform to *educate* people. To erase some of the myths. Just like you and your show," Provost said. Provost was the talker. Valenti held the briefcase and looked serious.

"We've already secured the participation of Jerome Macy, the pro wrestler, and we're in talks with a dozen other celebrities. *Name* celebrities. This is our biggest production yet and we'd love for you to be a part of it."

I'd met Jerome Macy, interviewed him on my show, even. He was a boxer who'd been kicked out of boxing when his lycanthropy was exposed, and turned to a career in pro wrestling where being a werewolf was an asset. He was the country's second celebrity werewolf.

I was the first.

While working as a late-night DJ here at KNOB, I started my call-in talk radio show dispensing advice about all things supernatural and came out as a werewolf live on the air about three years ago now. Sometimes it seems like yesterday. Sometimes it seems like a million years ago. A lot had happened in that time.

Arms crossed, I leaned against a wall, away from the table where the two producers sat. I studied them with a narrowed gaze and a smirk on my lips. In wolf body language, I was an alpha sizing them up. Deciding whether to beat them up because they were rivals—or eat them because they were prey. They probably had been talking to Jerome Macy, because they seemed to recognize the signals, even if they didn't quite know what they meant. They both looked nervous and couldn't meet my gaze, even though they tried.

This was all posturing.

"That's great. Really," I said. "But what is this show going to be *about*?"

"Well," Provost said, leaning forward, then leaning back again when he caught sight of my stare. "We have access to a vacation lodge in Montana. Out in the middle of nowhere, a really beautiful spot, nice view of the mountains. We'll have about a dozen, give or take, well-known spokespeople for the supernatural, and this will be a chance for them—you—to talk, interact. We'll have interviews, roundtable discussions. It'll be like a retreat."

My interpretation: We're going to put you all in a house and watch you go at it like cats and dogs. Or werewolves and vampires. Whatever.

"So . . . you're not using the same model that you've used on some of your other shows. Like, oh, say *Cheerleader Sorority House*."

He had the grace to look a tiny bit chagrined. "Oh, no. This is nothing like that."

I went on. "No voting people off? No teams and stupid games? And definitely no shape-shifting on camera? Right?"

"Oh no, the idea behind this is education. Enlightenment."

Ozzie, the station manager and my boss, was at the meeting as well, sitting across from the two producers and acting way too obsequious. He leaned forward, eager, smiling back and forth between them and me. So, he thought this was a good idea. Matt, my sound guy, sat in the back corner and pantomimed eating popcorn, wearing a wicked grin.

I had a feeling I was being fed a line, that they were telling me what would most likely get me to agree to their show. And that they'd had a totally different story for everyone else they'd talked to.

I hadn't built my reputation on being coy and polite, so I laid it out for Mr. Provost. "Your shows aren't exactly known for . . . how should I put this . . . having any redeeming qualities whatsoever."

He must have dealt with my criticism all the time because he had the response all lined up. "Our shows reveal a side of life that most people have no access to."

"Trainwrecks, you mean."

Valenti, who had watched quietly until now, opened his briefcase and consulted a page he drew out. "We have Tina McCannon of *Paradox PI* on board. Also . . . Jeffrey Miles, the TV psychic. I think you're familiar with them?" He met my gaze and matched my stare. One predator sizing up another. Suddenly, I was the one who wanted to look away.

"You got Tina to agree to this? And Jeffrey?"

Both of them were psychics; Tina worked with a team

of paranormal investigators on prime-time TV, and Jeffrey did the channeling-dead-relatives thing on daytime talk shows. I'd had adventures with them both, and the prospect of spending two weeks in a cabin in the middle of nowhere taping a TV show was a lot more attractive if I'd be doing it with them.

"What do you think, Kitty? Do we have a deal?"

I needed to make some phone calls. "Can I get back to you on that? I need to check my schedule. Talk it over with my people."

"Of course. But don't take too long. We want to move on this quickly. Before someone else steals the idea." Provost actually winked at that, and his smile never faltered. Valenti had settled back and regarded me coolly.

"You're not scheduling this over a full moon, are you?" I said.

"Oh, no, certainly not," Provost said, way too seriously.

"Just one more question," I said. "Have you signed on Mercedes Cook?"

Provost hesitated, as if unsure which answer would be the right one. I knew which answer was the right one: If the Broadway star/vampire/double-crossing fink was on the show, I was staying as far away as possible.

"No," he said finally. "She turned us down flat."

Wonders never ceased. But they'd asked her. And she'd said no, so I might still do this thing. "Ah. Good," I said, and Provost relaxed.

We managed polite farewells and handshakes. Ozzie and I walked the two producers outside to their rented BMW. Provost continued to be gracious and flattering. Valenti stayed in the background. Sizing me up, I couldn't help but think.

After they'd driven away, we returned to the building. The late summer sun beat down. It had been a beautiful day, a recent heat spell had broken, and the air felt clean. Smelled like rain.

I turned to Ozzie. "Well?"

He shrugged. "I think it's a great opportunity. But it's up to you. You're the one who's going to have to go through with it."

"Right. I'm just not sure what exactly I'd be dealing with. What are the consequences going to be if I do this?"

"What's the worst that could happen?" he said.

I hated that question. Reality always came up with so much worse than I could imagine. "I could make an idiot of myself, ruin my reputation, lose my audience, my ratings, my show, and never make a living in show business again."

"No, the worst that could happen is you'd die on film in a freak accident, and how likely is that?" Trust Ozzie to be the realist. I glared at him.

"Who knows? At best it'll suck in a whole new audience. To tell you the truth, with people like Tina and Jeffrey involved, it kind of sounds like fun."

"You know what I'm going to say," Ozzie said. "Any publicity is good publicity."

So far in my career that had been true. I was waiting for the day when it wasn't.